"I know, Index.
After we eat lunch, I was thinking…
Wait, you're lost in Italy already?!"

Academy City High School student
Touma Kamijou

A Certain Magical

Index

11

KAZUMA KAMACHI

ILLUSTRATION BY
KIYOTAKA HAIMURA

"Kyaaah?! The weird stick went *vroom*, and hot air came out and attacked me…!!"

Nun managing the Index of Prohibited Books **Index**

"...You came to rescue us?
Did you think we would believe you?"

Sister belonging to the Roman Orthodox
Church's Agnes Unit **Lucia**

"......"

Sister belonging
to the Roman
Orthodox
Church's Agnes
Unit **Angeline**

"Wait… Where is *here*, anyway…?"

"Well, when all is said and done, it's a blessing in disguise."

Vicar pope of the Amakusa-Style Crossist Church **Saiji Tatemiya**

"You know all about what's going on here, right?"

Roman Orthodox sister
Agnes Sanctis

"...Then what exactly is that blood from?"

Former Roman Orthodox sister
(now an English Puritan) **Orsola Aquinas**

"It would be annoying, yes?
And I do so hate annoyances."

Roman Orthodox bishop **Biagio Busoni**

c o n t e n t s

Girl from the Amakusa-Style Crossist Church **Itsuwa**

A Certain Magical Index

VOLUME 11

KAZUMA KAMACHI

ILLUSTRATION BY: KIYOTAKA HAIMURA

NEW YORK

A CERTAIN MAGICAL INDEX, Volume 11

KAZUMA KAMACHI

Translation by Andrew Prowse
Cover art by Kiyotaka Haimura

TOARU MAJYUTSU NO INDEX
©KAZUMA KAMACHI 2006
All rights reserved.
Edited by ASCII MEDIA WORKS
First published in Japan in 2006 by KADOKAWA CORPORATION, Tokyo.
English translation rights arranged with.KADOKAWA CORPORATION, Tokyo,
through Tuttle-Mori Agency, Inc., Tokyo.

English translation © 2017 by Yen Press, LLC

Yen On
1290 Avenue of the Americas
New York, NY 10104

Visit us at yenpress.com
facebook.com/yenpress
twitter.com/yenpress
yenpress.tumblr.com
instagram.com/yenpress

First Yen On Edition: May 2017

Library of Congress Cataloging-in-Publication Data

Names: Kamachi, Kazuma, author. | Haimura, Kiyotaka, 1973– illustrator. | Prowse, Andrew (Andrew R.), translator. | Hinton, Yoshito, translator.
Title: A certain magical index / Kazuma Kamachi ; illustration by Kiyotaka Haimura.
Other titles: To aru majyutsu no kinsho mokuroku. (Light novel). English
Description: First Yen On edition. | New York : Yen On, 2014–
Identifiers: LCCN 2014031047 (print) | ISBN 9780316339124 (v. 1 : pbk.) |
  ISBN 9780316259422 (v. 2 : pbk.) | ISBN 9780316340540 (v. 3 : pbk.) |
  ISBN 9780316340564 (v. 4 : pbk.) | ISBN 9780316340595 (v. 5 : pbk.) |
  ISBN 9780316340601 (v. 6 : pbk.) | ISBN 9780316272230 (v. 7 : pbk.) |
  ISBN 9780316359924 (v. 8 : pbk.) | ISBN 9780316359962 (v. 9 : pbk.) |
  ISBN 9780316359986 (v. 10: pbk.) | ISBN 9780316360005 (v. 11: pbk.)
Subjects: | CYAC: Magic—Fiction. | Ability—Fiction. | Nuns—Fiction. | Japan—Fiction. | Science
fiction. | BISAC: FICTION / Fantasy / General. | FICTION / Science Fiction / Adventure.
Classification: LCC PZ7.1.K215 Ce 2014 | DDC [Fic]—dc23
LC record available at https://lccn.loc.gov/2014031047

ISBNs: 978-0-316-36000-5 (paperback)
       978-0-316-36001-2 (ebook)

1 3 5 7 9 10 8 6 4 2

LSC-C

Printed in the United States of America

PROLOGUE

A Trip to Northern Italy

Un_Viaggio_in_Italia.

Touma Kamijou was an unlucky person.

There was no need to look any further than the seven days of the Daihasei Festival to understand that. It was clear to everyone. The Daihasei Festival was an athletic festival–like event, where espers battled it out against one another. But for some reason Kamijou had gotten tangled up in a battle among sorcerers on the very first day, and he'd been the last one standing in a huge battle to prevent Academy City from subjugation. He was always getting caught up in crazy situations.

Even with that problem resolved, it didn't change the fact that he was fundamentally unlucky. He'd accidentally walked in on Miss Komoe changing, received a head-butt from Seiri Fukiyose's steel forehead when she fully recovered, been bitten by Index, faced gumballs pelted at him from wheelchair-bound Aisa Himegami, been dragged away by Mikoto Misaka to share a folk dance until Kuroko Shirai teleported from behind and drop-kicked him in the back of the head…Kamijou was absolutely exhausted in more ways than he could count.

But no matter how dogged his misfortune was, he never let it discourage him. In fact, he crawled back to his feet with a smile every time. He was special that way—but it didn't change the truth: He was hapless.

Once again, Touma Kamijou was an unlucky person.

He missed bargain sales at the supermarket by mere minutes. Manga magazines he bought at the convenience store would, on a regular basis, somehow be creased down the middle of the pages. Every scratch-off lottery ticket he'd ever bought had wound up being a losing one. Finding a "get one free" Popsicle stick or winning one of those vending machine roulette games were actual impossibilities.

Once again, Touma Kamijou was an unlucky person.

"The number you submitted for the visitor guessing contest was dead-on! Congratulations, you've won first prize—a five-night, seven-day trip to northern Italy!!"

Uh, what? thought the plain old high school student Touma Kamijou as he listened to the clanging handbell, his shoulders actually drooping in wonder when he heard the voice. The wind caught his spiked-up black hair, tossing it around.

The place was Academy City, a city taking up the western portion of Tokyo. The time was the last day of the Daihasei Festival, a gargantuan athletic festival held every year. He stood on an ordinary street corner near a homemade-looking stall made of plywood sheets, nails, and two-by-fours. A student from a girls' school called Kirigaoka-or-something Academy was running the stall. The students had organized a visitor-counting lottery here.

The rules were simple.

First, entrants bought a special card with actual money. Then they estimated the total number of visitors who would come to the Daihasei Festival, wrote the guess on the card, and gave it to the reception desk. The winners were ranked based on how close they came to the actual number.

Of course, people would always see programs on TV giving broad estimates, like "festival reaches ten million visitors" and the like. That made guesses easier for participants who played later in the week. But if more than one person guessed correctly, whoever first submitted the answer would win.

The stall employee, a girl wearing a short-sleeve T-shirt and red leggings, fumbled around in the storage space below the counter and presented an absurdly large envelope that looked like it might have contained blueprints or something.

"This wasn't actually planned for students, but essentially, you'll be going on a trip during the post–Daihasei Festival cleanup holiday." The girl smiled politely, the way cashiers always did. "The itinerary, sightseeing tours, and required documents are all in here, so please give them a look when you get a chance. If you have any questions, please direct them to the travel agency rather than our academy. Here, sir, please take this!"

She thrust the gigantic envelope out to him, but at this point, Kamijou was still under the false impression that there was some dramatic pitfall somewhere in the situation he had chanced upon.

He folded his arms and tilted his head in thought. "Umm, can I ask you something?"

"I may not be able to answer detailed questions regarding the trip. If that's all right with you, sir?"

"First prize, as in, like, *first* first prize?"

"I'm not sure I understand the question, sir."

"That prize is supposed to go to the luckiest person, isn't it?!"

"Umm, may I leave now?"

"No, wait! This is a trip to northern Italy, right?"

"That is a simple question, and I can answer that, but I think it's written very clearly in the documents."

"There's not gonna be any crazy plot twists where all of a sudden I'm on a plane and actually headed toward some shady scientific cult religion's private airport, right?"

"…Oh, I understand, sir! Is this your first time traveling abroad?"

She wasn't looking at him in annoyance—but instead in a sort of warm, cordial way. From a young lady of Kirigaoka's point of view, Kamijou was just a little kid afraid of what the big world outside the city might be like.

"Anyway, I need to announce the rest of the prizes now, so please direct your questions to the travel agency."

"Oh, wait! I mean, I get it! Something so irregular would almost never happen, I know! But doesn't it seem possible? Like the plane suddenly getting hijacked or waking up to find myself stranded at the South Pole?! I know, I know, I'm worrying too much, but I can't help but feel like there's some kind of catch here! Am I *really* going to be able to go to northern Italy with a friend?! Hey, answer me!!"

Getting first prize was stranger than any of that, so Kamijou figured he must have overlooked something important. And whatever that thing was, it meant he wouldn't be able to go on this trip.

"Oh, right! I don't even have a passport!" shouted Kamijou in his dorm room.

Index, lying on the floor, stared at him in response. She was about fourteen or fifteen, with long, waist-length silver hair and bright-green eyes. But after spending the entire Daihasei Festival out under the blazing hot sun, her skin had tanned a little. Still, she was a pale Caucasian to begin with, so instead of turning brown, she was a bit red. On an unrelated note, she wore a white habit with gold embroidery that looked like a teacup, with lots of safety pins on it—all very strange to him.

"Touma, Touma. What's a *passed port*?"

She spoke more slowly than usual because, for once, Index was full. She'd burst into Touma's class once the closing ceremonies were over and, after everyone accepted her presence there, proceeded to gobble up everything in sight. It happened so quickly it wouldn't have been hard to imagine she was a professional speed eater.

Without looking at Index, Kamijou continued to take out documents and pamphlets of all colors from inside the giant sealed envelope. "A passport is something you need to travel overseas. I think it takes, like, a month to actually get it after applying for one."

Actually, didn't Index come here from England? Why wouldn't she know what a passport is? Kamijou had his doubts, but Index lived in the world of magic and sorcery, where even international laws, to say nothing of Japan's constitution, often didn't apply. Maybe she'd come in riding on a magic carpet and slipped by the air-control radar network by flying super low to the ground. Kamijou began to seriously wonder about the defensive capabilities of their self-defense force. Meanwhile, he spread out all the contents of the giant envelope on the glass table before him.

From what the plans looked like, he'd be on a group tour. All the travelers were to assemble at the airport in northern Italy, then begin moving together. Which meant the schedule was already set in stone.

The date they were supposed to arrive and meet up was September 27.

That left only two days.

After the Daihasei Festival, workers would be taking everything down and security would be readjusting all over, so students would get a few days off from school. It probably seemed sudden because they'd looked for a travel itinerary that could fit into those few days, but…He could apply for a passport right now, but there was literally no chance of it getting here in time.

"…See how it is? I knew this would happen. I really did! So I'm not frustrated at all! I knew this was how it would turn out all along, and I was totally ready for this!!"

Kamijou hurled the giant envelope across the room. It whipped around, hitting the floor and rolling horizontally in place. He'd only meant to vent his frustration, but then he slammed his right ankle into one of the glass table's legs. He roared like a martial artist, and the calico that had been curled up nearby leaped on the bed to get away. Then it bounced up, stuck its claws in Kamijou's clothes hanging on the wall, and vaulted off them to the top shelf of his closet.

Then, it kicked with its hind legs. An object came falling down right onto Kamijou's upturned face—he was on the floor now—with a dry cloud of dust.

"Argh! Not even the cat gives me any respect! Wait, what's this?!"

Kamijou decided to see what had hit his forehead and grabbed it with his hand, bringing it in front of him as he lay there. It was a notebook with a red synthetic leather cover, about as small as the ones you'd see police officers using in TV shows. On the cover were stamped the words JAPAN PASSPORT.

His passport.

He suddenly lurched up and gave a dumbfounded groan. "B-but why? What's my passport doing in a place like this?!"

Kamijou and overseas cultures had nothing to do with each other. His textbook English was already getting failing marks. Filled with curiosity, he flipped through the booklet and learned that he'd apparently been to places like Saipan and Guam before. Maybe he'd gone on vacations there with his family.

"I guess the whole passport issue's solved...in a creepy way, anyway."

Touma Kamijou had amnesia, so he didn't remember any of it. Plus, he was hiding that condition from everyone. He couldn't slip up now. He glanced at Index, but she didn't seem very interested in his surprise discovery. Besides, she didn't know what passports were for, so she'd have no way of judging the situation in the first place. That's what Kamijou chose to think, anyway.

"Oh. Wait, Index, you don't have a passport, though, do you?"

"Touma, is a *passed port* that thing you're holding? I don't think I have one of those."

"Then we really can't go on a trip. If I left you here, you'd be lying dead on the floor after three days."

"Hey, why do you have to say it like that? I don't have what I don't have."

"...Wait, Miss Index. You've been very calm about all this. This is Italy we're talking about. An overseas trip! The normal reaction to this would be a desire to go, right?!"

"Touma, Touma." She looked at him, her eyes making it clear she was wondering why this was news to him. "Academy City is already a foreign country to me."

"Urgh! You deny any compromise so casually!!" He looked at the girl in white, his face astonished. "...Wait, what? So to you, every day is you living together with me abroad?"

Crash!! Index, lying down on the bed, rolled over suddenly and her head hit the floor.

She brought it right back up, though. "Wh-wh-what are you suddenly saying suggestive things for, Touma?! I...I'm a devout sister, and I don't think I can allow any comments that could be so easily misunderstood!!"

"Huh? But I..."

"A-anyway, I don't have that *passed port* thing you have! I think I have something like it, though."

"Something like it?"

"Yeah. This," she said, rummaging around in her habit sleeve and bringing out a United Kingdom passport. Kamijou was impressed by the overseas-passport design, which was different from his.

"Well, that makes sense. You may be with Necessarius, but obviously you still use airplanes to go on trips! That's good. Great. Sometimes I start thinking crazy things like you actually got yourself a camel and crossed through the Silk Road or something!"

"...For some reason I feel like you've been teasing me for a while. But anyway, Touma, how do you use this *passed port*?"

"W-wait a minute, Index. Let me see your pass— Wait, what the hell?! Why is this all totally blank?! You should at least have one stamp for leaving England!!"

Plus, the name on it was real: INDEX LIBRORUM PROHIBITORUM. As Kamijou shuddered at how fearsome state religions were, she yawned, bored. "Touma, Touma. I don't think it could possibly come with any Automatic Clerk effects."

"You little...You got Necessarius to print you a passport, and you just ignore it? You really did travel through the Silk Road, didn't you?!"

"Touma, you keep getting excited over strange things I don't understand. Anyway, does this mean that I can, err...go on the trip with you?" asked Index, her voice slightly nervous.

"…" *What?* Kamijou's eyes shrank to the size of pinpricks.

For now, he figured it was all right.

He had the impression they really *could* leave for a five-night, seven-day trip to northern Italy. Even though Touma Kamijou was unbelievably unlucky. Even though he was the least likely person in the world to experience something like this.

After going through this and that, they woke up the next morning.

After having vacation nano-devices implanted inside them, Kamijou and Index arrived at the special school district of Academy City, District 23—where all the city's aeronautical and space development was done. This was the international airport built for guests who came from outside the city for conferences and such.

The airport lobby was so big it felt like wasted space to Kamijou. The walls were made entirely of glass panes, and the sunlight was glittering by the runways outside. He'd heard inklings in the news about the place being crowded like rush hour during the Daihasei Festival, but there were still a decent number of people here getting ready to go home. Of course, the authorities had prepared a few extra vacation days in order to get all the guests back in an efficient manner. The noise and congestion in the lobby absorbed the sound of Kamijou's suitcase wheels rolling along the floor.

Kamijou was wearing his same old short-sleeve T-shirt and khaki pants, but the chain attached to his wallet hooked onto his belt, and he hid a spare wallet inside his pants, wrapped beneath a band on his calf. The nebulous anxiety he had talked about was plain to see. Moreover, the chain was a bit too thin—easily cut—and it displayed exactly where his wallet was to anyone who bothered to notice. Plus, reaching the spare wallet on his calf would force him to pull up his pants leg, and it would probably fall out while he was walking around. And despite all the care he'd put into his wallets, his passport was shoved most of the way into his other pocket. All in all, he certainly didn't look very used to overseas travel.

Kamijou also had only one suitcase, and Index had nothing. She had a few kinds of underwear and pajamas, but her habit was basically her only personal clothing, so all of it had fit in his suitcase. And before they'd left the dorm, Index had given him a small wicker case and, red-faced, told him to put that in there as well. Kamijou had wondered what was inside, but he figured asking would just provoke her to bite him, so he'd opted for silence.

As for other luggage, she was usually holding a calico in her hands, but the cat was now on loan to Miss Komoe's apartment. "K-Kami, going overseas? Are you sure you'll be all right?! I mean, well, in a lot of ways!! You won't have a teacher overseas, you know!!" she had said quite rudely. Who had asked her, anyway?

In the lobby, Kamijou searched for the departure gate's location. "Wait...I hope I didn't forget anything. Wallets, check. Passport, check. Airplane tickets, check. Documentation for the trip, check. Changes of clothes, check. Hair dryer, check. Cell phone, check. And I withdrew some extra money from the bank just to be sure...Okay. I guess I'm fine? At this point, there shouldn't be any sudden developments where I forget something and curse my misfortune."

"Touma, Touma. Why have you been such a worrywart lately?" Index fidgeted. Her excitement was making its way to the surface. Watching her made his vague gloominess seem silly.

"...You're right. Yeah, I guess I can have fun now! I'm always saying how rotten my luck is, so I guess I've been acting strange. But even I should have a little good fortune once in a while! Worthwhile vacations like this don't come around very often! Okay. For these five nights and seven days in northern Italy, I'll make sure to feel as happy as I can for the first time in a while!!"

He finally grinned, reinvigorated and free from his worries for now. Index smiled brightly. "That's the spirit, Touma." She nodded. "If you're that active and positive when you try to communicate, then I think you'll be able to get your point across even if you don't know most of the words."

"Gaahhhh!! They speak a foreign language!! I forgot about that!!"

That was the finishing blow. The suddenness of it almost made him fall face-first on the floor. After all, his English exam score had been twenty-two. His failure at learning a foreign language would have been more acceptable during Japan's period of isolationism centuries ago, but in modern times…

Having remembered his station, he slowly asked Index, "Umm, Miss Index?"

"What is it, Touma?"

"Would you, by any chance, just so happen to speak Italian?"

"Sure I can. But why are you talking like Orsola? What's wrong?"

"We are talking about Italian, the language spoken in the nation of Italy, correct?"

"Why are you asking me something so obvious all of a sudden? If there's anything worrying you about Italian culture, I can teach you."

"…Then please, if it isn't too much trouble, can we start with how to say *yes* and *no* in Italian?"

"Touma, Touma. This might sound rude, but why on earth are you going all the way to Italy, anyway?"

"I can't do anything about what I don't know!" This time, he actually *did* collapse onto the airport lobby floor.

Index sighed, feeling truly disappointed. "You know, Touma, in order to live properly in our current international society, you should learn how to speak at least three languages."

"A strange-looking sister just schooled me on *current society* and used the phrase *at least*!! But for now, let me just promise that I'll be relying totally on you when we get there! I don't even know how to say *yes* or *no*!!"

"Well, I guess I can translate for you. But Touma, this is a good opportunity, so maybe it would be faster just to learn a few words while we're there…"

"That logic only works for people who are good at remembering stuff! I only have a superficial knowledge of culture! If I tried, it would be absolutely terrible!!"

"You're exaggerating again…"

"That kind of sigh is something you only learn once you can speak multiple foreign languages like it's nothing! Wait, Index, you're inadvertently fluent in Japanese, too. Can you speak Italian like that...?"

"I'm still someone who has to go around the world to read 103,000 grimoires, remember? Italian is a piece of cake! The ones I have the most trouble with are language families that aren't structured into a coherent system. A lot of them are just random words written on slate with none of the actual rhythm or inflection contained, so I'd need to learn how to sing them separately. But that's something specific to the cultural spheres of certain island and deep-forest nations."

"...I didn't understand that at all, but does that mean I can rely on you for stuff?"

"Yep. I'm always getting you to take the lead, but now it's my turn. I'll support you as much as you need, so you can enjoy yourself to your heart's content and not worry about trouble!"

She confidently stuck out her modest chest. From Touma Kamijou's point of view she was the shining image of a saint. *Salvation is real! This is Index saying all this, so we'll be fine! All right, I'm gonna have as much fun as I can on this trip!* Kamijou pulled the suitcase wheels across the floor, feeling invigorated, and started off toward the departure gate.

"Then I'll be counting on you, Miss Tour Guide!!"

"Leave it to me! Touma, whenever we go into a shop there, the first thing you do is greet the shopkeeper."

"You mean they won't talk to you first, Miss Tour Guide?"

"Well, the point of stores is kind of to look for what you want with the shopkeeper. It's a low barrier. Hmm-hmm! If you don't at least know that, then you won't be able to live abroa—"

Beep!

The gate's metal detector made a strange noise, and before he knew it Index had been caught on either side by hardy-looking officials.

"Hmm?" Index frowned, questioning—looking indignant that they would do something like this to a tour guide.

The men who had apprehended the suspicious girl, however—their eyes twitched, and in a low voice, one asked, "Well…What are those safety pins all over you for?"

"Waah! Now that you mention it, it must look like she's packing a ton of weapons! But that's not what they are! If you take them out, her habit will fall apart and go all over the place!!" They hadn't even left the country, and Touma Kamijou already needed to save Index from a troublesome situation.

Index, though, was confused. She didn't know why the safety pins were bad. She didn't even know why a strange noise had come from the gate in the first place.

Actually, asking her for aid might not have been the best idea. Kamijou felt a chill run down his spine. He tried approaching the officials. "Well, I know those clothes are kind of bad! But what should we do about it? There's less than thirty minutes until the plane takes off…"

"Let's see…There is a shopping mall in the airport, so you'll just have to go there and buy some real clothes."

What mall?! Where?! Kamijou's eyes rushed along the guidance pane attached to the wall by the gate.

Shopping Area—1.5 km from current location

"It's too far!! I really feel like the District 23 airport is seriously wasting all this space! But our only other choices are to miss our flight or to ride camels across the Silk Road! Gah. Index, we're running! They won't let you on the plane without normal clothes!!"

"Huh? What, Touma?…Wait, are you going to buy me clothes?!"

"Damn it! Those sparkling eyes of yours are insanely aggravating! I can't believe I have to waste money before we even leave! I'm going to be unlucky this time, too, aren't I?!"

As he wailed, he grabbed her hand and scampered down the very long passageway that connected to the airport.

Twenty-eight minutes until liftoff.

The jet's engines would be nice and warm by this time.

CHAPTER 1

The Streets of Chioggia

Il_Vento_di_Chioggia.

1

The Marco Polo International Airport was famous for being the front door of northern Italy and, in particular, Venice.

The airport was located on the opposite shore from Venice, whose place on the Adriatic Sea earned it the moniker "City of Water" on the Italian mainland. For the most part, the airport was for tourists. Their journeys were broadly divided into two possible routes: taking a bus or train across the Bridge of Liberty, a nearly four-kilometer-long bridge and the only available land route to the main island, or using a boat from an opposite shore and taking the sea route.

Tourists could take routes to other places besides Venice's main island as well, such as Vicenza, Padua, Bassano del Grappa, and Belluno. Whatever the case, tourists traveling to northeastern Italy from abroad would always land at this airport, and the passenger jet Kamijou and Index rode on was no exception. Normally the airport didn't receive direct flights from Japan, but Academy City seemed to be a special case.

Several dramatic scenes unfolded, like Touma surmounting questions from foreign officials at the immigration gates and breaking into a cold sweat during the long wait for their suitcase. Despite it all, they eventually succeeded in exiting the airport.

Index had changed out of her simple blouse and skirt Kamijou had bought her in the Academy City airport and back into her normal white habit. They couldn't bring the safety pins onto the plane, so they had reconstructed the fragments of cloth with new joinery they procured as soon as they got into Marco Polo International Airport. He found himself worrying, somewhat seriously, about his status as a young man when they'd come all the way to Italy and the first thing that had happened was a girl pestering him for a handful of safety pins.

Even so, they *had* made it safely out of the airport and set foot on foreign soil.

Now they were supposed to meet up with the rest of their tour group—they'd come via a different flight—and begin their trip as directed by their guide. If northern Italy had anything to offer, it was the city of Venice, which was itself a World Heritage Site. But there were plenty of other noteworthy locations. Kamijou had actually read all the materials twice last night without sleeping, so he knew.

And when it comes to Venice, you've got St. Mark's Square, the Doge's Palace, the Ponte dell'Accademia, the Natural History Museum, the Naval History Museum, and the most famous theater in the world, the Teatro La Fenice! For souvenirs, there's glasswork and mask making! There's even a ton of places to see outside Venice, too, like the city where Galileo taught! This is all just secondhand knowledge from the guidebook, but still! That's all gonna be actual experiences and memories soon! Wah-ha-ha-ha-ha-ha-ha!! Amazing! This is gonna be the best!!

That's what he'd been thinking, anyway.

"Touma…They're late."

"Yeah. I don't even see the guide, much less anyone on the same tour…"

Over two hours had passed already since the arranged meeting time. He knew guides had a tendency to pick places good for tourists, even if there were many other places they wanted to go, but to think the very first spot would be a flop!

They were at the bus terminal in front of the airport now. Still, it was mostly indoors. The ceiling and pillars along the station were part of the airport, and it was lit not by sunlight but by rectangular light fixtures in the ceiling. The ground and ceiling were both entirely level, so it didn't feel like they were outside in the slightest. It felt more like they were in a parking garage specially designed to be lit up.

The buses passing through without stopping were distinguishable by color, like having a blue or orange frame. Kamijou had figured out they seemed to mark differences in service routes or systems. Still, it wasn't as though the service schedule was very easy to read.

I see. This must be what Orsola felt like when she was having trouble riding the bus..., he convinced himself, remembering the smile of the go-at-her-own-pace former Roman Orthodox sister. Beside him, the heat had gotten to Index. She was already starting to slump in exhaustion.

Europe's average latitude was about the same as Hokkaido's, which meant its temperature would be lower than Japan's, making for a comfortable time...or so it had said in the guidebook. It seemed like there were always exceptions.

Bordering the airport was the Adriatic Sea. Warm, salty winds blew in from the ocean, unceasingly mixing and whirling into the bus exhaust as they came and went. The temperature itself might have been comfortable, but the regional wind buffeting his face and body was still lukewarm. Enough time out here and his spirit would be eroded like crags hit by waves. The people walking around nearby—European tourists and businessmen, by the looks of it—were also glancing up at the sky and patting the sweat on their faces with handkerchiefs.

"Touma, have we been left behind?"

"Damn it...We were right on time, too...Man, calling them didn't work, either! We might have to go on our own for now."

He wasn't sure whether it was because his phone was made in

Academy City or just that phone companies were working extra hard lately, but his cell phone appeared to be usable in Italy, too. Still, he'd called the number they'd given him beforehand and heard nothing but an automated Japanese voice mail.

These guys really aren't picking up.

They weren't getting anywhere; both tour group and guide were nowhere to be found. Still, going right back to the airport and flying home wouldn't even be funny. For the moment, they did have today's itinerary and hotel rooms already.

"We have a sister good at being overseas with us, so I guess we'll be fine. There's no point standing around here—let's at least bring our stuff to the hotel. We're all staying in the same place, so we might run into the tour guide."

"Ah, aauuuuh…Touma, can't we take a break? Five steps after coming here and I think I'm already beat…"

"Don't worry. I was beat after only eight steps. But the hotel should have beds and an air conditioner, so we can take a rest and then go sightseeing."

She groaned. "That won't be enough to cheer me up. I don't think I'll come back to life without one of Italy's famous gelatos. I've never eaten one, but I've seen the name a lot, so it must be delicious."

"Is that how it works? Well, we're tourists, so I guess we're supposed to go for some famous stuff, right?"

"Yep. By the way, Venice is famous for squid-ink gelato."

"…If you don't mind my asking, is that *actually* famous?"

While noting that her requests felt oddly seasonal, Kamijou glanced over to the service schedule on a square board posted on a pillar. The first hurdle at the moment was what bus to get on.

"…No point in worrying about it. I'll have to just give up on reading it myself…Index! Sorry, but could you go read which bus we're supposed to take to get to the hotel?"

"Huh? Oh, sure, but…"

As he watched her scamper over to the board on the pillar, he sighed. Had it really been a good idea to choose her to accompany him? Frankly, he would have at least a few clues to go by if it was written in English, but with Italian he had no chance. *What if I'd been thrown into this all by myself?* he thought, feeling a sense of renewed gratitude toward the usually oblivious sister.

But then she spoke. "Touma, how do you read a bus schedule?"

"Gyaaahh!! I should have known! What a schoolgirlish look of confusion!!"

In the end...

...the two of them got cold feet and it took fifteen minutes to get on a bus.

2

The highlight of their five-night, seven-day trip to northern Italy was the main island of Venice.

The hotel they were staying in, however, was twenty kilometers south of the city in a beeline—they had to follow a curving path along the shoreline, so the trip was even longer than that—in a small town called Chioggia.

It hadn't been chosen to cut down on travel costs; on the whole, Venice's stores closed up early, and there wasn't much nighttime entertainment to be found. The pamphlet had explained that if the goal was to party all around the clock, most people would purposely reserve a hotel a bit farther away from Venice...but Kamijou, a high school student, didn't feel like that information applied much to him.

"We're close to the water again, huh?" said Kamijou to himself as soon as he stepped off the bus. His hand gripping the suitcase quickly grew tired as he pulled it along.

The airport had been on the sea, too, but all of Chioggia seemed thick with the sea breeze.

There was no beach here, though. Their "coastline" was a stone canal. The river of ocean water was a straight line, like someone had taken a saw and cut away the land.

Index, standing next to him, said, "I think it's more like we're surrounded by water than close to it."

"What do you mean?" asked Kamijou, stopping in the midst of people passing by. He was the only one with luggage here, so most of them must have been going to or from work or otherwise out to enjoy themselves.

"The center of Chioggia, where we are now, is an island town on the Adriatic Sea, split into three canals. It's really small—only four hundred meters across. There's no way to expand the land, so all the buildings are tightly packed. You can tell just at a glance. There's almost no gap between the houses here."

"Huh." Kamijou took another look around.

One of the canals she'd mentioned flowed in front of him. The seawater, blue with a tinge of green, split the town like a ruler. It was about twenty or thirty meters wide. A pair of roads ran in parallel on each side of the canal, but in the middle, houses suddenly blocked them off. The flat walls, beige and white, protruded all the way out to the canal as though they were levees. The gaps between each building were extremely narrow—it looked like something as small as a soccer ball wouldn't pass through. He wondered how they cleaned them.

Then a small motorboat floated by in the canal.

Many boats were berthed on either side of the canal, all packed tightly together. They took up about half the width of the canal. That was just how necessary they were for living here, and it went to show that the sea was incorporated at a fundamental level for transportation in Chioggia. The boats weren't polished like private leisure ones were; there were quite a few that looked well used. Another glance revealed some with items like rags and buckets carelessly thrown in.

Kamijou wasn't accustomed to things like that. "Seems like a pain," he said honestly.

But as soon as he sighed, Index simply concurred. "It's actually supposed to be a pain," she said. "Since the town is split up by all the canals, you would need to take detours to bridges if you wanted to walk everywhere. You could just use a boat, but then you'd have to go all the way up and down the canals, since you can't cross the bridges. Frankly, it would obviously be easier if they were all just roads." She gave a pained smile. "I think it's like Venice in that way. In fact, they say Chioggia still looks like what Venice looked like before it became a tourist attraction in the sixteenth century. In other words, they left the flaws here, too."

"..." Kamijou fell silent for a bit in spite of himself at the fluid explanation.

Index looked at him and frowned. "What's wrong, Touma?"

"I can't believe it...Index is actually useful for something other than sorcery..."

"Touma's making fun of me for some reason! Why do you have to make me so frustrated after all I did was nicely explain it?! If you're going to do that, then I think I'll have to bite you without mercy!!"

"'I think,' nothing!! And besides! Why bother saying you'll do it without mercy when that's no different from all the other times—but wait, no, don't test it out, I get it, it's gonna hurt even if you don't try it out!!"

Index chomped her teeth at Kamijou, causing him to take a step back. He was ready to use the suitcase as a shield if it came down to that, but he actually felt it would be somewhat dangerous—would she really have trouble gnashing through such a lame defense?

But contrary to the trembling Kamijou's expectations, Index surprisingly *didn't* attack him. Instead she relaxed and sighed. "Well, we're here to enjoy our vacation, so I don't think being angry will get us anywhere. Come on, Touma, don't hide behind the luggage. You can come out now."

"...You're not using nice-sounding words as a ruse and then planning to attack the hideout the instant I leave it?"

"No."

"And it's not a two-layered counter, where you say that, then launch your assault after I feel relieved?"

"No, it's not."

"Huh? Okay, but just to make sure one last time...Really?"

"I said it's not!"

"That's a lie! You're definitely mad! You can try to trick me with your girls-mature-faster-than-guys act, but I'm not going to fall for it that easily!! Ha-ha-ha, did you think I would be hopeful about this when I'm always unlucky?! It's obvious that at the end of it all, you're just going to bite me as hard as you can like you always do! Warning, caution! The savage sister Index is watching vigilantly for a chance to aim for the top of my head even as we speak!!"

"…"

"See, I knew you were mad! Your shady act is really starting to come apart now, isn't it…? Er, wait, are you, um, actually mad? Gyaaah! The gentle sister's mouth, very quietly opening up!! Crap, I knew it would turn out like this! It's just like I said it would be!! And that doesn't make this any betteeeeeeeeer!!"

The sound of flesh being bitten.

And at the same time, the agonized shout of the boy who got Index mad for no reason.

3

The first thing he'd been coaxed into after arriving in northern Italy was more safety pins.

The first memory he'd made after arriving in Chioggia was his head being bitten.

"…One word. *Why?*"

"What, Touma? You look like you're about to cry tears of blood."

Index looked at him blankly. Her ire from a few minutes ago seemed to have dissipated.

They were on a small road on the way to their hotel. He'd realized this after actually walking through a bit, but it seemed the roads in this town were for the most part separated into two sizes: extremely narrow or extremely large. They'd leave streets so small that cars would have trouble using them only to find much bigger roads, wide enough to be a town square, waiting for them.

Kamijou and Index were walking down one of the larger ones right now. It was big enough for a six-lane road, but there were no white lines on the ground. No distinction between where cars went and where pedestrians went, either, and people were walking all over the street. It was a lot like a pedestrian paradise in Japan. Though nearly every single person was a westerner, like in the movies.

Buildings of brownish red and yellow lined either side of the street. The ones that were around three to five stories tall looked like cafés and eateries, with tent-shaped sheets to block sunlight hung from the shops' second-floor portions, going all the way across the widths of the buildings and perfectly covering the entire open café spaces. All the places next to the road were using parasols and other things to block the sun, so each side of the road was like a shopping arcade made of fabric.

This was the part of the city where all the restaurants were.

There was a simple reason behind Index's improving mood: There was plenty of food nearby.

Simple was really the only thing to call the girl's reaction. Kamijou sighed. "We'll eat after we drop off our things at the hotel, all right?"

"Y-you didn't have to remind me! I already know!!" she shouted, flustered, her face growing red. Kamijou couldn't tell if she really understood or not—as soon as the words left her mouth, her eyes were already on several other storefronts.

"Right…You know, I like eating as much as the next guy, but we should think about seeing places we can only find here, too. For example, uhh, the church of whatever! I want to go there! Take a look at the pamphlet—I have no idea what it's for or anything, but isn't it cool?!"

"Touma, that's called Saint Mark's Basilica, built to preserve the remains of Saint Mark, Venice's patron saint. And the center of sorcery in the City of Water."

"Enough annoying explanations! I want to go there so badly it's killing me!!"

"Ooof! My kindness just bounces off you!"

"After we check in to the hotel, I'm gonna grab that stupid tour guide and we're going to Venice! Hooray for gondolas!!"

"Listen, Touma! Food isn't the only thing on my mind, either!!

…Wow, this isn't working! Touma, are you so enthralled by the Italian air that you're not listening?!"

Index waved her arms around as she spoke, but Kamijou didn't respond to her. He was a Japanese-made high school kid. All he could imagine in Italy was pizza, soccer, and combat nuns. Now all of a sudden he was actually there, in a place like in the movies. He was overwhelmed with excitement.

Just being surrounded by all the people clamoring and calling things out in Italian that he couldn't understand the meaning of—like "Quanto?" and "Posso fare lo sconto del dieci per cento"—was enough to make his vacationer senses explode.

"Vuoi?"

"Wow! I…I think that might be actual squid-ink gelato…?"

"Sto solo guardando. Grazie."

Wait, did I just hear Japanese in there? wondered Kamijou. But no, it had to have been his imagination. As he rolled their suitcase along behind him, Kamijou turned around to look at Index. "I know, Index. After we eat lunch, I was thinking…"

He paused midsentence.

All the way here in Italy, Touma Kamijou remembered the Japanese word for *speechless.*

There was a simple reason, really.

Index had been right there three seconds ago, and now she was nowhere in sight.

"Wait, you're lost in Italy already?! I guess that thing I heard about gelato was really Index!"

Kamijou looked around in blank amazement, but he couldn't spot her ridiculously ornate habit anywhere.

"Damn. Is she in the crowd? Did she go down a small street? I have no idea where the hungry sister has gone! Shit, food really *is* all you think about, isn't it?!"

No voice answered Kamijou's wail. No matter where he looked, he was completely unable to find Index. Kamijou was the one with the wallet, though, so there were only so many things Index could do off on her own. She would come back naturally even if he didn't follow her, but…For some reason, he had this feeling that if he didn't drag Index back by the nape of her neck, he'd be flung into even deeper trouble.

"Heeeey! Index!"

First Kamijou took a look around, then he carefully stepped onto a smaller street that branched off from the main one. He walked down it, gazing to and fro, and then lost track of where *he* was. He hastily ran farther down the path, and even though he thought he was running *into* it, he ended up right back on the same road as before.

He stood there, befuddled, time passing by.

"Wait, now I'm getting lost…?!"

Kamijou broke into a fairly cold sweat and then stopped for a moment.

M-my last resort is my cell phone!

But.

Once again and as usual, Index's zero-yen cell phone was powered off. (He'd turned it off before getting on the plane, and it was probably still like that.) At hearing the regular, synthesized voice—not in Italian, of course, but in Japanese—announcing that the number he called was unavailable, he forgot to put away his phone and instead literally crumpled to the ground in front of the suitcase, still clutching the handle.

Touma Kamijou's state of mind could be summed up in one phrase.

"Now what do I doooo?!"

The people walking by turned around at his shout, but Kamijou didn't have the time to even see that. Then, as he sat on the ground with his forehead pressed up against the suitcase, a woman who seemed to be a local approached him.

She smiled in a way that imparted a somehow *stirring* feeling, as though she worked with her hands for a living, and asked, "C'è qualcosa che non va?"

"Huh?"

The woman was only asking him if something was wrong, but Kamijou had no way of knowing that. Meanwhile, the woman, not particularly offended, spoke again, this time slowly and pronouncing each word separately. "Non puoi parlare l'italiano? La c'è un ristorante dove un giapponese fa il capo."

She had just asked if he didn't speak Italian and then suggested a Japanese restaurant nearby whose manager was also Japanese. Kamijou didn't have any clues to interpret her meaning, though. But just from her tone of voice and facial expression, he got the feeling she was friendly toward him.

I...I don't understand Italian, but if I let this chance go, I think I might really end up all alone in the world! Okay, so...I probably can't speak Japanese to her, but maybe I can at least get her to speak in English. But I can't even begin to imagine how to ask someone to please talk in English, in Italian! If I knew that, I wouldn't be worried about people speaking Italian at all!!

Kamijou was caught in a grand dilemma. If the woman could actually communicate in English, he could just say one or two words, like *please English*, and she'd probably understand. But Kamijou was so unfamiliar with foreign languages that his mind wasn't able to come up with such a roundabout path. Finally, as his brain started to overheat and he began to grow dizzy...

"Senta!"

...a female voice suddenly broke in from beside him.

"Lui è un mio amico. Ringraziate per la sua gentilezza."

At the smoothly spoken words, the woman made a surprised look. Then she said, "Prego!" in a cheerful tone, turning her back on Kamijou just like that and vanishing into the crowd.

Meanwhile, Kamijou, left behind, couldn't figure out what had just happened. "Gah! She suddenly gave up on me? Why you...I was all set for a dramatic two-hour-long tirade of sweat and tears, having created nonverbal camaraderie with that woman, all in order to reunite with Index!! Just who's the person who interrupted us, anyway?! I don't care if I am speaking Japanese and you don't understand! I'll make as many quips as I want!!"

He shouted in spite of himself.

The world's so big nobody's going to hear me shout, anyway, Kamijou despaired, mind half taken up by timidity and cowardice. However...

"Oh my. I appear to have done something inexcusable. You looked to me as though you were being troubled by the language."

Suddenly, he recognized that familiar way of speaking. It was Japanese, of course, but he knew this feminine voice from somewhere.

"You're..." He turned around. With the eight-hour time difference between here and Academy City, the one he bumped into all the way in faraway Chioggia was...

"By the way, earlier I told her that you were my friend and thanked her for her kindness...Perhaps it was somewhat presumptuous of me to refer to you in such a way."

"Orsola! What are you doing here?!" shouted Kamijou.

Even now, the mellow sister in the black habit was smiling.

4

Orsola Aquinas.

Formerly a Roman Orthodox sister, now an English Puritan after an occupation change. She had deciphered a grimoire called the *Book of the Law,* and she directly opposed the Roman Orthodox Church that had tried to stop her. The incident was already resolved, and she should have been relaxing in her new home in London right now.

Just like the previous time he'd seen her, all her skin from her head to her toes was hidden behind a habit. She wore white gloves, too, and her hair was completely covered by a wimple. The only skin visible was on her face. Inversely proportionate to her skin exposure was her feminine body; her plain habit actually brought out her curves, giving the sister sex appeal.

She spoke. "I might ask you the same thing. What are you doing here? If I recall correctly, you live in Academy City, Japan, correct?"

"Uh, I won a couple of vacation tickets. What about you?"

"My residence has been here until just yesterday, in fact."

"Wait a minute. Orsola, you should be living in London. You were there when you passed along info from the British Library during the Daihasei Festival."

"Yes, and I have been hurrying around moving from the Roman Orthodox Church to the English Puritan Church. I still had things left over here. Today I returned in order to have my household possessions sent to London."

"This is where you used to live?" asked Kamijou.

Orsola answered with a simple "yes." She did so in a casual way, but the fact that Kamijou was able to have a relaxed conversation with someone in this situation threatened to open his tear ducts a little. *I don't care if this is a coincidence or what! I'm saved!* he thought, mentally putting his hands together in a gesture of appreciation.

"Oh. Huh. I see you're still wearing the same habit as always even though you're transferring to English Puritanism. Won't the people from Necessarius get mad?"

"Yes, well. Despite my saying I would send the household goods there, I won't be carrying them. I hear I will be fortunate enough to have everyone from Amakusa help me as movers."

"Eh?! Oh, wait, you went back to the earlier topic?! Wait, so you mean *the* Amakusa Church? That's where that Tatemiya guy was, right? What's he doing these days?"

"In regards to my clothing, it is perfectly fine. The English Puritan Church is quite proactive in its integration of many different techniques and cultures as a means of combating sorcery. For the time being, I am the Roman Orthodox of the English Puritan Church. They did the same for those in Amakusa by allowing them to retain their identities within the Amakusa framework."

"And now you're talking about the habit!! You're not even completely ignoring what I'm saying, either, since you still mentioned Amakusa! I have to say the rhythm of this conversation is really hard for me to figure out!!"

Her way of conversing wasn't random; she seemed to be simply speaking in her own unique mental order of things. But that made it pretty hard for others to talk with her.

Meanwhile, Orsola hadn't noticed at all and simply tilted her head cutely. "By the way, are you out shopping?"

"Well, that…I got here fine with Index, but now she's disappeared somewhere, her head full of Italian gelatos! What should I do, Orsola? Do you think if I hung some ice cream on the end of a fishing line, she'd bite?! Keep in mind—for me, fifty-fifty odds are a good deal!"

"Now, now. Please regain your composure. I understand that you and Miss Index have come here on a vacation, correct? Not as any particular messengers for Academy City?"

"You're…Actually, you're on the same topic now. But I think halfway around the world is a little far to send someone to deliver a message."

"Whichever the case, you have a little bit of free time, do you not? Meeting you here must have been destiny. You came at the perfect time. To tell you the truth, we were short on people to help pack things up for moving. If you are bored and have nothing to do, I will make you some lunch in exchange for your help."

"Nope, not on track anymore! We came here to have fun on a vacation, and now it's being canceled for someone else's convenience?! B-besides, we were going to go sightseeing after this, and there are plenty of restaurants around, so you don't need to go through the trouble of making us food."

He thought he'd given a normal reply, but Orsola looked at him again, this time dubiously. Not at his face, really—his *clothes* were what she was staring at. She looked at his wallet chain and the suitcase in his hand.

"Oh my. Just so I'm certain, you are going to do so…like that?"

"You have no right to be telling me how to dress!!" he shouted. Though the summertime, and the heat waves that came at the end of the season, had passed, the weather was still just hot enough for him to have to think about whether to wear short sleeves or not. But this was coming from a nun dressed from top to bottom in a black habit.

But Orsola looked at him like that was a silly thing to say. "Unlike in Japan, there are many nuns in this area."

"A normal answer? From Orsola?!"

"More importantly," she continued, not noting Kamijou's surprise, holding out her index finger and pointing at one thing at a time. "Carrying a brand-new suitcase for luggage, holding a travel pamphlet in one hand, and in possession of a cell phone with a camera...Well. It is quite like you are saying this to swindlers and con artists: 'Hello, welcome. Would you like my wallet? Or perhaps my passport?'"

"Urgh!" Kamijou hastily closed the cell phone and put away the pamphlet. "I-it's kind of surprising to hear words like *swindler* and *con artist* coming out of your mouth, Orsola."

Orsola gave a sigh. "This is still a smaller city, so it's not a significant issue. On a global scale, however, large Italian cities are some of the most unforgiving to travelers. Eateries are much the same. Landmark cities are ripe with tourist traps. They could easily make you pay ten times the sticker price. If you make judgments based only on if an establishment is on a main road or if there is a greeting in Japanese written on the signboard, you will not have a good time traveling."

"Wahhh! This is your home, so now I'm scared!! Then what should I do?!"

"Why not come to the conclusion that my offering of food would keep stores from tricking you? I can teach you how to differentiate between those kinds of establishments as well. Come now, why stand here talking? You would need a place to meet with the forbidden index nun again, wouldn't you? Still, Chioggia's inner area is small: only thirteen hundred meters one way and four hundred meters the other way. It isn't an issue you need to think about so seriously."

Kamijou found himself convinced by her fluid, unhesitant words. Of course—he was in Italy, so relying on an Italian would be best. It was pretty much the most basic lesson of all. But then he thought of something. "Still, I'd like to focus on sightseeing..."

"No, no! Miss Index looks perfectly entertained at that gelato shop."

....*What?*

"Wait, Orsola. Did we skip part of this conversation?"

"I know. If you are here for sightseeing, then why not visit a normal person's house in Chioggia? You can go to all the famous beautiful sightseeing spots you want as long as you have the money, but on the other hand, seeing the natural atmosphere the inhabitants are immersed in isn't something you can find simply following after a tour guide."

"Wait! Don't go back to the topic *now*! I admit you have a point, but you just said something about Index...!"

"My word! You already understand without needing to ask. You lucky dog!"

"Ack! Did you jump ahead or back?! I can't tell!!" shouted Kamijou in spite of himself.

Orsola just continued to smile warmly. "If you're looking for Miss Index, I saw her a few moments ago with her face pressed against a gelato shop window."

"I would have really appreciated it if you'd told me that right off the bat!!...But then where's Index right now?"

"Like I said, I can tell you how to read the bus stop..."

"Bringing this back around right now—where's Index?!"

"What?" said Orsola, tilting her head in mild confusion. "Oh yes. That's right. I asked a friend of mine earlier to show Miss Index to my house."

"That little...She left me behind?!"

"When my friend spoke of lunch, she seemed to follow her quite happily."

"Damn iiiiiiiit!!"

I forget! Who was that nun again, who'd said I could rely on her in Italy?! Kamijou slumped to the ground.

"Nooo...*Sniff*...Orsola, what do you think I should do? I'm always the one getting bitten, every single time...but today, for once, it's my turn. Just you wait, Index!!"

Gnash!! He bit the suitcase handle.

"Now, now," said Orsola, beaming. "Would she not defeat you in the process?"

"Urgh?!" The strike brought Kamijou back to himself.

Orsola continued to smile broadly, her face full of happiness. "Whatever the case, if you'd like to meet Miss Index, coming to my house would be the fastest way. It would be bothersome for me to explain the rest, so in conclusion, you should kindly come with me."

Now that she'd said it directly, he felt like she was right: Going to her house would be the shortest route. Besides, if he refused, he'd just be alone again when he didn't need to be. "…I feel like my rotten luck is coming on again…"

"Now, now. Vacations overseas never do go as planned."

Whether that was life advice or an offhanded comment was unclear to Kamijou, but he nodded at Orsola. Thinking about it again, he felt like vacations were fun for that reason.

Though as an amnesiac, he'd never experienced going outside Academy City in the first place.

INTERLUDE ONE

A cart had stopped on the stone road.

Not a horse-drawn cart, though. Two donkeys were pulling it—sad creatures, once called fools' transportation.

The cart was mostly toned red, with golden decoration. A license plate was affixed to it, and various modifications were visible—its size, some of the finer details—that would allow it to travel on public roads. It wasn't very unusual to see carts like these for tourists. Just like the gondolas of Venice, if the visitors demanded them, there was business to be done, no matter how many hundreds of years old the vehicles were.

However...

The cart had stopped in the road horizontally, unlike the rest of the traffic. It looked as though it had slipped across the road, but it hadn't. Of the cart's four wheels, the front right one had come off and was lying on the ground. It was clearly unnatural. Someone had taken it apart on purpose.

Bam!! came the sound of a blunt strike.

A young man's shriek followed, but another violent noise appeared to cut him off.

Next, a tall nun came out of the shadows of the cart, shouting, "Urgh...You don't know when to give up!!"

Sister Lucia. A combat sister who used cart wheels as weapons, derived from St. Catherine's Legend of the Wheel. Her hands, tight and lean rather than femininely soft, were stained red.

Blood splattered.

Lucia's habit was mostly black, the sleeves and skirt of which could be removed via zippers. Right now, though, the skirt and sleeves she wore were yellow. This was not an approved color for nuns. The pieces were part of a Soul Arm called the Fetters of Forbidden Colors, which *converted her habit into a straitjacket.*

When the person wearing the Fetters tempered mana from their life force, the Soul Arm would instead use it for itself. Its only effect was to make the clothing light up; if an especially strong effect had been incorporated, the wearer might have been able to use that ability against the Fetters. This way, the mana would all go to waste, so no matter how much the wearer tempered, in the end they wouldn't be able to cast any magic.

But at the moment, the important parts of the Fetters of Forbidden Colors were dyed crimson, which was temporarily suppressing the mechanism of the incarcerating Soul Arm. Of course, it was her own blood doing the job.

"Sister Angeline! Are you quite finished?!"

She heard the voice of a young girl. "I—I think it'll be done soon, ma'am..."

Lucia took a look inside the cart. It was unbelievably filthy considering its extravagant exterior construction; it was dingy inside, and stains of an unknown nature covered the walls and ceiling. Within this dismal interior, a girl as short as her voice implied was struggling frantically at her work.

Compared to Lucia's habit sleeves, which were rather short, you could barely see Angeline's fingers under hers. Lucia wondered briefly to herself if they were still easy enough for her to do her work in.

"...I did it! I—I undid the surgical lock, ma'am. We can take out the contents!"

There was a soft, metallic *click*.

The small girl called Angeline removed a rectangular metal box attached directly to the inner wall of the cart. Inside were magical weapons meant to discourage escapees. Normally they were sealed so that only specific escorts could use them, but Angeline had forced it open.

"Good." Lucia nodded.

A glance outside the cart revealed that they appeared to be in a tourist destination. She could faintly make out emphatic calling and shouting echoing over to them. There was a uniqueness to the way the words, drifting to them on the salty breeze, were pronounced. Italian didn't have a sound for "th," but it was still mixed in. On the other hand, basic Italian phonemes like "gli" or "sci" were absent. She also heard words with "z" being pronounced like "s."

"The way they speak…We must be near the Laguna…but still quite far from the main island."

Carrying the long, thin metal box with both hands, Angeline said, "Which means…W-we really *were* about to be taken back to the *Queen*, weren't we, Sister Lucia? The *Queen*…What do they want to do with something so excessive?"

"We escaped to find the reason, Sister Angeline. Also, I'm worried about Sister Agnes. I'm uneasy with what she was left with to defend herself. First, we should go into hiding and ready our Soul Arms."

"Yes, ma'am," said Angeline, nodding a little.

After seeing the smaller sister alight from the cart, Lucia grabbed its loose wheel and picked it up. Her weapon was a technique based on legends from St. Catherine that exploded wheels and then re-created them.

The two sisters, respective weapons in hand, ran down the road without a peep. The bright yellow fabric on their sleeves and skirts fluttered in the wind, coordinating poorly with their black habits. One would think the bee-like warning colors would draw attention, but they blended into the scenery anyway, ignoring the handicap.

I will not accept this, thought Lucia as she ran. *Watching Sister Agnes offer her pure prayers gives even* me *chills. The Lord judging her a sinner? The Church discarding her like a mere tool? No, I am a follower of the Roman Orthodox Church—and that is why I will never accept such behavior.*

Her gaze had been lowering to her feet, but she straightened it, bringing her face up again and keeping her eyes forward as she ran, her entirely makeshift, unreliable weapon in hand.

Her resolve was firm.

But their attention was directed inward—and because of that, they lost track of what was happening outside.

Snap!! came an earsplitting sound.

"Ugh…?!"

Suddenly, as though she'd been stricken in the chest, all the oxygen was driven from Lucia's lungs. The foot about to take the next step drained of strength. Then she lost feeling in the fingers holding the wheel, and she let go. The cart wheel, her only weapon, now rolled lazily away and fell over with a *fwump.*

This feeling of pressure…Some kind of Soul Arm?! she guessed, but she couldn't draw in enough oxygen to say it aloud.

Unable to break her fall, her body fell limp onto the dusty stone path. Her soft cheeks hit the coating of dust on the ground. Next to her, Angeline had just suffered the same attack, and she'd already lost consciousness—not from the lack of oxygen but more likely from the initial impact.

As Lucia's vision grew hazy, she saw something glitter. She rallied all her strength to turn her head and saw a red light shining on the cart's ceiling.

The cart and our habits' Fetters of Forbidden Colors activated in sequence…A spell to prevent our escape? It probably triggers if we get a certain distance away from the cart or a certain amount of time after the cart is immobilized…

She coughed. There was no oxygen in the breath, just a useless bubble of carbon dioxide.

…Not…here…

She saw a new cart approaching them in her sideways view of the world. It was too quick a response to their Soul Arms activating. An emergency signal had probably been transmitted elsewhere before they took down the cart driver and their escort.

She wanted to counterattack, but her fingers would no longer move. She couldn't focus her mind enough to use sorcery. The wheel was on the ground, right beside her. She could reach out and make it her weapon.

But now, without any way to resist, as her consciousness blinked away, she thought of one thing.

The name of one person.

Sis...ter...Agnes...

A moment later, she blacked out completely.

Then a hand grabbed her habit collar and threw her in the back of the cart like a cloth bag.

CHAPTER 2

Preparations for London

Un_Frammento_di_un_Piano.

1

The house Orsola had been living in was right down a small road that turned off of a larger one. Just nearby flowed a seawater canal, and the water's smell drifted toward her home. Small shells hugged the stone street.

She must have been renting a single apartment, as she stopped in front of a rectangular building with five floors. It had not been constructed recently; it had no auto-locking doors or heated floors. Instead, the walls were made of brick, painted light beige. It had character, sort of like a historical building. Only the television antenna sticking up off the roof spoiled the impression.

"All the buildings here look like this, huh? Like, old-fashioned or whatever."

"They're not old-fashioned, actually—they are simply old. Personally, I found myself overwhelmed by Japan's cities and all their shiny buildings. Treating places not even twenty years old as run-down... In my opinion, time in that country seems to go a little bit too fast."

"Did your ancestors all live here, too?"

"No, not at all. I simply happened to be assigned here, so I was just renting an apartment."

"Pretty much the same as me and my dorm, huh? Oh, another

thing—why are all the buildings these different bright colors, like blue and yellow?"

"This is a town on the ocean, so I believe the reason for the distinctive colors is to let one spot one's own house even from a boat far away. Of course, nowadays, whether the building is on the water doesn't have very much to do with it."

Apparently the town needed such identifiable coloring because people launched boats directly from their own homes, rather than having all the boats gathered at one large port.

Orsola guided Kamijou into the apartment complex. She lived on the fourth floor—but of course, there were no elevators. Climbing the metal stairs for a while with a heavy suitcase was a little demanding.

"Here we are," said Orsola.

Kamijou looked and saw her standing next to one of the many doors in the hallway. It, too, was an old-fashioned wooden door, but the lock on it was unnaturally shiny, as though it had been replaced recently.

Orsola rummaged in her habit sleeve and retrieved a key. Before she could put it in, though, the door opened on its own.

Four people came out, all of Asian descent—well, actually, they were the sort of young Japanese men and women Kamijou was accustomed to seeing. They wore similar clothing, but there were subtle differences in color composition and the way they wore them. He was the one standing out here; their clothing matched exactly what the people in this town wore, but he had the strange wallet chain from his belt to his pocket and his hidden spare wallet on his calf. Orsola must have originally been tasked with some shopping, as with a smile, she handed them a paper bag the color of French bread containing a smattering of daily necessities.

They began to greet the two of them, but before Kamijou could return the favor in his haste…

"Ah! It's Touma! Touma, Touma!" came a familiar female voice from the back of the apartment. It was followed by approaching footsteps not very suited to indoors, sounding as though she were still at the Daihasei Festival.

Pushing through the small crowd of young men and women to reach the front door was Index. She had ice cream in her arms. Yes, both arms—four or five square cases of it, cradled like a stack of comic magazines. She stuck a professional ice-cream scoop into a mountain of vanilla and said, "Touma, the gelato here is all so delicious, but it's really, really cheap on sale! Yum!!"

"You little...I was worried about you, and now I see you stuffing your happy, sticky little face with ice cream! No, we'll leave the fact that you left me behind for later. You can't just come into someone else's house and eat all the dessert you want!!"

"Huh? But they said they wanted me to help clean out the freezer, since they're moving."

As he watched Index's beaming smile, Kamijou's face started to break down, like he was on the verge of tears. "Damn, that actually makes sense...But I'm still not satisfied that you're the only one who looks ungrateful about it!!"

All Kamijou could do now was stamp his feet in frustration as Index dug into the ice cream with her scoop. Orsola smiled sympathetically at him, while the four young men and women stared at him, not saying much at all.

Were they the ones who brought her here? Is there a Japanese part of town somewhere nearby? "Oh, wait—you said the friends who came to help you out were from Amakusa, didn't you?"

The Amakusa-Style Crossist Church: originally a sect of Crossism taught in Japan but currently an organization the English Puritan Church had taken under its wing, just like Orsola. *I see...They did seem to specialize in keeping up with the times and blending in,* he remembered, impressed. He could tell with one look at their clothing.

Or so he thought.

He listened a little more closely and heard them talking in hushed tones in a way that *didn't* match their surroundings.

"...So that's the gentleman our vicar pope yielded the palm to... But how strong is he really...?"

"You doubt because you weren't part of the mission to rescue Orsola..."

"…This gentleman is the one who declared war, by himself without a single weapon, against two hundred and fifty of the Roman Orthodox Church's proud combat sisters…"

"Also, I just received this info from the vicar pope, but he stood up to our priestess with the Seven Heavens Sword in Academy City with his bare hand, punched her in the face, and flung her to the ground…"

The Amakusa members' conversation stopped abruptly.

The young man who had first begun to speak turned his head slowly toward Kamijou. "…A monster?"

"Hey! The first thing you think of after seeing me is that kind of twisted evaluation?!" asked Kamijou, the edges of his lips quivering. The Amakusa group members paled and retreated farther into the apartment.

Actually, he had lost his memories, so he didn't know what they were talking about when they mentioned Kanzaki. And he was afraid he'd reveal his amnesia if he carelessly asked about it. *What were you doing punching a girl in the face, Touma Kamijou?!* he asked himself, filled with trepidation.

Orsola sighed and turned back to Kamijou. "…Please, you mustn't scare them too much."

So she said, but from the door, he could hear them say, "Also, I heard he saw the priestess's naked body around the end of summer, and after she slammed him with the Seven Heavens Sword's sheath, he didn't even need to be bandaged up!" and "What?! Against a saint appointed by the Lord?! How much training has that gentleman been through?!" They sounded brimming with curiosity more than anything else. Were they actually scared at all?

"I just want to sit on the floor and do nothing…"

"I would rather you not suddenly grow exhausted, so please come inside soon."

Orsola had the door open and was gesturing him inside, so Kamijou and Index moved past her and into the apartment.

The place she was renting wasn't a single room like Kamijou's dorm; there were several rooms made for a family to live in. Most of Academy City's residences were student dormitories made for one or two people each, so this kind of place was fresh and new for Kamijou.

"Wow, must be nice to have such a big apartment…Wait, you even have a second floor?!"

Orsola chuckled. "That goes to an attic. I suppose it is rather like floor four and a half. We only use it to store cheese; there isn't enough space to stand up without bumping your head." This all appeared to surprise Kamijou, so she smiled a little. "In any case, I will first go and prepare some food," she said as they went into the living room, one of the several rooms in the apartment.

Index's eyes glittered, but Kamijou frowned just a bit. "Wait, you were going to treat us to lunch to thank us for helping with your move, right? We haven't done anything yet."

"Now, now."

"What kind of response is that?!" shouted Kamijou instantly, but Orsola was already diverting the conversation.

"First I must be a good hostess to the two of you. Besides, it will be time for dinner when we finish all the work, so if we pack everything into moving boxes now, we won't be able to get the cooking tools back out. We would have to wash them in the sink again, too."

Oh, okay, thought Kamijou in understanding. He looked around again. Folded cardboard boxes were piled on one side of the living room. The helpers from Amakusa were probably leaving Orsola in charge of deciding which things she would get rid of now and which she would take with her to London. She was right; if they let the chance go, they probably wouldn't have easy access to all the household goods later.

2

After Kamijou spent a while staring at the strangely shaped Italian power outlets and Index spent a while pressing each button on the TV remote control in order, Orsola came out of the kitchen with a tray in both hands, stacked with dishes and eating utensils.

The main course was pasta with Manila clams, with cold soup containing crabmeat and a plate that had only some kind of gooey, jet-black squid ink on it. Orsola explained that you kneaded corn-meal into soup to create something called polenta, and then dipped the result into the squid ink and ate it directly.

As Kamijou took a seat, the Amakusa girl who had carried the plates with lunch on them into the room with Orsola held out a moist white towel, asking, "Would you like one?"

"Oh, thanks." Kamijou bowed his head and took it. The girl said, "Not at all" and hurried back out of the room. He noted that her eye-lids stood out; they had epicanthic folds. On the other side, he heard more voices. "Itsuwa, how did the towel mission go?!" "Idiot. It's too soon to expect results. You have to keep removing the obstacles between you." "Don't you think this is a little roundabout?"

Kamijou wondered what they were talking about. Weren't they going to eat with them? He asked after the four young men and women who weren't coming to the table. "Umm, what about the people from Amakusa?"

"I believe they said they're currently training, and said their bod-ies would grow dull unless they used specific ways of eating specific ingredients..."

"After all, Amakusa uses the trace religious ceremonies present in daily activities like eating, sleeping, bathing, and walking. I think depending on the case, they may only be able to eat certain things," Index put in.

"Well. They do seem quite picky."

After Orsola arrived at *that* slightly off-kilter conclusion, she urged them to eat. Kamijou and Index thanked her for the food.

"Whoa! What is this? I never knew pasta could taste so good!"

"Yep! This might be five hundred times better than the kind Touma makes all the time!"

"You don't have any right to say that when you don't help me cook! But it's so good I don't care! Mmm!!"

Orsola smiled drily at the evaluation of her cooking and the subtle hostility mixed in. "I simply threw together whatever I happened to have on hand."

"You can just *throw together* something like this...? I was planning on going around to a bunch of stores with my guidebook, but now it feels like I already accomplished what I wanted to do."

"...Touma, I think I already made the biggest, most important memory of this vacation."

The two tourists were already satisfied, not even sparing a glance for the floating World Heritage Site twenty kilometers away. Even Orsola, the subject of all the praise, found herself in a supporting role. "B-by the way...Am I correct in assuming your goal in coming to Italy was not here but Venice?"

"It was supposed to be. That's what the vacation plan said, but I can't get in touch with the local tour guide. We still have a hotel to check in to, but then I don't know what we'll do. Venice is the most worthwhile spot for a trip, isn't it?"

"Go to Venice to look, and go to Chioggia to live—or so they say. You can't use a car in Venice, and there are issues with moisture, mold, and chills...Most importantly, the monthly rent there is many times higher than it is here."

Orsola spoke fluidly, with no particular hesitation.

"But even with the disadvantages, it *is* worth seeing. After all, it is the City of Water, the Queen of the Adriatic, the Bride of the Adriatic...It's such a pretty place that it has all kinds of names extolling its virtues."

"I guess there's a whole Adriatic series of names, huh?" Kamijou dipped the polenta, which was the color of a cheese block, into the black squid ink and brought it to his mouth. The squid ink looked thick, but it had a light, plain taste.

"Well, originally, the militaristic maritime nation of Venice controlled the Adriatic Sea, so it was appropriate for them to receive such treatment. Once a year they would have a national ceremony called the Marriage of the Sea. The doge—the head of state—would throw a golden ring into the Adriatic as a wedding ceremony to bind

Venice and the Adriatic Sea. That is how close and important the sea was at the time."

"Huh? Venice was its own country once?" he asked.

After scooping up some of the cold soup containing crabmeat, Index answered. "Touma. What we think of as Italy only came about in modern times. Until then, the vast lands of the Italian Peninsula were divided into a bunch of smaller city-states. Kind of like how the Sengoku era was in Japan, I think."

"..."

"What? Why did you get quiet?"

"...No reason. I was just thinking you know a lot of stuff."

"Mgh. Wh-why does it sound like this surprises you?" Index glanced at her soup bowl. He thought he saw her cheeks reddening a little bit, too.

Orsola continued to speak, twirling pasta onto her fork. "Venice was one of the strongest city-states. They despised being ruled by others, so they opposed the pope of Rome and even ended up being excommunicated. That isn't the amazing part, though. It was the fact that the city continued to prosper even though it had been deemed an enemy of the Roman Orthodox Church. It also has a history as a powerful nation. During its height in the fourteenth century, it took over powerful city-states in northern Italy one after another, such as Padua, Mestre, and Vicenza."

"And *here*, too?"

"Yes. Chioggia was once a rival marine city-state to Venice, but after a string of battles, it fell. At the time, there were plenty of other city-states on the water like Venice that got their power from trading in salt and foreign goods, but their numbers fell due to war, politics, disasters, and many other factors. In the end, only Venice was left."

"Huh," said Kamijou as he followed along.

That meant it would have taken only a tiny coincidence in the past and Chioggia would have been the one to leave its name in the annals of world history. Kamijou, who lacked much historical knowledge, found this a little impressive. It was like playing a Three Kingdoms or Sengoku-era video game.

"In any case, if you've come all the way here, I think you should see Venice. For a Crossist disciple such as myself, the city has extremely fascinating styles of architecture, among other things, but even without them, Venice is quite simply beautiful. Chioggia has motor-boats but no gondolas. You can see things there that you can't see here. In all of Italy, Venice is the only city where you can go about your business without needing a car."

"Huh, that sounds interesting! Thanks, Orsola. Anyway, Index, after we get our luggage squared away, do you want to go to Venice?"

"Hmm…This food is all I need. I think I could stay here forever."

"Index, that's a pretty unreasonable request to make of someone moving out tomorrow."

3

"All right, let's get on with the packing."

With that, Kamijou and Index headed for the household supplies' location.

There were several rooms in Orsola's apartment, so everyone went into the same one as her and asked if she wanted to bring each item as they packed them into cardboard boxes. After that was finished, they carried out the larger pieces of furniture, like her bed and shelving, then cleaned the ceiling and walls. Finally, they'd move to the next room; that was how they did the work. Orsola and Ama-kusa had already finished a couple of rooms.

For now, Kamijou and Index decided to clean up the living room first, having finished their lunch. Kamijou wrapped the plates and utensils in newspaper and placed them in cardboard boxes, then brought the table and chairs outside the building. They loaded the things into a truck parked outside the apartment building with a canvas covering the flat-bed. The lady driving it was apparently a member of Amakusa as well.

With this and that, they had been working for about an hour now.

"Wow. Touma, I think my habit's getting kind of dirty," said Index, who had been engaged in close-quarters combat with the dust behind the bookshelves.

Kamijou sighed. "You know, you should have expected to get a little dirty while helping her move."

"Now, now. That certainly is true, but still...," Orsola broke in from the side, mediating.

Kamijou looked over at the sudden voice just in time to see Orsola patting the dust off the chest area of her habit. The action, of course, made various womanly bits start to sway. Kamijou sputtered and whipped his head back around to look away. He wished she wouldn't start talking to him while doing something like that. Index shot him an irritated glare.

Orsola, of course, didn't appear to be bothered by it in the slightest. "You must have spent many long hours on the airplane to get here, right? If you haven't even gone to your hotel yet, it is only natural to worry about such things. If you like, you may take a shower here," she said proudly as a huge ball of dust atop the fluorescent lampshade fell on her head, sticking to her black hood. She smiled. "Come, come, Miss Index. The bathroom is right over here."

"Hey, wait! I think *you're* the dustiest one here right now!!"

"Do you think so?" asked Orsola, cutely tilting her head. The giant, fluffy ball of dust remained on her head as she took Index's shoulders from behind. "In either case, Miss Index may go first. Umm, the dryer is right over here."

"Dryer for what?"

As they left the room talking, Kamijou's shoulders drooped tiredly. "Oh, right. Orsola, where did you keep the newspapers again?"

"They're right over here. Why?" came her voice from outside the room. Then he heard a door slam shut.

...She's so worried about sweat and dust. I guess it's because she's a girl? He felt like Index would bite him if she knew he was thinking about it, but despite his insignificant impressions, he returned to cleaning and tidying the room. He started sealing the packed boxes with packaging tape and carrying them to the front door. There were big, expensive-looking decorative plates on the floor nearby,

so he decided to wrap them in newspaper to help soften any impacts during moving and place them in a box, when...

"What's this?" he said suddenly. He'd run out of spare newspaper.

I don't know how much these plates are worth, but I think it's a lot...Wouldn't want to leave them on the floor and then accidentally step on them.

He stood his mop up against the wall and looked around the room. He thought Orsola had told him the spare newspaper was behind that door over there.

But when he actually went through it, there was a short hallway instead of a room with two white doors of the same design on one side of the wall.

Which one is it? I guess I should just go into the closest one first. And so, without really thinking about it, he put his hand on the doorknob before hearing something from the other side.

"Hmm-hmm-hmm-hmm, hmm-hmm, hmm-hmm-hmm. ♪"

Along with the cheerful humming, he heard a watery sound like rain falling.

*Th-this combination of the voice and the water...*Kamijou stopped dead in his tracks. *Is it the shower...? Ack, that was close! This is what I call the bathroom trap! Man, I was about to fall for it. And get totally beaten up!!*

He breathed a quiet sigh of relief and took his hand off the door-knob. By process of elimination, the other door had to be the one where Orsola kept the newspapers, like she said.

However.

"Hmm-hmm, hmm, hmm, hmm-hmm, hmm. ♪"

I hear a voice from here, too...What the heck? What's going on here?! N-neither bathroom has a plate on the door to tell me...Wait, I wouldn't even know the Italian word for bathroom *if I saw it.*

As one mystery led to another, Kamijou's heart rate actually increased a little because of the innocent humming. But he had to stay calm. He knew one thing for sure: There couldn't be two bath-rooms. Orsola had said the newspapers were here, so one of them

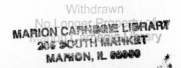

had to be a normal room. And the two doors couldn't possibly lead to the same room.

That meant one thing.

The walls must be thin, which is why I can hear voices from both doors...? One of them is what I want, and one of them isn't. Shit! These are the kinds of choices that could lead straight to a game over!!

He listened closely and carefully to the sounds coming from each door.

Right...No, left? No, this is...It's the left one. I can hear both the shower and the humming from the left one but only humming from the right one! Which means the sound is actually coming from the left one, and the softer sounds of the shower aren't getting all the way to the right-hand door; it's all logical, which means that's why I can only hear humming from the right side!! Everything's fine! Kamijou wouldn't ever encounter so many intimate events!!

"I've got it!!" His ears guiding him, with absolute confidence, he threw open the right-hand door.

In front of him was a steamy bathroom.

"Oh?"

And the one with the startled voice was actually Orsola Aquinas. The shower curtain was open; she was currently reaching for a bottle of shampoo on a shelf. Hot water poured down her large chest, which was usually hidden behind a thick habit, and he saw drops tracing a path to her navel. He saw everything.

"U-ugyaaahh!! This was the bathroom?! There's even a shower here!! Sorry, Orsola, but my ears told me the dangerous one was on the left...!!"

He was so rattled that he unthinkingly forgot to close the door as he fled toward the left door.

And then.

This time, from the left-hand door, he heard the motor of a hair dryer go on.

A moment later...

"Kyaaah?! The weird stick went *vroom*, and hot air came out and attacked me…!!"

The left door slammed wide open from inside, and a naked Index stumbled out. She had a towel in her hand, but it accomplished nothing. She hadn't dried her slightly reddened skin with the towel, either; every time she waved her arms, droplets of hot water flung from her body. Her long hair was still wet, too, and the moisture was clinging to her modest chest.

He looked to see that behind the left door was *also* a bathroom.

Kamijou stood dumbfounded at the sight.

"The right door was a bath *and* the left door was a bath?! That's bull! Hell was waiting for me no matter what I did!! This isn't fair! Why in the world are there even two bathrooms in one apartment?!"

No longer having anywhere to run, Kamijou sank to the floor. Even Orsola was slightly embarrassed by this, as she pulled the translucent vinyl curtain to cover herself and hunched down a little before speaking.

"W-well. There is a story where Saint Barbara once renovated a bathroom into a room for baptism. One is for daily life and the other for religious use. Its baptismal functions aren't active because I'm moving right now, so I was simply using it as a normal shower."

"Another stupid story from the unscientific magical world! I'm so sick of this!!" he shouted, pounding his fist against the floor that didn't belong to him.

Then…

"…Why are you even here in the first place, Touma?"

Index had looked down and sunk to the floor as well, actually wrapping the towel around herself with slow, precise movements.

"Huh?"

"…And why don't you say you're sorry for seeing someone naked?"

"L-look, Miss Index, that's not it! I, Touma Kamijou, had just discovered decorative plates left over in the room from before and was kindly informed that the newspaper for softening impacts during the move was here…Wait, that's right. Orsola, where're the newspapers?!

Don't tell me you store them in the bathroom! That's not usually where they go!!"

"Umm. They aren't in a room but rather on the floor in the hallway."

"Gah…?! Damn it, they really are in the corner over there, all tied into a bundle! Shit! Why didn't you notice them there before, Touma Kamijou?! Then you wouldn't have gotten in so much trouble…"

Kamijou began to whine and complain, and finally, the stark-naked Index's temples twitched.

"I! Said! Why does your brain place such a high priority on people's naked bodies?!"

"Gyaaaaaaaaaaaaaaaaaah! For some reason you're, like, twice the Index you usually are!!"

Touma Kamijou experienced his second instance of skinship through biting in these foreign lands. He could only sincerely hope Orsola wouldn't mistake it as a strange part of Japanese traditional culture.

4

As Kamijou rolled around the floor, clutching his chomped-upon head, and Orsola continued packing up more dinnerware, the sky grew completely dark.

"Once again, thank you very much."

Orsola bowed in gratitude, and the canvas truck rumbled, shook, and drove away. It was shaking pretty hard, and Kamijou worried about the slightly fragile tableware.

In any case, this was the end of the moving job.

There was nobody nearby, though he didn't know if all the streets of Chioggia had emptied out or just this one spot. In the near distance he could hear the household sounds of eating and uproarious laughter.

Orsola picked up her suitcase with the bare minimum that she needed. "Thank you very much for your help, both of you. I apologize for keeping you here so long."

"Nah, it's all right. What are you going to do now, Orsola? We're heading back to the hotel and then going sightseeing. Do you want to come with us?"

"No, I couldn't." It was a casual question, but for some reason, Orsola put a hand to her cheek and flushed slightly, looking away. "Are you asking me to come with you to the hotel now?...They do say three is a crowd."

Kamijou suddenly sputtered and coughed.

Index, though, frowned. "??? What do you mean, three is a crowd?"

"You don't need to ask! And you don't need to know, either, Index!!" Kamijou stopped Orsola just before she was about to politely explain. Index still had a question mark on her face, not understanding.

"I am here on a break from my job in London, so I can't stay for very long. And..."

"And?" asked Kamijou.

Orsola's lips moved very slightly into a smile. "I'd like to go around Chioggia to say good-bye...And I don't want to show that to either of you. I may not be very good to look at."

Oh. Kamijou finally realized it. This was where Orsola's home had been, and now she didn't live here anymore. And she wasn't moving out because she wanted to. If not for the nonsense with that big group called the Roman Orthodox Church, she wouldn't have had to move.

Kamijou had convinced himself he'd saved Orsola after the incident with Agnes. That wasn't strictly mistaken, but it certainly hadn't come without a price. The rescue had been successful only after she'd lost her usual way of life. Still, the compromise was better than it could have been.

"...Sorry for not being considerate, Orsola."

"No, please don't be. It's not as though this is the last time I will ever see Chioggia. Now, now, please don't make a face like that. I am as interested in London as I am Chioggia."

In front of the apartment complex, lit up by light from the moon and stars, it was now Orsola smiling and showing consideration. Index, standing next to him, silently nudged him in the gut with her elbow. She was probably telling him not to go any further. Even Kamijou understood that much, though. He had to.

"Good-bye, then. When I have the opportunity, I will invite you both to my home in London."

"Sure. And if you ever come to Japan again..."

"Touma, I think you'll need to clean your room before thinking about that."

The three of them laughed before beginning to go their separate ways on the dusk-fallen road.

But after just one step...

...suddenly Index's face shot up.

"Wait...*Is this...?!*" she shouted. "Everyone get down!!"

Kamijou and Orsola looked at Index blankly. *Get down? Why?*

Then he heard a metallic sound in the distance. Index's face immediately became serious.

"GTTR!! (Go to the right!!)" She stared almost directly overhead.

Bang.

With a strange sound, Orsola's suitcase went flying away.

"What?" Mystified, Orsola gawked at the hand from which the suitcase had been wrenched. It fluttered through the air and fell to the ground, undoing its metal clasps and opening up like a bivalve mollusk. Combs and tubes of lipstick scattered all over the road. An ironed black hood, probably part of a change of clothes, hung just over the edge of the canal flowing along the road.

Kamijou watched the wide-open suitcase slide across the road.

An unnatural square hole, about one centimeter on each side, had been bored into it.

"Touma, get away from there!!" came Index's strained cry.

If she's the one alarmed...then was that sorcery?

He was about to turn back to her and ask, but he ground to a stop halfway there. Orsola's habit—the surface was slightly sunken in, like it had been compressed with a stamp. The point on the clothing silently moved from her shoulder toward her chest.

Like a laser pointer to help someone aim.

A ranged…"Sniper?! Orsola!!"

Kamijou let go of his own luggage, pushed the idly standing Index to the ground, then rushed toward Orsola's chest. He tackled her down to the road.

There was a soft, metallic *clink*. Then Kamijou felt a pain on his back, going in a line from right to left. Something was scraping against his skin.

Where are they?! Who are they?! And how?!

He endured the stinging pain and looked around. The only things he saw were rectangular buildings around five stories tall and the straight canal. Being the amateur that he was, he couldn't tell whether it was a suitable environment for a marksman. A simple glance around wouldn't let him spot someone with a humongous rifle, either. Whatever it was had probably come from the opposite direction the suitcase flew in, but all he could see that way were building walls. Index *had* seemed to see it coming, but—

"Touma!!"

His thoughts interrupted, as soon as Kamijou directed his attention outward, a cold, wet hand grabbed the back of his neck. He turned around in alarm as an arm reached out from the canal alongside the road. A black arm in a long sleeve. Someone had crawled up from the surface of the canal and now had Kamijou's neck from behind.

"Umph!!" Before he could react, the stranger pulled him with a sharp jerk.

He lost his balance as it tore him off Orsola and into the canal. The cloudy seawater burned his throat. The scrape on his back exploded with pain. His vision was murky due to the light refracting irregularly, but he saw someone trying to climb their way back up to the road as he fell. In their right hand was a shining metal object.

A knife—or a sword.

Shit…Who the hell is that?!

Kamijou stuck out a hand to grab the attacker's leg, but it slid out of reach just before he grabbed it. He paddled, giving himself upward momentum, and then his face burst above the surface.

Because it was high tide, perhaps, there were only a few dozen centimeters from the water's surface to the road. But that small height difference was preventing Kamijou from seeing anything.

"Urgh!" He put both hands on the canal's edge and hauled himself up.

Then he saw Orsola there. She was in an unnatural pose, squatting on one knee. She must have been getting back on her feet after he'd shoved her down. There was more surprise than fear plastered on her face.

And…

Standing directly in front of her was the assailant. A man dressed head to toe in a habit black as night. Like Orsola's, there were zippers on the shoulders to remove the sleeves. Kamijou couldn't see the man's face, since he was turned away, but he saw his distinctive hair—it was dyed purple.

Contrary to his expectations, his soaking-wet hand was holding neither a knife nor a sword. It was a spear. The wooden handle was painted black and only seventy centimeters long, looking like it had been cut short, while the sharp blade measured ten centimeters.

If he stabbed someone with that, they'd die. The man lifted it up with both hands. As though he was about to drive a stake into the ground.

Kamijou had to stop him right this instant, but he had just managed to crawl up from the canal and was still lying on the road. It would take a few seconds for him to get to Orsola and Index, who were meters away. Meanwhile, the assailant raised his lance and then thrust it downward.

"Die, asshole!!"

Kamijou grabbed the hair dryer that had fallen out of Orsola's suitcase and hurled it at the man. It struck the defenseless attacker in the back of the head.

His lance swerved off course, barely scraping by Orsola's face before its tip crashed into the ground.

"!!"

The assailant whipped around. Deciding to get rid of the nuisance before his actual target, he dove for Kamijou. His blade glittered in the night, a strange orange light like the evening sun. It must have been sorcery. Kamijou, still on the ground, tightened his right hand into a fist.

"DTBTTI! (Direct the blade's tip toward itself!)"

A moment after Index's odd-sounding shout, the spear in the man's hands broke apart like a chopped vegetable. The sudden dismantling of his weapon made the man in the habit freeze.

"!!" After getting off the ground, Kamijou dove for the man, his posture low, aiming to come upward into him. He flung his right fist at the man's face. The diagonal impact from below shook the man's head.

"Agh!" he groaned, trying to retreat.

Kamijou hit him again with his fist. With a *bam!!*, the strike, all his weight behind it, plunged into the middle of the man's nose, this time driving him to the ground. He landed on his back and stopped moving.

He had no time to breathe yet.

"Ack! What about the sniper?!"

"It's okay," said Index lightly. "I *already dealt with them.*"

"Dealt with what?!" shot back Kamijou, more confused than before.

A moment later.

"Agagagagagagahh!!"

From somewhere far away, the shout of a large man drifted. Kamijou's ears perked up, and Index's voice began to slide into them.

"If he was aiming at us from a distance, then the enemy knows exactly where we are. No matter where he is, if I use spell interception, it will hit him."

Index seemed to have done *something*, but Kamijou couldn't exactly tell what.

He heard the sole of a foot tapping on the road. He looked over to the street corner and saw a male figure leap out. He was holding his hands to his temples, and he was moving unsteadily, like an explosion had just gone off right next to his ears. It was too dark to make out any of the man's features. He ran—not at Kamijou but straight at the seawater canal.

"Abbandonate l'avanguardia! Ora prendete la barca ritiro! Uccidete quella donna sulla nave!!" *(Abandon the vanguard! Take out the retreat boat now! Kill that woman on the ship!!)*

After shouting something that sounded Italian, he jumped without any hesitation off the edge of the road—the canal—and into the water.

Is that guy running away the sniper from before?! Shit, do I follow him, or would I be going too far?!

As Kamijou wondered what to do, he heard the sound of water churning.

However—

It was an extremely loud roar, far too much to have been a single person diving in.

Crash!! went the water's surface as it parted.

The seawater flew into the air like a waterfall in reverse, and the man landed atop the object that had come out.

"What…?!" Kamijou almost stopped breathing.

A sailboat had emerged from the bottom of the canal. An old-fashioned one with four masts, the sort you could imagine sailing the seas during the Age of Exploration. But it differed from other boats because of its material. The vessels built to cross the oceans in search of new lands were made of wood—but the one that just sprang out was semitransparent and felt *cold.* It looked like it was made out of crystal. Even the sails and the ropes looked the same. It certainly seemed doubtful that it could even function as a boat like that. The lights from the town and the moon illuminated it so that it gave off a faint whitish color like a lightbulb.

But.

The stranger thing was the boat's size.

"Ack!!"

"Touma!!"

The canal was only twenty or thirty meters across. But the boat that came out was so wide that it broke the canal walls on the road on both sides, *then grew even bigger.*

"How the hell did they hide something like this?!"

The motorboats, lined up like bicycles in front of a train station, were smashed and either sank to the bottom of the waterway or crashed into the translucent ship hull and flew into the air. With a punch, Kamijou blocked a boat fragment going for Index's head, but a moment later, a surge of water like a flash flood swept out his feet. It was the same as a child slipping in a bathtub. Kamijou toppled over like a floating washbasin as he slid and fell.

"Ow! What the hell is this?!"

He looked overhead from his new vantage point on the water-soaked ground and saw that the triangular masts already reached forty meters high. And the ship was *still* continuing to come up out of the water.

It was too strange. He'd been pulled into that canal earlier, and it was only three meters deep at most. There was no space under there to hide a boat of this massive size.

Crash!! The ship's hull sprang up yet again.

The ship's deck had been just about at road level before. Now it crashed upward once more. Not a moment later...

"Kyah...!!" Orsola, hanging on to the edge of the boat, was lifted up off the ground as it rose. Kamijou had no time to watch, though, as another shock came from underneath him. Like an uppercut, the edge of the glimmering ship drove up into him.

Roar!! howled the wind.

He experienced a moment of weightlessness; his feet were already off the ground. No sooner did he feel his body sliding than he and the ship were hauled straight up twenty meters.

He wouldn't stand a chance falling from this height. "Urgh!!" His hands flailed, grabbing the edge of the ship. That was his railing now.

The wall of the ship's hull, which had just been under the water, was now a towering cliff over twenty meters tall. It was probably about seven stories high. He could see over all the surrounding apartment buildings now. As he hung there, he looked to the side and saw Orsola hanging on like he was—and the ship's hull, over one hundred meters long, continuing on.

"Orsola! We have to get on the ship!!" *I'd rather not get on something so strange, but it's better than the alternative!!* he told himself bitterly, grabbing the strangely slippery, almost-white construction material and managing to climb up onto the ship's deck.

The ship was enormous.

Over one hundred meters long and just under twenty meters from the deck to the ship's bottom. Everything from the deck to the tops of the masts was made of the same translucent material, giving off a faint whitish glow. Kamijou and Orsola were near the center of the ship, but the front and back led to staircases, with the cabin on the same level. They were essentially in the middle of an earthenware mortar right now.

Three levels above and probably five levels below, making eight stories in all. This ship was bigger than Kamijou's dormitory building. The shores of the canal were cracked open, the seawater pushing up through them into tiny streams, flowing farther and farther out.

"This is insane…How can something like this suddenly pop out of the canal?"

The hull of the ship was also made of the strange translucent material. All the light from the moon refracting every which way inside was giving it the dull white glare.

This…I thought it was glass or crystal, but it's not. It's almost like ice.

Out of all the practical buildings made of ice, the domed igloos built and lived in by the Inuits in Canada were famous—but this was on an entirely different scale.

Kamijou ran his fingers along the deck to check. It certainly looked like ice, but it had none of the chill that lingered on your skin. It was lukewarm, almost like plastic…The rule that water froze at zero degrees Celsius applied only under a certain pressure. Given the correct conditions, the boiling point and freezing point of water could be changed, so there were instances of ice being twenty degrees Celsius and water boiling at eighty.

It must have been created through sorcery.

Despite the ground being ice, his feet didn't slip on it. He'd heard before that people slipped on ice because there was a film of unfrozen water on the top, which reduced friction. Ice with an altered melting point wouldn't melt when touched by human skin, so maybe it couldn't create that watery film. Though it was sorcery, Kamijou's right hand touching it wasn't enough to break it. Maybe it had some kind of trick like Stiyl's Innocentius.

Then, one last time, the boat heaved upward. He felt a shock come from below. Orsola's hands were too slow, and she fell off the edge of the ship.

"Kyaa?!"

"Grab on!!"

He immediately stuck his hand off the deck, managing just barely to catch one of hers. She weighed only as much as a girl might, but supporting that weight with his unstable posture made it feel several times heavier. He broke into a cold sweat but somehow managed to drag Orsola up onto the deck.

She came over the edge and they both toppled down to the ice.

"Touma!! Are you okay?! Touma!!"

He heard a worried shout from Index, far below the cliff-like ship hull.

Kamijou had no time to answer her. *Ga-clunk!* No sooner did the boat shudder than he was thrown back. He coughed as Orsola's body, still on top of him, pressed into his chest.

He took a look around. They were the only two here. The giant ice ship was silent, but it presented one answer to Kamijou.

Is it actually moving forward? You'd think with this thing's size, it would get caught in the canal and stop. Isn't it basically just a beached jellyfish now?!

But contrary to his surprise, the giant sailboat was in fact moving smoothly forward. Like a curling stone sliding across a sheet of ice...And then it hit him. If this glimmering ship was made of ice with an altered melting point, maybe it was able to create a temporary film of water only on the bottom of the hull to reduce friction.

"Are you okay, Orsola?"

"Y-yes...," replied Orsola uneasily, suddenly realizing she was lying on top of him. The usually easygoing lady pulled away with a jerk—and then lost her balance and fell back.

Kamijou himself was a little out of sorts—her womanly scent was now clinging to his sticky, soaked shirt—but now wasn't the time for that.

He grabbed hold of the edge of the ship—a slightly higher wall that acted as a guardrail—and spared a furtive glance below. He shuddered; he was so high it was like leaning over the top of a lighthouse. The ice sailboat was still pushing itself through the canal, widening it and eating through one parked boat after another as it advanced little by little down the stream.

"What the hell is going on?!" he yelled, though it didn't change what he was seeing. Eyes peeled, he looked for something, *anything* that hinted at a way out. "Over twenty meters from here to the ground...And even if I jump into the water, I'll probably still break bones. Wait, since the ship is bigger than the width of the canal, is the bottom of it actually made of stone? Damn, can I only see water from here because the boat is pushing up all the seawater?!"

The seawater appeared to be flowing inside buildings from the cracks under their front doors. He could hear panicked noises coming from some of them—and then they stopped, dumbfounded, as they witnessed what was causing all of it.

"?! No, please, wait!!" cried Orsola, abruptly leaning over the railing. Her eyes opened wide as she stared ahead of them. "Oh no... How terrible..."

"Wh-what is it, Orsola?"

"This boat seems to be forcing its way through the canal in an attempt to escape north out of Chioggia and into the Adriatic."

Before Kamijou could ask what was wrong with that, she continued.

"Please lower yourself. The Vigo Bridge across the canal is coming up! The boat is going to break through the stones and leave!!"

"Are you kidding me?!" Kamijou hastily grabbed Orsola's back as she leaned over the railing.

A moment later, a heavy *wham!!* split through the air.
The boat destroyed the bridge in one hit.

"Urgh?!"

Kamijou's hand slipped away from Orsola's clothing. As he crashed down onto the deck, the impact drove out all his breath.

Gah...! What about...Orsola...?!

He pushed off the deck and unsteadily stood again. Fortunately, Orsola had been knocked toward the inside of the ship and was lying there like Kamijou. Honestly, that was more a relief than anything. If she'd been knocked in the other direction, it would have been a twenty-meter drop.

Damn it...Even against the monumental situation, he forced himself to think. *Some weirdos attacked us. Now I'm on a strange boat made of ice. Index and I have been separated...Seriously, what's going on?*

Orsola looked past the ship's wall, then said in a daze, "It seems... we are leaving land."

"Yeah. Where in the world could this boat be going?" he said with a cough, catching his breath, watching land grow smaller and smaller.

But not even this silence lasted very long.

From far away—but from inside their boat this time—he heard multiple sets of footsteps running around.

"Cerca. Loro devono essere a bordo!" *(Search. They must be on board!)*

It was a large man's shout. Kamijou shivered. He didn't know what the words meant, but he definitely heard the hostility in them.

Orsola lowered her voice. "What should we do? They seem to be looking for us..."

"I know! We can't exactly jump off and escape. We wouldn't be able to tell what direction we were going in with how dark it is."

There was a chilling lack of anything nearby on the sea. *We went that far already?* he thought hopelessly. He got the feeling that the ship had been getting shorter as they made their way farther out to sea. Before, it had been riding on the bottom of the canal, but now it was actually floating along the water. Boats were generally built so that around half their height was underwater. That meant from their point to the surface of the actual sea were about ten meters.

But more importantly, you needed special skills to do long-distance swimming in rough waters with your clothes on. He could struggle all he wanted, but in all probability he'd drown before reaching land.

From what he could tell, this icy boat was modeled after an old-fashioned warship; some dozen or so translucent cannons protruded from the walls of the hull on either side. Without an oxygen tank or a snorkel, he'd have to swim with his head above the water's surface. But those on the ship would spot the irregular ripples in the water and discover him immediately. If those cannons could actually fire, he'd die as soon as they saw him.

He watched as land grew smaller and smaller, but Kamijou and Orsola were unable to disembark.

"Shit...!!"

The clattering footsteps from inside the boat were coming closer. Up here, there were no safe places to run. The light source of the boat itself wasn't very strong. The ice's surface was faintly glimmering; only darkness lurked in the air above.

Weak as it was, however, light *did* radiate from the floor, the walls, and everything else. The silhouettes of Kamijou and Orsola would be clear as day. Blending into the darkness would be difficult.

Perhaps the only good thing about all this was that the boat was large, over one hundred meters long, and seemed to have many obstacles and cabins they could duck into.

"Orsola, we're going inside. They'll find us for sure if we stay here. We should look for an opportunity to hide for now."

"Y-yes! I understand."

Kamijou grabbed Orsola's hand. He ran across the icy ship's deck, crouching.

Their presumably fun-filled vacation to Italy was starting to show unexpected complications.

INTERLUDE TWO

Going back a few weeks before…

The cart's wheels rattled sharply over the slight bumps and dents in the road, causing the cart to shake a bit. Though it rolled along at a relaxed pace, the rocking gave the ride a subtly sharp and angular impression, providing nowhere near enough peace for the passenger to sleep.

Agnes Sanctis sat in the back of the cart. The interior was not covered with a cloth canvas supported by a frame; instead it was a real room with walls made of oak.

Her age was, perhaps, somewhere in the mid-teens. She was somewhat shorter than other girls her age. Her skin color was white, and her eyes were the hue of lemon tea. Her hair, between brown and blond—what most would call red—was parted into several braids, each about the thickness of a pencil.

She wore a jet-black habit and thick-soled sandals thirty centimeters high. Her clothing had been created with highly functional material, but it was almost unnaturally clean at the same time. Normally clothing accumulated wear and tear over time as it was used then cleaned, but there was no trace of that. If there was one thing that stood out about what she wore, it was that.

The small nun looked out the window.

The square window was even smaller than a food tray. And just on the outside there were intersecting pieces of lumber attached like a fence. The window was still closed, but the faint smell of salt still reached her nose. Past the glass that lay between her and outside was a satellite city benefiting from an international tourist attraction. She could see parents and children dragging suitcases along and café shopkeepers calling out to them.

"This your first time here?"

The voice came from the front of the cart—from the coachman's seat. Though Agnes couldn't see him from here, as the oak wall blocked him off.

The somewhat large, middle-aged man's voice was distinctive, and he mixed in French-sounding words with his normal Italian. She idly speculated that he might be from Milan.

"Yes. I haven't had reason to visit. When I'm in the north, it's usually Milan."

While her Japanese was rather rough—she'd had difficulties learning the language—her Italian was quite polite. After she responded to the coachman's words with the same intonation, he immediately softened.

"Oh, that's nice. If I had to choose, I like the inner lands better. It's like, the air there is nicer, you know? Crisper, I guess. Around here you've got a lot of good places to visit, though. This is how I make my living, but the idea of going around to see new places is attractive. I really am glad I work in Italy—everywhere is unique. I'd get bored of what other countries look like."

Agnes smiled weakly, still staring out the window. "There are plenty of nice places even outside the country."

"Really?"

"Yes. I may sound like a fangirl, but you know about World Heritage Sites, right? When you actually go to them, you'll realize why they were worthwhile enough to add to a list like that. The gardens of Fontainebleau are pieces of art of water, green, and relief sculpture created during the Renaissance, and the Cologne Cathedral is a grand gathering of buildings with pointed tops sticking up into the skies. Though in Asia, thoughts of beauty or ugliness were always preceded by a feeling of mystery."

"Is that right?" replied the coachman, not sounding very interested.

The cart proceeded at an unhurried speed. The slowness was likely not only because of the coachman's driving but the fact that the cart was being pulled by donkeys, not horses. They had literally no horsepower.

"People who have been all over the world sure have interesting things to say."

"No, not at all. I feel more like I've mostly focused on Europe."

"For me, there's no *mostly* about it. Never been out of Europe myself. I mean, this is my job and all. Only so far you can really go in a cart."

"Does everyone use airplanes to travel far?"

"Seems like it. But I still think land roads are more reliable. When you get involved with science, I hear you can't prepare spells to prevent people from fleeing…Whoops, this must be hard to talk about right now. Sorry about that."

"No, don't be. I do agree, though, that the airplane did feel quite cramped."

"Really? I knew it. It's like they're trying to just brute force everything into the air with airplanes. I mean, I hear if there's a hole in it, the difference in air pressure will cause the whole thing to fall apart in midair. I know there are different rules when you're really high up, but it's still scary. Balloons, on the other hand, are something I'd enjoy a nice, relaxed trip in."

"Balloons *are* a very similar form of air travel to airplanes."

"Oh, really? Well, either way, that's *their* field, so I guess I won't have much to do with them, anyway. Ah, looks like we're here."

The change in inertia caused Agnes's body to wobble slightly. The donkey-drawn carriage had stopped. Her eyes moved from the window to the double doors in the back of the cart.

As she stared at the still-unopened exit, she said, "So that's where we were going…*La Regina del Mare Adriatico*…and the Queen's Fleet."

Then, as though that were the password, the door unlocked.

CHAPTER 3

On the Ship of the City of Water

Il_Mare_e_la_Sconfitta.

1

Ice on the outside, and ice on the inside.

The hallways, walls, and ceilings were all made of a semitrans-parent ice. Everything was made out of it, even the doorframes, the knobs, and every single screw in every hinge. Some of them didn't even seem like they should actually work. The interior of the ship was ice, through and through, and the walls and floors dimly shone with the same white glow as outside. Was it taking in moonlight and diffusing it everywhere?

The illumination wasn't as strong as an electric light. Despite the clearly visible outlines of the walls and ceiling, the space itself was dim. It resembled a movie theater with the weak light from the screen shining in it.

After Kamijou and Orsola opened the hatch linking the deck to the interior, they dashed into the nearest room. No lookouts had actually been there to stop them—it would all be over the moment they were found, anyway. But even without anyone here, there was this invisible feeling of pressure coming from farther down the hallway. Part of it came from wanting to hide somewhere safe immediately.

As soon as they entered the room, closed the door, and pressed themselves against the inside walls, they heard the hatch outside opening and closing. The sounds of multiple pattering footsteps and indecipherable shouts drifted over. All he could tell was that they were men. And he couldn't understand them, which meant he couldn't understand the present situation—which got on his nerves even more.

"Damn it, what's going on?" he said to himself.

He'd come all the way here because he'd won a vacation trip to Italy. And then some weirdos attacked them, and now they were on some huge stinking boat? He was sick of it.

The room he and Orsola had hidden in appeared to be a room for controlling one of the cannons—the ones lined up all along the walls of the ship's hull. They must have each had a single, small, separate room for it.

They could see inside the cannon from here. Several chairs sat in front of it, with a shelf along the wall and a big barrel in the corner of the room. All of them were made of the same translucent white ice. But on the other hand, that was all. No cannon powder or volleyball-like shots were in that barrel. Was the cannon purely an imitation? Or was it a magical cannon that ignored the laws of nature? Kamijou couldn't tell.

Everything inside the ship, from the interior walls to the furnishings, was giving off a weak light. It all had flat textures, giving the entire setup a smooth, slippery impression. It was a strange space, where there was light everywhere but it would be difficult to read words on a page.

"I am concerned about this ship as well, but why would they need to use something so outrageous to attack us…?" said Orsola uneasily. Her anxiety was understandable—they were out to kill her. She and Kamijou couldn't plan to fight against something they didn't understand.

Suddenly, Kamijou remembered the man who had appeared from the canal with the short spear. "That idiot who attacked us…His clothing was like your habit, but remade for a man to wear."

"Yes. Those were indeed the garments of a male priest. It might be appropriate, then, to assume he was from the Roman Orthodox Church."

"Which means this is all about the *Book of the Law*? I can't think of anything else that would cause us trouble."

"I was under the impression that incident had been settled with my moving to the English Puritan Church…If they buried me in the darkness now, they would be the ones to be incriminated." She paused. "Would they go through the trouble of making a warship out of ice, destroying a canal in Chioggia, and ruining the Vigo Bridge?"

"Yeah, it seems a little theatrical…" Kamijou clutched his head.

All the sorcery-related incidents in Academy City and Japan felt arranged specifically to keep sorcerers out of the public eye. But this ice warship was nothing like that. It didn't hide its appearance, its destruction, or its retreat. Was Chioggia in a state of panic right now? Of course, nobody would believe someone who said a giant ice sailboat appeared in a tiny canal and destroyed part of the city. And even if they did, it wouldn't lead them to realizing the existence of sorcerers…

"Where's this ship headed?"

"If we are moving north out of Chioggia, we are likely headed toward Venice. As long as we don't go south, we will not go to open sea, but…Oh, there's a window over there."

Orsola pointed to an observation hole for aiming the cannon from inside the room. But all they could see out of it was a dark ocean. The flat seas went all the way to the horizon, and after that it was an equally black sky. There were no clues as to their current location.

And then.

Crash!! The water's surface exploded. With a water-splitting roar, like a killer whale breaking the surface, came an icy sailboat of equal size to the one they were on. As they watched, five—no, ten—translucent warships broke through the water's surface. They could see in only one direction from here, but the same thing was probably happening all around them.

The Adriatic, which had been clear to the horizon, was now being covered up with innumerable ships.

The sea surface, which had been naught but dark, was now being dyed in a pale whitish light. The light from this ship wasn't all that

strong on its own, but with so many other ships gathered, it was a different story.

"...I suppose this means this ship was not the enemy's base but merely a single part of it."

"Was the main fleet here all along? Could they just not all deploy near Chioggia because it was too small?" Kamijou gritted his teeth.

They were up to their necks with just one boat, and now there were even more. He felt like the slight hope of escape was quickly vanishing. Maybe he would have to abandon his idea of getting off the ship in the middle of the sea and wait in hiding until they arrived at a port somewhere.

"Jeez. I'm sure Index is fine. Her cell phone...doesn't work. I'd love to praise Academy City for making phones that can survive being dropped into the ocean...but her zero-yen phone is probably still turned off from before we got on the plane. Wait, would the waves even reach out here on the ocean?"

"Well. I believe all my luggage has been perfectly washed away. My suitcase opened up and its contents were strewn about the road, after which this boat forced the canal water up..." Orsola seemed slightly embarrassed about it—she must have had things she needed as a woman in there.

Kamijou sighed, but he was a little impressed at the same time. "...You're pretty tough, thinking ahead to what'll happen after this is over."

"Oh, but squid ink isn't a Venetian specialty but a Chioggian one."

Kamijou completely deflated as Orsola swung the topic in a strange direction without listening to him, but that didn't last too long, either.

Ker-click.
The room's doorknob suddenly turned.

"?!" Kamijou and Orsola, standing near the door, were startled. They quickly turned around. It wasn't only one knob they heard.

Click click click click click!! Several dozen of them went off at once. Had all the doors on this floor—or the entire ship—opened automatically? The noise came at them from the right and stampeded down to the left.

There was nowhere to hide in the room.

And on the other side of the door—in the hallway made of ice with an altered melting point—a person, who had been hastily looking through each room, stopped right in front of Kamijou.

It wasn't a person he could see shouting in such a guttural voice, like the kinds he heard on deck.

Outside the opened door was a sister. Her most unique feature, perhaps, was her red hair, tied into many braids, each about the thickness of a pencil. She was even shorter than Index, with eyes that betrayed a hint of childish mischief. She wore a black habit like Orsola, but it looked more like a dress and exposed a lot of her skin. To top it all off, he saw thirty-centimeter-high sandals on her feet.

"Agnes?!" he shouted in spite of himself.

Agnes Sanctis: a combat sister in charge of an entire unit in the Roman Orthodox Church and the nun who had once attempted to assassinate Orsola Aquinas during the incident involving the *Book of the Law*.

Wait, is this some kind of joke?! What is she even doing here? She already attacked Orsola once. Is she involved in this?! It was so sudden and unexpected that he couldn't find any words to say.

"..." She didn't seem to have thought she'd find Kamijou and Orsola behind the door, either. She stared at the young man's face standing next to her, eyes widening a little bit, and then...

Bam!! She wasted no time hammering her fist into Kamijou's cheek from the side.

"Gah...?!"

His vision swam. Orsola gave a quiet yelp. The strike dizzied him—not out of pain but out of being unable to react to the abruptness of it. Meanwhile, Agnes took another step in and wound up another punch. Kamijou tried to focus on protecting his face, but as if she'd read his thoughts, her small fist swung low diagonally and dug into his side.

Whop!! came a dull noise like a hammer hitting a leather bag.

Kamijou's body made a nasty creaking sound as he doubled over in pain. Then Agnes brought her fist down from above. He collapsed, helpless, to the icy floor as she took a side step to put distance between them. She glanced at Orsola.

"Wait…I would appreciate it if you waited a moment…?!" Orsola put her arms out, frantic. Agnes narrowed her eyes a little but didn't open her fists. Then, as she continued to be cautious, she heard…

"…I'b sowwy I'b so sowwy though honestly my heart skipped a beat because I mean your habit is like I can see your back through it and I can even see a little of your butt and your stomach too your clothes are cut along it like it's reaching arms around you and all I can see is skin and…"

…the usual nonsensical chant-like stream of words coming from the boy's bent form.

In the small room, Agnes placed herself to be an equal distance from Kamijou and Orsola, then…

"!! There!!" she cried, stamping her thick sandal sole into Kamijou's calf. Then she pulled up his pants leg. "I knew it! You smuggled a weapon onto the *Queen of the Adriatic*—!!"

Agnes's cautious voice cut off before she finished.

Attached to his calf by a band was a spare wallet, practically screaming that he was not at all used to overseas travel.

"…" Agnes fell silent, less out of embarrassment that she'd been wrong and more out of caution at not being able to read his intent. Once again, she shuffled over, repositioning herself against the two of them.

She didn't let down her guard, but the standoff held, telling them that they could conduct conversation without her using physical force. Orsola let out a quiet breath, and then strung together more words than she usually did.

"Well. No sooner were my moving preparations complete than people from the Roman Orthodox Church attacked. As fate would have it, we ended up on this boat. The *Queen of the Adriatic*…Might that be this ice ship's name?" she asked in blank amazement.

Finally, Agnes relaxed. She looked at Kamijou, who was on the floor, though her gaze still didn't show any signs of letting down her guard. "That…Is this a problem with her personality, usually?" she asked, rather exasperated.

Kamijou wasn't listening to anyone right now. "…And so I'm sorry Agnes and forgive my confession in the middle of my apology but from the first time I met you I actually thought you looked really hot in that tight habit miniskirt and— *Gwoh?!*"

Thirty-centimeter soles dug into his side, sending Kamijou reeling away. Agnes asked the exact same question again. He sat up and, coughing, responded.

"Well…Wait, uh, why are you mad? Did Orsola say something weird again? The *Queen of the Adriatic*? What's that? I feel like I've heard it before."

"Oh. I must insist that I listen carefully to what others say."

Nobody could tell what words that response had been in answer to, so the other two didn't even bother engaging Orsola. Agnes slumped, this time seeming to have let go of her caution for real. "…This fleet's called the Queen's Fleet. This boat is one of its escorts. It looks like you really don't know crap. You're bad at bargaining—it's written all over your face. Though if it's all an act, it's pretty damn impressive."

"What are you even doing here…?"

"You're one person I don't have to explain myself to. But I'm here helping search for the infiltrators." She continued with something crazy. "Never thought it would be you two, though. Maybe I can use this. I was having a rough time. That problem was more than I could solve myself. But with you two, it'll be solved quickly—"

"Hey, wait a minute," interrupted Kamijou. *Problem, rough time, use, quickly*—none of those words sounded very good. "I don't like this. Orsola was attacked, and we were forced to get on this weird boat. We've been pulled around this whole time. I don't know what you're trying to do here, but—"

"If you insist on whining and complaining, I'll start yelling. If you want to get out of here, I think you'd better not get on my nerves. If you want to know how to depart the Queen's Fleet, anyway."

Kamijou and Orsola looked at Agnes with surprise.

She didn't care much. "If you don't want to, that's fine. I'll just go and call someone over, and you can deal with the rest however you want. Why not try jumping overboard and freaking swimming to land? Don't know how many kilometers it would be, and if you make splashing noises in the water I think they'll shoot you with cannons without question."

Now that it had been said again, Kamijou had no way of arguing. They were in the sea. If he thought about it normally, he'd realize there was no escape. Swimming obviously wouldn't work, and even if they stole a life raft or something like that, they'd easily be sunk.

As Kamijou mulled it over, Orsola spoke. "...By saving us, what would you gain?"

"A reward, I guess. Just think of it like that," answered Agnes immediately.

The situation was already baffling, and now it seemed about to get even more tangled. Agnes was on the same search team as the men with the deep voices. Did she have a different goal?

Orsola sighed and looked at Kamijou again. "For now, we must do as she says. Either way, I don't believe we'll find a way to escape without cooperating, and if we make Miss Agnes mad, the other people will arrive."

"Heh. So you do get it." Agnes smiled belligerently.

Kamijou clicked his tongue. He could feel the situation growing more and more chaotic. Offhandedly, he said, "I don't like this, but let's hear what you have to say."

2

"What's the Queen's Fleet, anyway?"

That was the first question Kamijou asked in the small cannon room.

"Well, it's a fleet meant to keep watch on the Adriatic Sea."

Agnes's tension had finally gone away, and despite not getting any closer to him than she needed to, the energy was draining from the tips of her hands and feet.

"Its goal is to collect data from stuff like the stars, the wind, and the surface of the water to see where and how much mana is being used on the Adriatic. Unlike on land, we can't simply put guards on the ocean. But it'd be a problem if people were doing weird sorcery experiments on the water."

"...Keeping watch on the Adriatic...," Orsola repeated, looking around the icy room with doubt on her face. "Is it necessary to build something so tremendous for that?"

"At this point we probably could've made it more compact, but, err, the Queen's Fleet was made hundreds of years ago...back when peace and order on the Adriatic was so unstable that they *had* to patrol it constantly," Agnes explained, bored. "And part of it is to scout out other religious sects, I bet. The organizational diagram of the groups on the sorcery side has started shifting around lately, so they wanted a big event to fix all that."

Which meant that the English Puritan Church and the Russian Catholic Church would know about the *Queen of the Adriatic*'s move. If not, they wouldn't be able to meet their goal of showing it off. Kamijou noted as much to her.

"Right, well, I'm sure the higher-ups knew and just kept quiet about it, yeah? Fooling around with scouts isn't going to cause waves, and if their underlings stupidly run out ahead and react too violently, that'll cause a much bigger problem. Like what's happening right now."

"...Wait a minute. I still don't get what's going on. We didn't know about the *Queen of the Adriatic*, and now that we know how dangerous the situation is, it feels like we're not really..."

"You think they give a crap about you two? What I'm saying is..."

Agnes stopped.

They could hear the pattering of footsteps from outside the room. Agnes pressed her ear to the icy door and waited until it quieted down. How many people were on this ship? The man in the habit who attacked them and the men with the deep voices yelling instructions on the icy deck couldn't have been part of Agnes's unit.

"But I don't recall ever hearing about this while I was still a Roman Orthodox."

"I didn't know until getting here, either. I mean, the Church's got two billion followers. Which means there's an insane number of disparate units. We only know about the places and things we use regularly and the super-famous people all the way at the top."

"…Now that you mention it, I don't even know how many units there are in total," Orsola replied, thinking back to her old post and the group she belonged to.

But…

"Hey, is this fleet really just set up for keeping watch?" Kamijou turned to Agnes, suspicion on his face. "Look at the facts: Some guy attacked us, probably from this ship. And then a huge freaking boat came up and broke the canal. Next thing we know, we're in the middle of a huge fleet. Why do we have to suffer through all this?"

"Hmph," sniffed Agnes for some reason. "I'll ask one more time. You two are truly unrelated to the *Queen of the Adriatic*, right?"

"Yes, like I said, I was in the middle of moving. And now that I think of it, I do wonder if everyone from Amakusa is all right," said Orsola, somewhat worried.

Agnes sighed tiredly. "Well, then you simply got caught by those keeping watch, didn't you? You two destroyed a Roman Orthodox Church project in the past. You're obviously on a blacklist, stupid. Plus, one of you came all the way from Japan and the other came from London with a combat brigade of Amakusa people with her. With everyone who took part in the battle over the *Book of the Law*, it's no wonder they thought you were up to something again."

"Is that right?" said Kamijou, confused. In all honesty, he couldn't imagine what a "normal" response from the sorcery side would entail.

Agnes grinned. "But anyway, you're pretty sharp to notice something wrong with this all being just for observation."

"Huh?" replied Kamijou.

She continued. "The whole thing about it being just for keeping watch is a front."

"Whatever do you mean?"

"The real reason for it is, well, this is basically a workers' facility." Agnes's smile darkened. "They round up all the sinners and failures like me and make them pay off whatever they owe the Roman Orthodox Church. So most of the people on the boat are the sisters from my unit…or rather, my former unit. The rest are mostly people overseeing the work and stuff."

Did that mean Agnes was working here? Maybe looking for infiltrators was part of their job. But the air here felt oddly dangerous, what with the people who suddenly attacked them and the fact that they'd been hiding themselves.

"What exactly do you do here?" asked Kamijou.

"The work itself is simple. Anyhow, they ask for as many hours of labor as they can get. We're worked around eighteen hours a day. For the sisters who aren't used to stuff like this, it seems like hell."

He was startled. *Wasn't there a form of torture like that…?* Overwork was banned as a form of punishment right now. It was a method of wearing away a person's mind by forcing them to continue doing simple, fruitless labor over long periods of time. The more meaningless the work, the more it stung. The feeling of all your work not being good for anything was probably like telling a marathon runner that time would be reset after they finally reached the goal, making them do it over and over again.

"Anyway, this is the important part. In exchange for my letting the two of you escape…I want you to rescue two of my subordinates. Their names are Sisters Lucia and Angeline."

Lucia and Angeline. They didn't ring a bell at first, but when Kamijou thought hard, he realized it was the sisters he'd seen during the incident regarding the *Book of the Law* and Orsola. He felt like they'd beaten him to a pulp in Parallel Sweets Park.

"But however shall we rescue them?"

"Right…Well, this is going to sound like karma, but…" Agnes sighed. "The two of them broke out of the Queen's Fleet. Apparently, they plan on breaking out the other sisters and me. All I can really tell them is, 'Yes, yes, good work,' though. I'd rather they get out for now, then actually prepare something to rescue the rest of us."

Agnes's answer was bored, unenthusiastic.

"How did they say they did it, again? I think it was a spell that used the Queen's Fleet's searching characteristics against it…Well, in any case, they really did escape. That much is trustworthy information."

Before Kamijou could open his mouth to ask why she wanted them to save the ones who had already broken out, he came to the answer. They had run away once—and then been caught again and dragged back.

"So they got brought back here and now they're in detention?"

"Detention? Well…," Agnes said in a bored voice. "This is a prison, so. Including myself, all the nuns here are Roman Orthodox prisoners. The most important thing they need to do is plug any potential escape holes. So stopping spells for breaking out comes first. Still, this isn't an execution site, so they're not gonna just up and kill 'em to keep 'em quiet. At most they'll be dealt with so they can never use that spell again."

"Dealt with?" repeated Kamijou casually, but Agnes took a moment before speaking.

Instead, Orsola gave an uncharacteristically bitter frown, then asked her, "…Preventing the use of sorcery means robbing them of their ability to think. Meaning, *they will break down the structure of their brains*?"

That unnerved Kamijou, who still sat on the ice floor. She hadn't suggested a concrete method, but that only let terrible ideas spring up in his imagination.

Agnes, too, gave a sigh. "It's not like they're corpses for Vetala sorcery. And a labor force without minds would be horrifying to look at. That's why my request is that you rescue them before that happens." She started to scratch her head in annoyance. "…Just you two for now. The other sisters have the bare minimum of food, clothing, and lodging right now. And they probably don't have the willpower to resist even poorly. Sisters Lucia and Angeline. If you get to them before their brains are wrecked, you'll probably get the spell they used, too."

"But is this escape spell not already known to the Roman Orthodox Church?"

"The Queen's Fleet has something big coming up. Only the people higher up know the details, though. As long as they have enough people to spare for that, they don't give a crap about one or two people breaking out. The Roman Orthodox Church isn't dumb enough to let something this important go wrong because they were paying attention to something minor."

Agnes collected herself a bit.

"So if they're going to get away, now's their only chance. If you two will act, this will be quick. I'll go to the Queen's Fleet's flagship to create a diversion, so get the job done while I'm there, please."

If she was going to the flagship, then did that mean there was a way to cross over there from this escort ship? These were magical facilities, so maybe there were some weird warp devices or something.

"...So you're saying you'll help us?"

"Not help you—use you. If you don't like it, I won't go to the flagship. Instead I'll just turn you in." Agnes's lips twisted into a mean smile, but Orsola smiled.

"Now, now! There is no need to be so embarrassed about it. If you had no intention of cooperating, you wouldn't have approached us about it."

"Mgah?! H-hey, what are you hugging me for?!"

Agnes found her face buried in Orsola's arms, massive goodwill, and enormous chest, so Kamijou instantaneously turned his head and averted his gaze. He heard a nasty-sounding *grrk*.

But that wasn't important right now. "While you're there...But you'll be captured, too, won't you? We should break out together," he said from his spot on the floor, looking up at Agnes.

However, after escaping Orsola's bonds, Agnes quickly responded, "No, I have a symbolic role."

"Umm, that was really vague. I don't get it."

"I'll explain it real nice and simple. Most of the people captured in this fleet are from my unit. The managers here are afraid of a laborer revolt. Basically, I'm like a mental safety switch to prevent that. Let's see…For example, I'm like the boss of all the prisoners." She smiled thinly and sardonically. "By getting me, the most influential person in the whole former Agnes Unit, to obey and never resist, it makes the others think that, well, if she couldn't, then what chance do we have? …Of course, that's all basically just an illusion." She exhaled a little.

The fact that she was moving on her own instead of with a supervised group was probably due to her having the authority to do so. Agnes seemed to have come to check on Lucia and Angeline while she searched for them, though.

"I'm a prisoner, but I have the right to walk around freely in the fleet. I'm also exempt from manual labor. They allow me the luxury of having three meals a day and the option of coffee or *spremuta* after eating. Pretty good deal, right? Everyone else needs to work for me to have it, though."

"…"

"They're treating me like a guest. From my point of view, what Sisters Lucia and Angeline are doing is a waste of time. They're, like, idiots. All the other sisters are being really obedient. If they were going to fight back, they should have just run away by themselves. But they came all the way to my tightly guarded room and told me they'd rescue me someday."

There wasn't much seriousness in Agnes's voice. The words were simply tumbling out, and that was all.

"Besides, I don't need to do any labor, so I don't have to break out. I can just laze around on a couch and eventually I'll be back at my post. They're pathetic, huh?"

Agnes's words ticked Kamijou off a little. Maybe it *was* a nuisance for her personally, but he didn't think she had to put it like she had.

"Whatever you two want, it'll be freakin' important to assure their cooperation to find out how to get safely away from this fleet at sea. Might have to rough up a few people. Anyway, I guess just do the best you can manage."

"What do you mean 'best we can manage'?"

"Just my honest opinion. If you want my thoughts on it, in case you're lucky enough to get out of here, never get involved with the Roman Orthodox Church again."

He didn't like her decisive tone, either, but she was still right. They couldn't hide out in one place forever. If they were going to flee, it had to be soon. And they had a way out right in front of them.

Kamijou, still sitting on the floor, let out a massive, spiritless sigh. "…All right, fine. But if we get seriously outnumbered, we're not going to have much time."

"You picked a fight alone against two hundred and fifty sisters before, and that's what you have to say now?"

At the moment, she seemed to acknowledge Kamijou's strength *as her enemy.* The corners of her lips pulled up into a sardonic smile as she bent over and offered her hand as if for a handshake.

She must have been telling him to stand up. "Oh, thanks." Kamijou amenably grabbed her hand with his right. In addition to her slender fingers, his hand closed around her habit's baggy sleeve, and a moment later…

Thud.

The seams in Agnes's habit broke apart and it fell straight down.

"Oh my," said Orsola, putting a hand to her cheek. "Well. I had thought it was a somewhat odd design. Your revealing habit was a special garment meant to act as a countermeasure against anything magical?"

That was beside the point.

Most importantly was that Agnes now stood bent over before him in only her underwear, and though they were full of lace like last time, the white panties were somehow cute. And also, she wasn't even wearing a bra because her clothing had had a wide-open back. Then there was her modest chest, slightly and charmingly emphasized because she was bending over.

Agnes's face, at first, seemed to wonder what had happened. Then she looked down...and then to herself, as though to reconfirm what she was seeing. "Ky—" Eventually her throat perked into motion.

"_____???!!!"

Before she could start screaming, Kamijou and Orsola put her in a full-force nelson hold, covering her mouth.

3

Index was standing in the darkened streets of Chioggia.

The small town on the sea was a scene of chaos. People were in turmoil not only because the historically significant canal and stone bridge had been destroyed, but also because nobody could figure out *how*. Those looking at the disaster began asking questions, listening to the voices answering in stammered words, growing increasingly dubious, and going through the whole thing again.

Seawater had flooded into the road farther than one hundred meters away from the canal and had even started dripping into another canal parallel to it. The boat was gone now, so the dirty water was trying to go back into the canal. Even so, some houses had seen it coming in from the gaps around doors. Business buildings especially, like restaurants and cafés, were starting to light up, the sounds of frantic cleaning drifting toward her.

Amid it all.

Index stood quietly, her gaze fixed in the direction where the ice sailboat had disappeared.

"The *Queen of the Adriatic*, allegedly deeply involved in the history of northeastern Italy..." The words she spoke possessed support in the form of her immense stores of knowledge. "No, one of the Queen's Fleet aiding it?"

A whirlwind of information from the 103,000 grimoires in her head began to coalesce and organize. She drew out the necessary knowledge, blocked out the unnecessary knowledge, and began to investigate whether her speculation was true or not. Finally, she confirmed it.

Which means it had to have been the Roman Orthodox Church. But why did the Queen's Fleet attack?...Orsola Aquinas and Amakusa. Maybe these two being here together was the cause. Touma and the rest of them don't absolutely need to be eliminated to move the Queen of the Adriatic!

Then she began to think about possible countermeasures.

I can't go by myself to the Queen's Fleet without being able to use sorcery. No, the enemy is greater than a single sorcerer can hope to stand against. But at this rate, Touma and the others will...In that case...

Index brought her face up. She cast her gaze around and, before long, took off running toward the destination she had in mind.

4

Kamijou and Orsola were battled out of the cannon room.

After borrowing the sewing set from Orsola's sleeve, Agnes had said in a very low voice, "...Anyway, I'll be found out on the spot unless I at least put my appearance back to normal. Just get out of here now, please." Then she had begun to move the needle in and out of her custom-made habit. She would most likely head for the flagship when she was finished.

There was no point in thinking about her.

Kamijou poked his head around the passage corner and looked ahead.

The straight hallway, made of ice with an altered melting point shining with pale-white diffused light from the moon, was, in contrast to the ship's scale, extremely tight and narrow. Maybe it was a trait of warships. It seemed to him like if a few more people were here, they'd probably get stuck and be unable to move.

All the ship's interior surfaces were like screens in a movie theater; the floor and walls were clearly distinguished, but it was very difficult to see in the air of the passage. Kamijou found himself squinting a little to stare farther down it.

"...Nobody here."

"Just as Miss Agnes said."

After their short exchange, they walked around the corner. It had taken quite some time to confirm even that. That first step required reckless courage.

According to Agnes, "Control of the fleet's navigation and weapons relies mostly on sorcery. The greater part of those on board are from my former unit, and asking any of them for help could cause them to be framed, so that's out. There are around two hundred fifty in the unit, but there're close to a hundred ships. You do the math: Each ship is close to empty. That's what it takes to have a few overseers manage a lot of laborers, basically. It does mean it's a weak point, though."

But if the ships are all on autopilot, what work are they doing here?

She'd said they were doing simple physical labor meant to wear them down, but he didn't think she went into details. Whatever the case, it could wait until they got off the ship with Lucia and Angeline.

Even though he made sure there was nobody actually around, he still couldn't completely rid himself of anxiety that someone would attack. Behind all the doors in the passage, right around the corner…He could all too easily imagine someone waiting somewhere for their opportunity.

Agnes had also told them that Lucia and Angeline had been taken up three stories above the deck. Normally stragglers were brought down belowdecks to the ship's hold, close to the bottom, but apparently, the mind-control equipment to "make it so they could never use their escape spell again" was in the upper levels.

They headed up via a steep, cliff-like staircase.

The passage on the third floor had windows along one side. Belowdecks there were cannon rooms packed tightly together, but those weren't needed in the upper part of the structure, so the hallway was positioned closest to the outside.

"Oh my," said Orsola casually as she cast her gaze out one of the windows.

Kamijou's eyes followed hers, and then he gasped. "…Yeah, this isn't going to be easy."

They were on the third floor—but only counted up from the deck. There were another ten or so meters from the deck down to the water. It was like looking down from a fifth floor or higher.

It felt like seeing a town from the top of a tower, but instead of a town he was seeing a big fleet of ships. Giant hundred-meter-long sailing warships made of ice like this one were blanketed over the water like a school of fish. Just from their one window they could see over fifty of them. The faintly glimmering ships, radiating with the off-white color of a lightbulb, cast a film of light over the dark ocean's surface.

"Huh?...I guess Agnes is on the move, too." Still alert to his surroundings, he focused on the view out the window.

An icy, arched bridge began to crackle into existence between two of the boats. Standing on it was a lone figure. As it crossed the bridge, the ice bridge began to crackle out of existence behind the figure again. Agnes seemed to be beginning her diversion.

Her destination must have been the flagship she mentioned. A few hundred meters or so in front of her, at the center of it all, floated a much more enormous sailboat, surrounded by all the other ships. Both its length and width appeared to him to be twice the size of this escort ship. It was as though he were gazing at a tall castle from the town around it.

Kamijou looked away from the window again. "Don't even want to count them all...World's biggest religion, huh? This is all so far out of our leagues."

"...The entirety of the fleet is the size of a small city."

Kamijou resumed his walk down the passage, thinking. Their first priority definitely had to be slipping away without anyone noticing, not standing up to all of it. As for Lucia and Angeline, whose spell held the key to escaping, they—

"...Ack?!"

His thoughts froze as he approached the corner. He grabbed Orsola's hand, then pressed both of them against the wall. Very slowly and carefully, he poked his head out to look.

The room Agnes had told them they were after was about ten meters down the hallway.

And there was somebody right in front of it.

Wait, was that really a person? It *looked* like a suit of armor over three meters tall, made of ice, blocking the door like a boulder. It, too, radiated a pale-white light, so it wasn't very transparent. And it looked heavily armed from head to toe. In its hand, it gripped a... mace, he thought. Probably a type of staff or club, anyway. But it looked like it was holding a squarish steel frame, chopped up into round slices.

Kamijou pulled his head back and turned away from the faintly glimmering corner of the wall. *Damn it. Trying to silence it in one hit would be too tough...If it calls its friends while I'm wasting time fighting it, it's all over for real right then and there.*

The passage was narrow, with few avenues for escape. If a dozen or so people came into either side of it, there would be no slipping past them. They would just have to wait, with a numbers advantage, for him to lose the battle of attrition.

Shit, he cursed to himself, his eyes flying over the passage again, rechecking how narrow it was, when...

Bam!!

A moment later, with a loud noise, his vision was filled with the pale ice.

Kamijou didn't understand what he was seeing at first.

The ice armor guarding the door around the corner had zipped down the passage, turned the corner, and now stood in front of him...It took him a few seconds to realize what was happening.

Its legs were quickly sliding to the side. The ice had a different melting point, so it didn't melt—which meant it shouldn't be sliding. Upon closer inspection, the armor's feet were linked with the floor. It was almost like it was swimming through the ice.

But Kamijou couldn't be calm as he noticed that.

What...?!

His eyes widened with surprise; the ice armor's arm was already whipping around at him. A brutal strike, bottom to top. The steel frame–like club easily slipped through the thick floor without losing momentum, appearing to be drawn toward his torso.

It had enough weight and speed to crush a cargo container like an empty soda can.

"!…Ah-gahhhhh!!"

When he went to evade the strike, he felt a burst of air on his cheek. His bangs swung as he instinctively realized he couldn't dodge it. His right hand moved, mostly out of reflex. His palm swung down in a reckless pounding motion at the incoming attack from below.

Bgweee!! A high-pitched noise echoed through the ship.

Suddenly Kamijou's palm broke out into a severe, cold sweat, which went up to his elbow and then to his shoulder.

"…Urgh!" grunted Kamijou unintentionally.

The armor in front of him was motionless.

With a few *snaps*, the ice armor's club split right down the middle. Then, the shoulder holding the club broke apart, sending fissures vertically down from its chest to its abdomen, cracking apart its thighs and knees, finally causing it all to topple over sideways.

Clatter, came the noise.

The pale light enveloping the armor's body disappeared, as though the ice breaking had changed the degree of light refraction.

Orsola, who had been holding her breath nearby, finally spoke. "A-are you quite all right…?"

"Think so." Maybe it was just him, but his wrist hurt a little bit. "I busted it up…Was this like a robot that moved with sorcery?"

"Well…It doesn't appear to be a golem, where a caster is delivering clear orders to it. Rather it seems more accurate to say part of the ship altered its own shape. Following the way warships attack, it was possibly…like a cannon, facing inward." Orsola stopped before the fallen ice sculpture and ran her hands over it, speaking lowly and clearly.

"Part of the ship…?" Kamijou tapped his right hand against the nearby wall. The thick ice didn't break, though.

…*They're different, I guess. The armor was always moving via magic, but the boat's walls have already changed completely*, he thought idly, but there was no time to investigate the details. *Still, though…*

He breathed a genuine sigh of relief that magic had been used. If he'd let himself be pulled into a regular hand-to-hand fight...Well, he wasn't sure even a modern tank could have beaten the thing. Kamijou would have been killed within seconds.

Whatever the case, he'd gotten past the hurdle not with raw strength but with grit.

Kamijou turned the corner, this time with nobody out there. "All right, let's go save Lucia and Angeline. This is a pain."

"There is one thing about that," said Orsola somewhat worriedly. "Would it be possible that Miss Lucia and Miss Angeline are the only ones in that room? There should be at least several casters administering their magical procedure. If we open the door, I believe things will get ugly."

As she spoke, Orsola picked up a fallen piece of ice. It was the club the ice armor had held, broken in two. She held it with both hands like an instrument case.

"My weapon," she said with a smile—both things were out of place. To add to that, she went around picking up more, saying this one or that one seemed stronger. Mostly the ice armor's portions of leg. Would they have about the same attack power as a weighted stone?

"...Right." It didn't seem very helpful to Kamijou, but he accepted it for now. "Guess this time we'll have to fight when they come out. We can only pray they don't come out scattered."

"Yes. Well then, let us be off."

Kamijou and Orsola nodded to each other and ran down the passage. It wasn't that they wanted to fight while they advanced. Stronger was the more negative feeling of not wanting to be spotted by anyone *else* in the passage.

They made it to the door in one spurt. Kamijou grabbed the doorknob. It didn't seem locked. To be honest, he felt scared, but hesitating would get him nowhere. Without a second thought, he threw open the door.

Bang!! echoed the loud noise.

"Urk!" It was a clean room. Maybe it was their version of an infirmary. Even so, the beds were made out of ice, too, so he couldn't tell how much good they'd do for a patient.

There were around seven men and women in the cramped room. Two were sisters wearing habits with yellow sleeves and skirts. They were Lucia and Angeline. They each wore a golden circlet outside the cloth on their foreheads, but it also looked like they were digging into the fabric. The other five people were all unhealthy-looking men, slender as wire. They could have been researchers, but each wore a deep-black habit with a cloak. On an icy table next to them were lots of metal sticks made of something other than ice, which Kamijou couldn't surmise the usage of. Their tips were sharpened like pens, making them seem somehow eerie. The strange movie theater screen–like illumination wasn't helping, either.

No ice armors in here.

But one on five was still a plain old numbers disadvantage.

Shit…!! If he took on every one of them at once, he'd lose. It was all up to how much of a surprise attack he could get in while they were frozen in surprise. He almost took a long step into the room when…

…a shadow stepped between them first.

"Don't move."

It was Orsola Aquinas. She awkwardly threw the ice piece she was carrying underhanded. It clattered and rattled as the wrecked club slid across the floor. It was less a throw and more of a bowling ball roll, but…

Gulp.

The Roman Orthodox men with the advantage of numbers all stopped moving at once.

"How do you think I destroyed that?" she declared confidently, her hand moving toward her sleeve.

Kamijou glanced at his own right hand. Then he finally realized what she was trying to do.

They didn't know about the Imagine Breaker.

"Oh. I misspoke and used Japanese accidentally, but I see you understand me. Though it is perfectly fine if you do not. If you won't listen to my warning, I will simply have to use *this*," she said, hand going into her sleeve.

"Wait...," one of the men said in Japanese. Now that they were talking, it meant they'd already begun trying to compromise. "...You...What sort of Soul Arm are you hiding?"

Before Orsola could respond, another man opened his mouth. "There's plenty of ice out there. You could have just broken a piece and brought it here."

"Oh my. Do things like *this* happen to grow naturally on this ship?"

Orsola threw the next piece with a *bonk*. This time it was a piece of the ice armor's leg. Unlike the fragment of the club, this one had a finer, more lifelike construction—and it was shattered around the knee.

"..." The men took a step back.

With strength, Orsola took one forward. "As for your previous question, if you would like to know how I did so, I would not mind showing you. But please make sure not to turn to cinders before you see it. Oh my, oh my. *Will you be able to block this relying only on your arms to guard yourself?*"

She lightly shook the hand inside her sleeve, and the men all tensed up so nervously it was funny. Slight fear was visible even on Lucia and Angeline's faces.

Kamijou was astonished. A bluff was a technique you could use only when you already had an accurate idea of the opponent's strength.

"Then I apologize, but please, bind these men," said the nun in question to Kamijou with a smile.

5

The Roman Orthodox men put their hands up without argument.

Because of Orsola bluffing that she had a secret weapon, she couldn't carelessly approach them. Instead, Kamijou bound their hands and legs. The whole boat was made of ice, so there was nothing to use for rope. Without a choice, he had to use things like their belts. The experience of loosening a man's belt made him genuinely uncomfortable. He really hoped this was the end of it.

After checking the knots tying the men up, Orsola finally relaxed and removed her hand from her sleeve. She breathed a sigh of relief; she was probably more nervous than she was letting on. Directing her attention to Angeline and Lucia, she said, "We are here to rescue you."

The two of them instead took a half step back. They seemed to be dumbstruck at how suddenly Kamijou and Orsola had appeared.

A dynamic duo if I ever saw one, thought Kamijou. Angeline was the shorter and Lucia was the taller...or so he thought. Angeline's face had gone pale, and she was looking at him as though she was about to burst into tears. She was holding the waist of Lucia, who was standing next to her. Lucia, for her part, had a hint of red hostility on her light-colored face, glaring at him with a sharpness that would find any opening. One hand was wrapped around the clinging Angeline's shoulder.

Both of them wore as a base the same black habit Orsola did, with long yellow sleeve and skirt pieces attached. Maybe it was the uniform of the people working on the ships. Lucia's smooth, fair arms were slightly visible through her sleeves, which were on the short side. Angeline's baggy sleeves exposed only her fingertips, though.

"...You came to rescue us? Did you think we would believe you? The only reason the two of you were thrown into a place like this is because you failed."

The low, cautious voice had to be Lucia. Angeline couldn't even get her mouth to close. Kamijou was more apprehensive about *her* attitude than the hostility being directed at him. "Umm, we're not on this ship because we wanted to be. We just have Roman Orthodox people after us for no apparent reason. Our first objective is just to get out of here." There was no point hiding it, so he revealed what they were after. "From what Agnes told us, you can use a spell that lets us do that. If we want to run, we need your help, so she said she wanted us to come help you before they did some weird stuff to you."

"S-Sister Agnes...She said that?"

The familiar name caused the twinge of fear on Angeline's face to disappear. She seemed to brighten right up with only that. Maybe she was actually an animated girl at heart.

But Lucia's sleeve swung out and she pressed on Angeline's head from above. "Sister Angeline, these are the words of a heretic. Please at least consider the fact that this may be a trap."

"I-I'm sorry, ma'am! But, well, if these people met Sister Agnes, then maybe, maybe she's…"

"Once again, you are being too hopeful! They know our connection to Sister Agnes. They could be feeding us good-sounding lies because they know that!"

Angeline continued to shrink away under Lucia pushing down on her head, but she occasionally threw a glance toward Kamijou.

Shit! This would go so much faster if Agnes had just written a note or something. He sighed. How was he going to explain this? The real problem was that their alarm was justified—Kamijou and Agnes *weren't* very friendly with each other. There was nothing harder than bringing someone over to your side using only words.

As Kamijou fretted, Orsola opened her mouth to speak. "Then I will ask you this. Why do you think we came here?"

"What?"

"As you say, this is the enemy's base. We came in here only after felling the guards. Is there any other merit to taking such a risk to come here other than to rescue you?" said Orsola, sparing just one glance toward the men tied up in the corner of the room.

"…Well, that's…," she managed reluctantly. But she couldn't put together her thoughts, so her words stopped before she said anything else.

"Do you think we came all the way here to make enemies of you? The damage would have been done even if we had left you here. What reason would we have to rescue you, even using Agnes's name? I find myself having trouble thinking of one." Orsola glanced at the corner of the room again, where the men were tied up, after she and Kamijou had taken that risk.

"…" This time, Lucia was silent.

Instead of pointlessly explaining the unanswerable question, she created a situation in which the person she asked wouldn't be able to answer. *That was smart*, thought Kamijou, inwardly surprised. She hadn't said a word of compromise or made a single excuse in their defense, and yet she'd just silenced Lucia. This didn't feel like the way Orsola usually did things.

Then she brought her mouth close to his ear and whispered, "...It *is* my job to persuade those in heretic lands who do not know the Lord."

Oh, that makes sense, thought Kamijou in frank admiration. Maybe negotiating with her life on the line was something she was really good at.

After looking at Kamijou and Orsola in turn with a searching gaze, Lucia said, "So if we didn't have any value in rescuing, you would have left us here...What luxury."

"Sister Lucia!"

Angeline's baggy sleeves pulled on the cloth around Lucia's waist. The taller one sighed tiredly. "All right. Your words do have *some* truth to them. Also, Sister Angeline, how many times have I told you not to do that? You're rubbing against my thigh."

Kamijou almost looked away when those smooth words came out lightly. Did they not really care, since they were both girls?

His cheeks reddened in spite of his intent, and Lucia's eyebrow twitched. "Are you having any ideas?"

"N-no! Not at all, no, ma'am!!" he said, using every ounce of spirit to try to be cool. Then he forced the topic back on track. "Well, I mean, we'd like to get out of this crazy ship as soon as possible. How do we go about doing that? Oh, you know, I hope they didn't confiscate any tools you needed to do it."

"I-it's all right. If the spell could be guarded against by taking a few instruments, I don't think our fellow Roman Orthodox followers would have been this rough..."

"Sister Angeline, if you are serious about that, then you need a pat on the head," said Lucia, very casually dealing with Angeline's pouting. "The conclusion is that it is impossible to evade the Queen's Fleet's security by water, such as swimming in the sea or stealing a lifeboat. And if we are discovered even once, we will be fodder for countless cannons."

"…Wait a minute. You two got out of here once before, right? Did you fly through the sky or something?"

"Even if we did that, we'd simply end up waiting for anti-aircraft fire…Anyway, it is too bothersome to explain. We will show it to you right away. Sister Angeline?"

"Yes, Sister Lucia. Ah, err…Whatever your intentions, th-thank you very much. Our spell and minds both were about to be destroyed if things had continued much longer."

Angeline bowed her head in thanks, but Lucia said her name again and she quickly got to work.

Lucia and Angeline put their palms together. Not evenly, though. A closer look showed that they appeared to be giving detailed consideration to which fingers were touching and which weren't.

"Normally, tools used for magic are ones a caster prepares based on his or her specialties…," said Orsola, a bit impressed. "But instead, they're using the clothes binding them as a temporary substitute. By channeling mana into the two binding spells via different routes than normal, they gain the effects of an entirely different sorcery. I am very impressed you thought of such a thing given how restrictive your environment is…"

So maybe it was like using something really trivial, like a spoon or a shoelace, to its fullest potential to break out of an impenetrable prison. As Kamijou thought about it, before his eyes, it happened.

Lucia and Angeline raised their joined hands horizontally. It looked like a social dance. And their fingers were pointing to where a cabinet, made of off-white glimmering ice, rested.

Whhrmm.

Like a pupil opening up, a big hole, about one and a half meters across, appeared in the semitransparent cabinet.

"With a spell that belongs to a subset of the one that created the boats using ice, we can open up a cavity like that one. By applying it, we can harden seawater and create a roller coaster on the seafloor. We can get out through there."

"W-we shaved off little bits of the ice walls and tried really hard to figure out how they worked. The Queen's Fleet is amazing at guarding the sea, but it's not so good at things underwater...Ow!"

Angeline winced as the big hole in the cabinet suddenly shrank and closed up. Their joined hands drifted apart. A bead of sweat trickled down her temple.

She slowly shook her head. "I—I guess they must have added an interception spell to these clothes. Oww...," she said, rubbing her temples—right about where the golden circlet was wrapped around the part of the hood on her forehead, digging into it.

"We will just need to destroy part of what's restraining us. It's magically using the way this fabric was sewn together and where its seams are, so if we break the seams in order, it will be nothing." Lucia picked up off the table an impractical-looking pen made of ice.

Break them? Kamijou cast a glance at his right hand. "Hey, if that's what you need to do, then wouldn't it be quicker to—? *Gwah?!*"

Before he could finish, he felt a soft impact on the back of his head. He turned around. Orsola had one hand to her cheek and the other balled into a fist. "Now, now. You don't honestly intend to render even them stark-naked, do you?"

"Ow!! Sorry, Orsola, you're right, I was wrong! But why are you so mad...? Ow, ow! That hurts!!"

Lucia and Angeline looked at them askance as Orsola delivered a series of surprisingly accurate knocks on the head to Kamijou. Then they began stabbing the ice pen into the yellow sleeves restraining them, poking holes. The work looked detailed and delicate in the difficult low-light conditions where only the walls and the ceiling glowed, but their hands moved with fluidity.

"A roller coaster on the seafloor? Like a chute? If we go too slowly, won't the Queen's Fleet catch up to us?"

"No, i-it actually goes pretty fast. Its maximum speed...i-is about three hundred kilometers per hour."

"On average it is only ninety kilometers per hour. The friction does slow it down."

Kamijou blanched at their words. He was pretty sure bullet trains traveled at three hundred kilometers per hour. For one thing, would they be able to breathe? He also wondered how they would slow down. Lucia and Angeline had already tested this once before, and they looked good as new, so there probably weren't any issues. *Really hope it's not some occult brake using some insane magic theory*, he thought, glancing at his right hand. Hopefully he wouldn't have to break the coaster before then, but…

Kamijou's eyes caught back up to the nuns' work. "Either way, we can get out of here right now with that, right?"

"…Actually, it's a little more complicated," said Angeline simply. "We have to use seawater to create the seafloor coaster. That means we have to get to the bottom of the boat first."

"We will make a hole in the floor of the ship, then create the coaster out of water. After we go in, we'll seal the entrance behind us, cutting ourselves off. That way, it will be difficult for the Queen's Fleet to track us."

So we can't rest easy yet. Kamijou sighed, but Lucia and Angeline both seemed to think optimistically about it.

"Sister Lucia, we'll be able to get out with Sister Agnes this time!"

"If possible I would prefer it not end there, but our first priority is to secure Sister Agnes. If she doesn't move, nobody else will, either. W-wait, Sister Angeline, don't make a hole there!" Lucia quickly grabbed Angeline's hand.

They'd been feeling less and less cautious as time went on. Their behavior wasn't quite haphazard, but Kamijou could sense their emotions. It was a subtle change, but he thought he could see anticipation hidden under the surface.

"I—I wonder when we'll be able to meet Sister Agnes."

"It likely won't be easy. She's probably doing things for us as we speak, as secretly as she can."

And that was why Kamijou wavered on whether to say it. He thought back to Agnes's words.

"I have a symbolic role."

She *had* told them to rescue Lucia and Angeline. But the words were somehow cold, like she was watching others from afar, where they couldn't affect her.

"Pretty good deal, right? Everyone else needs to work for me to have it, though."

Those words were less her consideration as their ally and more her sympathy and pity. That would cause only pain for Lucia and Angeline, who sought a position by her side, wouldn't it?

"They're treating me like a guest. From my point of view, what Sisters Lucia and Angeline are doing is a waste of time."

How did it come to this? thought Kamijou. Lucia and Angeline were slowly starting to break into smiles, and that sight pained him to no end. Weren't people supposed to smile? They weren't smiling out of malice. They smiled out of heartfelt care and goodwill.

"...Sorry," said Kamijou. "But I don't think Agnes is coming."

Lucia and Angeline stopped dead.

Their expressions died away.

The small seed that had finally begun to sprout in the earth had just been stomped on and crushed.

The first one to open her mouth was Angeline. "Why...is that?" she said. "You met Sister Agnes, didn't you? She asked you to save us, right? A-and also, where is Sister Agnes now, anyway?"

Lucia said nothing, but she turned an inquisitive gaze at Kamijou.

"Agnes is..." Kamijou saved himself the trouble and skipped right to the facts. "She told us she was going to create a diversion so we could rescue you. She said you're the ones in the most danger right now, so we should prioritize rescuing you instead of her. She went to the, err...the Queen's Fleet, right? She went to its flagship."

"She...The flagship?!"

Surprisingly, the startled voice was Lucia's. Whether out of anger or panic, her already pale face drained of color.

"This is not a joke! Why does she think we thought up ways of breaking out to the point where we risked our own lives?! It was to prevent this from happening! The one in the most danger *is quite obviously Sister Agnes, isn't it?!*"

Wait a minute, thought Kamijou. He felt a kind of temperature difference between himself and the two nuns. He could sense that each of them was working off a different premise to begin with.

Angeline's face returned to its almost-crying expression. "Besides, d-did you even understand wh-what the Queen's Fleet is for?"

"Umm…To keep watch on the Adriatic Sea, right?"

"Miss Agnes did say that was a front, didn't she?" said Orsola, knotting her brows. "…We heard from her that it was a manual-labor facility to work those who have brought detriment to the Roman Orthodox Church…"

"That's ridiculous," said Lucia, almost short of breath. "The Queen's Fleet is an escort group headed by the *Queen of the Adriatic*, meant to protect large-scale sorcery of the same name and its ritual site. The 'labor' we're being made to do is all in preparation for that. They would never need something so grandiose for the simple task of observation and labor!"

"The *Queen of the*…?" repeated Kamijou. When they'd reunited with Agnes, he remembered hearing that term at some point. "What… the heck? So this gigantic fleet is all just a warm-up act for the *Queen* or whatever? And what kind of magic is that ship even trying to cast?"

"I don't know…Only the overseers managing the laborers—high officials of the Roman Orthodox Church—know the details."

"A-all we know is that the large-scale sorcery, the Queen of the Adriatic, will be performed on the flagship. And that there's another spell, called the Rosary of the Appointed Time." Angeline counted off each fact on her fingers.

"A-and finally, that Sister Agnes is needed to use the Rosary of the Appointed Time."

Kamijou was dumbfounded. He thought at first that Angeline wasn't overly familiar with Japanese so she had misspoken somehow, but…

"We don't know the details, either. However, we are certain they will use her and that it will at the very least destroy her brain. The procedure's effects will be much more wide-ranging and difficult compared to what they were going to do to us. Sister Agnes…might be reduced to nothing but a beating heart."

Lucia's additional explanation was all too precise and cold. Kamijou felt a shudder move over him, up his spine, and to the very core of his head, all at once. She didn't have only a symbolic role. She had a certain degree of freedom secured for her, and it was a good environment to live in…What had all that been about, then?

"Never thought it would be you two, though. Maybe I can use this."

Agnes's words came to mind. She'd said them to herself. Now he finally understood what she meant.

"I was having a rough time; that problem was more than I could solve myself. But with you two, it'll be solved quickly."

The rough problem wasn't the security situation. If Agnes had rescued Lucia and Angeline and then told them to run away themselves, they would never have agreed.

He should have seen it before. What Agnes Sanctis had done to Kamijou and Orsola during the *Book of the Law* dispute was difficult to call benevolent, but she had just as much right to act out of consideration for others.

Lucia and Angeline had told them the entire Queen's Fleet was a warm-up act for the Queen of the Adriatic. Agnes was the key to the huge, large-scale spell activating. If she escaped with Lucia and Angeline, they would pursue them to the ends of the earth.

"The Queen's Fleet has something big coming up."

But Agnes had said this, too.

"Only the people higher up know the details, though. As long as they have enough people to spare for that, they don't give a crap about one or two people breaking out."

If that was true, then when she said she'd go to the flagship, she really did mean it was to create a diversion. To abandon everything for the allies who had tried to save her.

Kamijou wondered what she was feeling.

"While you're there…But you'll be captured, too, won't you? We should break out together."

In that very last moment, what had she felt when she said those words?

And…

What had she felt when she lied about everything to guide Kamijou and Orsola to Lucia and Angeline?

"You picked a fight alone against two hundred and fifty sisters before, and that's what you have to say now?"

The emotion buried in that lighthearted comment…
Realizing Agnes's unspoken wish, Kamijou stood there, dazed.
And then, into the useless boy's ears…

Grasshh!! Suddenly, the explosive sound of an ice wall crumbling split through the air.

The sound and the shock wave were enough to throw them all to the floor. The ice wall must have taken a hit from outside and broken. The side of the room farthest away from them had shattered into a rain of ice shards like glass. Just above them, a stray piece of wreckage hurtled past at a dreadful speed.

"…Ow!!" cried Kamijou, not at having fallen but from the throbbing pain inside his ear. "What was that…?!" It was like he was hearing the others' voices through headphones. It seemed like the sounds were coming to him from far away.

"A-an attack?!" said Angeline, voice trembling. "From where…?!" She had immediately been safeguarded under Lucia as she dropped to the ground. Lucia's face was baffled as well—that was only natural. This escort ship was surrounded by many of the same. Was an outside attack even possible?

Then Orsola, also on the floor, abruptly lifted her head. "Could it be…?" She looked past the destroyed ice wall—to the nightscape seen from five stories aboveground. "…*One of our own ships fired on us!!*"

You have to be kidding me! Kamijou wanted to shout. "This is their own ship, isn't it?!"

"No," said Lucia through gritted teeth as though in pain. "The escort ships are made of seawater. As long as the Adriatic Sea still has water, they can destroy as many as they want! Repairing and rebuilding isn't an issue!!"

Lights blinked in the distance, past the broken wall. It was fire, spurting from the lips of many cannons. Unlike normal artillery fire, the gunfire was like a wave broken up into fine pieces, carried along by the wind.

"...Urgh!!"

The delayed storm of noise came a moment later, like thunderclaps.

Before Kamijou could take any action, the swarm of cannonballs destroyed the entire face of the ship, not only the room they were in. The pale light disappeared from only the parts that had been smashed. The bound men near the wall began to fall into the night sky. Before he could think about reaching out to save them, a fragment of ice crushed by a cannonball collided with his temple. Strength immediately drained from his limbs. The fleet was in a close formation during these bombardments, so follow-up shots mercilessly pelted the ships nearby as well. Masts broke, cabins were smashed, and he could see beyond the broken wall those boats desperately freezing seawater to repair themselves.

But this ship was different.

Its automatic regeneration didn't activate, and the ship began to list heavily.

Orsola, who was clinging to the ice floor, said, "Ouch...The workings of the cannons appear to be conforming with the legends of Saint Barbara..."

"Urgh!! It's sorcery, right? Then I'll use my right hand!!"

"It isn't possible to block all the cannonballs! The ship is too big!!"

A whole host of additional explosions drowned out her shouting. The overlapping sounds of firing came together to hit them with a shock wave like lightning. Kamijou was pressed to the floor, but the quake from below still sent his body a few centimeters into the air. The continued onslaught of cannonball strikes caused the entire floor to tilt. Maybe a supporting pillar underneath them had been smashed. A moment after, the walls and floor started to rotate, along with his vision. There was a *pshhhh* sound like sand pouring nearby. It was the water's surface parting.

They were sinking.

By the time Kamijou got a grip on what was happening, the vessel of ice had already been mercilessly shattered like a small model boat hit with a hammer.

INTERLUDE THREE

Her parents had been killed.

Many a twist and turn had followed, but in the end, that was the catalyst for Agnes Sanctis beginning her life on the streets.

Food wasn't that difficult to come by, as long as she didn't care about the quality. It was hard on her until she accepted restaurants' discarded dumpster trash as food. More dreadful, though, was the frigid winter. Whenever a continental cold snap came over Europe, the chilly skies transformed into a harbinger of death.

She had resided in the business area of Milan as a young girl. The townscape, where everything was arranged a little too perfectly, never saw even a single newspaper or rag fall on the street, nothing that could serve as protection against the cold. The afternoon warmth from the centuries-old stone buildings and thick asphalt roads never lasted by nightfall, and the days would slowly turn the world into a hard, sharp freezer.

Even scavenging through trash cans would sometimes yield only "food" so stiff you could hammer a nail with it.

That was what the Roman Orthodox Church had saved Agnes from.

She thought many others besides her, of all sorts—adults and children, men and women—had been taken in as well. Each had his or her own reason, but none of them seemed to have been embroiled in incidents like Agnes or lived on the streets, where every day was a battle for survival. It seemed to her that the greater portion of them had been living normal lives and felt lucky to have been chosen by the Church.

There was no way for Agnes to have known at the time, but the Roman Orthodox Church was the largest religion in the world, with over two billion followers. For many reasons, it was "just quicker" to take in people with talent from the beginning than average people with no talent and groom them into professionals. Calculations suggested that one talented person out of ten thousand would allow them to secure two hundred. Perhaps that was a numerical victory.

Many conditions seemed to govern whether a person was chosen, but it was difficult to ascertain what they were.

"Wh-what will happen to us now?"

A girl named Angeline spoke those words. She said she used to live in France, but her parents had taken her to Milan, then abandoned her. It seemed possible for her to return home if she wished, but when asked, she would simply respond with a pained smile, saying, "What good would that do?" She'd been better off than Agnes, but she had a relatively severe past among the group, too.

"There is no need to question. If the Lord says something is necessary, it is the duty of His followers to answer Him."

The stiff, formal words came from the mouth of a girl called Lucia. She was a few years older than Agnes and Angeline and apparently had worked of her own volition to be chosen by the Church. Agnes had also become acquainted with two other girls, named Agatha and Catherine.

"I don't know," said Agnes.

She certainly believed in God. But God wasn't the sort of being who would come to you as soon as He was called. Her father had been a priest, and he'd died praying. The murderer had killed him and flung him off before Agnes could ask what his name was. If God had been nearby, that wouldn't have happened.

"More importantly, I'm worried about dinner tonight."

In the present time, Agnes came off as rather rough because of the peculiar way she had learned Japanese, but in her mother tongue of Italian, she spoke properly.

On the other hand, Lucia responded, "What do you mean 'more importantly'? There is nothing in this world more important than the Lord..."

"I-I'm worried, too. The secret ingredient has been olives for the last twelve days. I'm tired of it. Or...Ors...I can't remember her name. The really nice apprentice sister. She's definitely forgetting about it when she plans her repertoire. And our baths are strange. They're a little too hot. Don't you agree, Miss Lucia?"

"The secret ingredient doesn't matter! And our baths are only a bit lukewarm!!"

"R-really? Come to think of it, it doesn't seem to bother the grown-ups much...Umm, which means, with your age...Miss Agatha and Miss Catherine over there are older, and they were saying it was really hot. Does...Does that mean you're...even older than—"

Lucia sent a chilling glare where Angeline pointed. The girls over there hastily looked away.

With the sounds of bickering in her ears, Agnes narrowed her eyes and just faintly smiled.

It didn't seem like God was nearby.

He wasn't a handyman who would come to help as soon as you called.

But...

Lucia, Angeline, Agatha, and Catherine—if the Roman Orthodox Church was to thank for her chancing upon people like them, Agnes felt like she could give genuine thanks to God. And start trying to believe in the teachings of Crossism.

Not only that...

If her only blessing was that she was given the chance to meet them, she would protect that blessing with her own two hands.

No matter what happened.

She would make the absolute most of the chance God had given her and use it to prove her faith in her own way.

"What's the matter? You look strangely serious."

"M-Miss Lucia, Miss Agnes is trying to say she can't put up with how hot the baths are, either. I-if you want to negotiate with them, I'll go with you! See? Miss Agatha and Miss Catherine stood up, too!!"

"Yes," said Agnes with a curt nod to the mistaken assessment.

If this was going to be her home from now on...

...then first, maybe she should try to make it a place she could call comfortable.

CHAPTER 4

Battle of Fire Ships and Cannons

Lotte_di_Liberazione.

1

Agnes Sanctis was in a room on the Queen's Fleet's flagship, the *Queen of the Adriatic*. Everything about it was already different from the other escort ships, but this room was even more conspicuous.

The room had four walls.

Each wall was close to twenty meters long, and it appeared to be a perfectly square room. But if you looked closer, you could see that each of the four walls was ever so slightly leaning in toward the middle. It wasn't a cube but a quadrangular pyramid. If you looked up along the walls, glimmering in their pale off-white light, you could see its pinnacle far overhead.

From here, it looked like it was roughly one hundred meters high. The sailboat wasn't actually that tall, of course. Either this space was governed by magical rules to fit inside the ship anyway, or there was an optical illusion involved.

That wasn't the only strange thing about the room. The pale-white pyramid room was made entirely out of equilateral triangular panels of ice. You couldn't actually create a proper quadrangular pyramid using only equilateral triangles, so there had to be panels of other shapes somewhere to make it all fit.

But despite a lot of looking around, she didn't see anything like that.

The figure was an armchair theory—it seemed impossible in reality. But it had been created anyway. It was a straightforward indication that this was hallowed ground, a space inexplicable using the normal laws of the physical.

Nothing adorned the room.

The perfectly flat surfaces, made of ice that gave off pale-white light, seemed to be rejecting all others. It was cold to the point of being called absolute, and its outer reaches were emitting a heavy, invisible pressure on the inner portion.

Agnes looked at the center of the room.

A transparent ball of ice, about seven meters across, sat there, somehow fixed to the floor. The strange, empty object was like a soap bubble—and was the prison she was supposed to be inside.

*Whrrmm...*A low vibration reached Agnes's ears.

She frowned. "Saint Barbara's Divine Cannon...? Who on earth are they firing at?"

Her voice echoed through the vast pyramid.

A few moments later, the one standing in the vaguely glimmering room with his back against the ice orb answered. "You do not know, Sister Agnes?"

The figure was a man.

He wore heavy, dragging clerical garments and four necklaces around his neck. They looked like the rings in a tree stump. Dozens of crosses were attached to them. *A menorah*, thought Agnes. *Another expression of the Sephirothic Tree, a symbol of the four planes using seven candles.*

"Bishop Biagio."

Suddenly, a third voice interrupted them. It came from one of the crosses the man wore.

"Ship Thirty-Seven has been sunk. We may want to cease our attack...Any more and we may incur interference from land. The fleet is already deployed in Veneto's—"

"Let the proper departments handle the attention," he ordered. "It is not our jurisdiction." The man called Biagio ran a finger over one of the crosses around his neck. The person's voice cut off, as though the cross was a switch to turn a communication spell on or off.

He looked at Agnes and smiled. "I have been in many departments, but talented subordinates are not easy to find, are they?"

"I believe it is an officer's job to take care of subordinates with no talent so as to draw it out."

"Mere idealism. And that is the reason your life was a failure, Sister Agnes. You don't take care in selecting your subordinates, and that has brought you here."

"I bet," said Agnes, brushing aside the comment.

Biagio clicked his tongue bitterly. "…I *did* order Ship Thirty-Seven not to approach the rest of the fleet until those rats were found. To think you ended up using even the 'connecting bridge.' What would you have done if the rats had moved to a different vessel? None of this will work if something happens to you."

Agnes wrapped her arms around herself. It probably couldn't hide the fact that her habit's functionality had been destroyed.

It was specially made for her, its highly revealing design incorporating the Crossist tradition of punishment. Public humiliation was the goal, and included in the garments were defensive mechanisms to prevent death by any cause, whether suicide or homicide. Her life was not protected out of kindness—but to lengthen her suffering for much longer. It couldn't be used for long periods of time, though, because of the immense strain it put on her.

"It is quite ironic, you know."

"Be quiet, Sister Agnes," said Biagio with a chuckle. "To think an apostate like you is the only one with the affinity for this grand spell that has protected the Adriatic since the early days of the Church."

The Rosary of the Appointed Time was the key to activating the Queen of the Adriatic. Agnes didn't understand the exact inner workings or effects of it, but one of its functions was apparently that it would destroy her mind.

"Humans use their minds to temper mana within their bodies. The Rosary of the Appointed Time, however, does not function properly with mana created by normal humans. And that is where you come in, Sister Agnes. Put that talent of yours to its utmost use."

Grandiose words, but essentially all they said was that in order to create mana that wasn't normal, they had to reshape a person's mind into something that wasn't normal—in other words, to turn them into a living husk. Agnes's innate qualities—the way her mind would be broken—were well suited for the spell.

It was infuriating, but she knew saying that wouldn't change anything.

She'd been prepared for something like this since she set foot here.

"Anyway, what did you mean by Ship Thirty-Seven sinking?"

"You want meaning beyond those words?"

"…I would think your own subordinates, the overseers, were aboard as well."

"I am the one who decides how to use people. Am I wrong?"

Agnes fell mum. Then she considered the possibility that their group had gotten off the ship before it sank, but…

"Don't you think that having such faith in *their* escape spell is rather too optimistic?"

"…What are you talking about?"

"Showing you their corpses would be fastest, but collecting all their scattered fragments in the Adriatic would be backbreaking work. It would take some time to confirm their identities as well. Yes, so how should I deal with the situation?"

Agnes grated her teeth. The faint sound caused a satisfied smile to cross Biagio's face.

And then…

"Bishop Biagio! We have an emergency!!"

One of the dozens of crosses around his neck interrupted them with an urgent voice.

Biagio frowned. "What is it?"

"We detected a giant structure *beneath* the Ship Thirty-Seven wreck! It appears to be gathering the ship's wreckage…"

Biagio spat. "A submerging spell…From the sea's floor again, like Sister Lucia did before? We clearly need to rethink the Queen's Fleet's surveillance. And a giant structure? Not the sort of thing an individual could prepare…Which means the 'group' really was in Chioggia. That's why I said to crush them early. I gave the orders, but my subordinates have failed me once again. First we fail to deal with this 'group,' and now the infiltrators can escape…"

Biagio looked at Agnes. This time, he wasn't smiling. Instead, a hint of irritation was starting to creep into his eyes. "…Really. Every single one of you is absolutely useless."

2

The burning taste of seawater slowly roused Kamijou.

He was underwater.

He saw his limbs drifting loosely in front of him. He couldn't tell how far underwater he was. The night sea seemed to be closed off by a curtain of darkness, and all he saw upon looking up was the surface covered in blackness. The fleet of ice ships was sure to be surrounding him, but he couldn't see any light at all, like a thick film covered it up.

Blub. White bubbles left his mouth, the pockets of air breaking apart and floating ever higher.

What…about…Or…sola…and…the…others?

Names of people tugged at the back of his mind.

There wasn't even any rubble from the ice ship anymore. The special ice had probably reverted to seawater. Perhaps a new ship had been created somewhere else.

Lucia…and An…geline…Are they…?

He knew he had to get himself to the surface, but his thoughts weren't leading to any physical action.

His mind was yielding to the overwhelming sleepiness he felt. His thoughts weren't connecting that goal to actions or results.

He coughed.

More air bubbles leaked from his mouth, floating ever upward.

This...is bad...I really...might die...

It was a long way down to the seafloor.

He even started to feel like he was staring at an opening high above from the bottom of a ravine.

...That's...

As he looked, the black color of the sea spread out before him suddenly separated.

He thought an orca or a shark was coming near him, but a moment later he realized he had mistaken how far it was. It was very, very distant, and it boasted a length of at least thirty meters.

Could that be...?

Before he could think...

Grble. The side of the long, thin structure facing him opened up into four parts like a flower—as though it were a giant mouth about to swallow up the drowning boy.

3

On the wooden floor, Touma Kamijou, dripping wet all over, lay faceup.

Looking down on him was Index. There was a rectangular travel bag and a suitcase on either side of her. She had secured both those things as they were about to be carried away by the canal's seawater in the town of Chioggia.

They were in a long, thin, dimly lit space. Its height and breadth were around eight meters and its length about thirty. The walls and ceiling weren't squared off but curved like a tunnel. It was like the blackish, hollowed-out inside of an ancient tree. Its creation had been very carefully calculated, too, like a wooden roller coaster support beam.

"Don't need to look so worried, there. He'll wake up on his own soon," came a man's voice from the side. "When that enemy ship got blasted off the map, it definitely scared me a little. But man, looking at the results, we should be thankful it wasn't worse."

That's not the problem, thought Index.

And the man probably knew that, too. He made his next words short. "See? He's up."

Index immediately perked up and turned around to Kamijou again.

His eyelids, somewhat hidden behind his wet bangs, opened slightly. "Index..." After saying her name, he slowly sat up on the floor.

"Are you hurt, Touma?" That was the silver-haired, green-eyed girl wearing the pure-white habit. She seemed to be relieved upon seeing Kamijou's face, but that quickly returned to a look of exasperation.

And next to them was..."S-Saiji...Tatemiya?"

"Yup. Been a while, eh? Vicar pope of the Amakusa-Style Crossist Church, at your service. Currently under jurisdiction of the English Puritan Church, though."

His hair, originally black, had been dyed jet-black again, giving his spiked-up locks the sheen of a stag beetle. He also wore a baggy shirt and jeans. He was tall, but compared to his clothing size, he was extremely slender. He wore four small electric fans looped through a string around his neck, and for whatever reason his shoelaces were over a meter long.

Kamijou breathed a sigh of relief. He was another person he knew from the incident with the *Book of the Law*, like Agnes and Orsola. "Which means...Amakusa's here?"

He knew they'd come to Chioggia to help Orsola move out. Had Index been running around the town looking for them after being separated from him and Orsola?

Kamijou reached up to wipe the sweat from his brow, but his hands and clothes and insides of his pockets were all sopping wet. As he sat there at a loss, he suddenly saw a white towel being held out from beside him. He turned to see the girl with the epicanthic folds in her eyes standing next to him.

"Here, take this."

"Oh. Thanks."

Kamijou took the towel and watched as the girl said, "It's not a problem" and withdrew.

"Wait, so…why are you all the way out here…? And where is *here*, anyway…?" he asked, rather confused by all this.

Upon looking around, he felt ten or twenty people farther back in the dark room with their eyes on him. Amakusa's main force must have all been in this wooden, tunnel-like place. They were saying things like, "Itsuwa, how did it go?" and "You should have stayed with him longer." What were they talking about?

"Oh yeah…! What about Orsola and the rest?!"

"No worries, man. They're here, at least. We identified Orsola, Lucia, and Angeline, if I remember their names right. Also, we found a man tied up and a Roman Orthodox nun. All sorts of people. We're in the middle of questioning them separately."

Not knowing exactly how many people were actually on that ship was troubling, but for now Tatemiya's words came as a relief. Kamijou took a look around. "So is this Amakusa's secret base or something? Wait, how did you even get to me after I fell into the sea like that?"

"Ha-ha-ha!" laughed Tatemiya. "I guess it might be a little hard to imagine. First things first: This ain't a building, man. It's a vehicle."

"Huh?" Before Kamijou could give voice to his question, he felt a sudden burst of inertia. His body slowly began to slide backward. The entire tunnel-like facility was moving.

Struck dumb, he stiffened. "Wait, so this is a…?!"

"A submarine? Heh, that'd be nice, but it's not *that* advanced. It's more like a wooden canoe that can just barely go underwater," said Tatemiya in an almost crooning tone. "Basically…"

"…It's just a submersible."

Crash!! He heard the roar of the tunnel breaking through the layer of water. His vision swayed heavily up and down. Before his still-disbelieving eyes, the ceiling of the tunnel began to part completely from the center. It was like double doors opening, its wood scraping and creaking all the while.

What he saw was a sparkling yellow and white night sky.

The smell of seawater drifted to his nose. His footing rocked and swayed like he was riding a boat.

"Maybe it's still tough to get. Heh. I mean, who would believe it, right?"

Tatemiya followed the utterly unimpressive wooden wall.

There was a huge *rattle* as the entire floor, which must have been thirty meters long, began to rise up. The clunking of gears moving in unison reverberated, and in about forty seconds, the floor reached the height of the opened ceiling. Essentially, the floor had become the ceiling of the tunnel.

He saw the night sea.

Kamijou was standing on a giant structure shaped like a rugby ball, thirty meters long and eight wide. The opened ceiling was spread out to either side of it like wings. It had crept up above the water: a small man-made island built from tons of wooden materials.

"This is insane…," muttered Kamijou.

It certainly appeared to be a submersible, but it didn't have an engine room, or a command room, or fuel tanks, or even a communications room. It was just a vague, empty tunnel on the inside of this "submersible." Even assuming it burned wood for fuel made no sense. It was like a moving hunk of papier-mâché.

"…So you brought this *thing* with you to help her move?"

"Eh? We're originally a group of hidden Christians. Of *course* we've got a weapon or two hidden up our sleeves. And given where we come from, we specialize the most in marine warfare." Tatemiya grinned. "Paper is made from trees, which you can also use to make boats. If you know how to use the connection there, you can easily have something this small."

As he spoke, he took what looked like a stack of bills out of his baggy jeans pocket. It was a pile of Japanese paper, casually bundled up with a rubber band. Was he saying those all changed into boats? Kamijou thought for a moment some strange incantations were written on them or something, but they were actually just blank pieces of paper.

Sorcery…is just insane, thought Kamijou, looking away and exhaling before moving on to what was around the submersible underneath him.

He could just barely make out land near the horizon. It could have been Chioggia...but then again, maybe not. He thought he saw more lights from this one.

Meanwhile, in the other direction, he could see a band of pale-white light floating on the dark sea. It could have even been giving off stronger light than a town would...and it was probably the Queen's Fleet. Looking at it from afar, the immense scale stood out much more easily. Kamijou had no knowledge of the world of sorcery, much less marine warfare, so he didn't know if they were in a safe place or not.

He'd walked right into enemy bases before. But whatever those bases were, they never had more facilities inside them than he could count on one hand. This time, though, was different. There were almost a hundred military structures all clustered together.

...*Agnes*...He frowned a little, recalling the face of the girl who had implied she would stay in a place like that by herself.

Index watched him, then said, "Whatever we do now, we have to ask what's going on first. I want to know how far away we have to get until we're safe...And you look like you really want to say something, too."

"Well..." Kamijou found himself a little lost for words. "I didn't understand much about that run-down ship, either. I think Lucia and Angeline would have a better explanation than I would."

"..."

"Wh-what?"

"Nothing. I was just thinking how Touma is still Touma even when he's right in the middle of enemy territory."

"That was uncalled for!" he shouted again.

Index had her annoyed, pouting face on, though, and wouldn't answer him.

They were getting nowhere, so he took a quick look around, trying to move the conversation along. *Oh, right. Where are those two, anyway?*

Then, the crowd of young Amakusa men and women standing a little bit away from them parted.

From the other side of them came Lucia and Angeline. They seemed ready to back right out again, but Orsola pushed their backs from behind, smiling.

"Oh, I guess...you're all right, too. We're all lucky to be alive. Maybe no cannonballs hit us in the face, but we still fell into the sea from five or seven stories up."

Kamijou addressed them casually, but Lucia's and Angeline's faces reddened and they looked away without a word. *Huh?* His expression froze—he was making no progress with this conversation.

Orsola chuckled and said to the two Roman Orthodox sisters, "Now, now. You don't have to be so embarrassed about it."

"P-please don't say something so unreasonable so easily!!" Angeline snapped back, halfway to crying, swinging her baggy sleeves everywhere. Lucia hadn't raised her voice, but she closed her eyes, murmured something, and surreptitiously crossed herself. Maybe she was trying to calm down.

"???" Completely bewildered, Kamijou frowned.

"Ha-ha-ha," laughed Tatemiya upon seeing his confusion. "Well, there were dark curtains on every side, so I don't know *exactly* what happened inside them."

"...That was a super-creepy comment."

"What I mean is, Lucia and Angeline, their habits were kind of different from Orsola's, right? You know, the yellow on their sleeves and skirts. Those are restraining garments the Roman Orthodox Church gave them. When they wear them, they're like chains and collars, basically saying they can only get a certain distance away from a certain point. Or so they said. They broke out once before, so they were the only ones they gave 'em to."

"So what are you trying to say?"

"Oh, come on! Get a clue, man. If they were intact, their magical effects would've taken 'em down. That would be no good. So, sorry about this, but *we used your right hand while you were passed out.*"

"Huh?" Kamijou's eyes became pinpoints.

"I'll say it even more simply. Their habits went..." Saiji Tatemi-ya's lips turned up into a vulgar smile and he pointed at Lucia. Her expression was blank, and the vicar pope had one solemn word.

"...*poof*!"

Lucia's face immediately reddened, and with her hands inside her shortish sleeves, she held Angeline and turned her away. It was like a mother trying to use her own body as a shield to protect her child.

He looked more closely and saw a handful of safety pins attached to each of their habits, like Index's. The golden circlets tight around their foreheads were gone, too.

Kamijou had a good picture of what happened, and it took him a minute to react. "Wait...Such an amazing—I mean terrible—event happened while I was unconscious?! And how am I supposed to deal with Index being right next to me now that she's remembering and starting to get angry?! I mean, I didn't see anything, and you're the ones who did it!! How is it fair to get mad at *me*?!"

Even as he argued with his words, he was already moving into the early stages of a groveling position. Index was quiet to the wailing Kamijou, but that only made her slow, silent movement of lips and baring of glinting teeth all the more terrifying. The bloodlust in the air audibly whirled around her. Even the veterans of Amakusa started to flee in fear. The entire submersible was wrapped in chaos.

Meanwhile, Angeline pulled her face from Lucia's stomach and escaped her arms, then seemed to remember something. "O-oh, that's right! This isn't the time for...Sister Agnes is still...! Umm, we owe you all a debt for saving us, so we should at least explain the situation...!"

But her stammered, quiet words didn't reach the ears of Kamijou, currently putting up the defense of his life, or those all around him.

"You're just always like that, aren't you, Touma?!"

"But you're always like *this*, Index! I'll admit that there are times people should get mad and lecture others on their faults. But why the heck do you always come in with a biting attack like you're chowing down on seafood or something?!"

"Umm, excuse me..." Her audience wasn't listening to her, and

Angeline waved her hands in the air, flustered with a worried expression. It was a lot like a bad school debate the way it was going. "Well, umm, we still have a goal to accomplish, so if we could explain about Sister Agnes, that would be really...ahh..."

"It *is* strange! It's totally strange! Besides, if you have such a powerful biting attack, you should be using that against sorcerers, too! 103,000 grimoires? That bite is way more dangerous than them!!"

"Touma, Touma. I don't think I'm easy enough that your plan to act defiant will work!!"

Kamijou, for a change, had turned his back to Index trying to bite him and was running away. The sister in white jumped after him, and the two of them tumbled down to the ground. The girl with the epicanthic folds found herself rolled up as well, and she yelped as she fell to the deck. The white towels she was holding flew everywhere. From nearby he could hear the Amakusa people shouting things like "Itsuwa, now's your chance! Go for it!" and "Go for a little kiss on his earlobe!" and "At least try to push your chest into him!" and "Shut up! First thing is getting rid of the powerful enemy in the index! Itsuwa, if you're a woman, then use all your might to kick her out of there!!" Tatemiya laughed as he watched, and Orsola put her hand to her cheek with an "Oh my." Lucia just sighed in exasperation.

Frankly speaking, not a soul was listening to Angeline.

"Umm, uummmmm, excuse me...!!"

The pace of Angeline's fluster began to accelerate steadily.

At the moment when it reached its highest peak, her eyes snapped wide open.

She'd made up her mind. Lucia was standing right next to her. She grabbed Lucia's skirt with both hands.

"L-look! Everyone pay attention!!"

She vehemently flipped up the skirt of Lucia's habit.

Suddenly.

Everyone stopped talking.

Beginning with Lucia, everyone was startled at the earsplitting

silence that followed. Lucia frowned as everyone looked her way, starting to get suspicious of their silence, reminiscent of when the pope waved his hand out the window of a palace. Then, she noticed the odd draft at her legs and looked down, mystified.

"?!"

Approximately two and a half seconds later, her face exploded into full-on redness as the skirt floated in the air of the night sky. She used both hands to push the cloth back down.

Without a word, she turned her head to look at the small sister at her side.

"...S-Sister Angeline?"

"W-well! This is always how our unit was, wasn't it?! So, it was, umm, just like, a habit, that's all!!"

Angeline probably meant that to defend herself, but Tatemiya and the boys among Amakusa then grew as red as Lucia and averted their eyes in additional embarrassment. And Kamijou froze in place while being held down by Index, which gave her the perfect opportunity to take a bite out of his head.

4

Amakusa seemed to have enough common sense not to go near land with their giant submersible. First they headed toward land in it, and then Tatemiya removed a bundle of papers from his pocket and threw them in the other direction, toward the sea. They transformed into nearly twenty small wooden boats. They all split up to board the boats, with Tatemiya finally returning the submersible to paper form. Without pausing to pick up the Japanese paper, it melted into the seawater and vanished.

The paddleboats headed for a nearby source of light. Kamijou wondered for a moment if it was an island, but, focusing his eyes more in the night's darkness, he saw that it was actually land. It appeared to be a place jutting out to sea at a sharp angle.

"Welp, now we're back in Chioggia. Though this area is separated from the central part where the lady Orsola lived by the sea."

Apparently, it was called Sottomarina. When they reached the shore, the members of Amakusa turned the paddleboats back into pieces of paper again. Then they scattered another bundle of paper, which this time created wooden chairs and a table. There were even wooden spoons, forks, plates, and cups, so they must have been setting up the table to eat food.

Then, the tall Lucia looked around them nervously. "I would love to join you, but we must now go back to where Sister Agnes is."

"There's no point going now," said Tatemiya, flat-out rejecting her. "We'd just throw the whole place into confusion. They'll all still be on high alert. We need to kill some time first."

With that, preparations for a late dinner on the dark sea began.

No actual food came out of the strewn-about paper stack, of course. Someone took out metal cooking utensils for camping, and the young men and women of Amakusa began to speedily start making food. As Kamijou watched them, he noticed they seemed to be doing unnecessary things in the process. Maybe it was some kind of ritual that obeyed Amakusa's rules or forms or something.

Angeline, who was also looking at the people making the food, said, "Coffee and black tea are okay, but I like *cioccolata con panna*."

"What's that?" Kamijou asked, looking at her.

"Oh, you don't know? It's a chocolate drink with fresh cream piled on top. Normally you use espresso for it, but I like chocolate bet— *Mmph?!*"

Before Angeline could finish her proud explanation of the supersweet drink, Lucia pushed down on Angeline's head from beside her. "Sister Angeline…You've seemed to be lacking a fair bit of caution lately. We are only cooperating with them temporarily. And also, I thought I've warned you to get rid of that attachment to such sweet food and drink."

Kamijou was the one who was confused by Lucia's anger. "You don't have to go that far. I mean, aren't all sisters basically the same way? You know, always letting others know what they want?"

"What basis do you have to make such a statement?! Please do not take Sister Angeline, a nun *in training*, to be representative of the entire Crossist Church!!" she shouted. Her face looked like she could absolutely not believe what she'd just heard.

Index looked away awkwardly. Incidentally, Orsola, next to her, had already picked up the thinly sliced fresh ham they'd brought from their chopping block and was munching down on it saying how "quite good" it tasted...Yes, all of them were basically the same way.

In the meantime, the cooking was finished.

Upon Tatemiya's urging, Kamijou and the others sat down at the table.

Then, suddenly, he found a white towel being held out toward him. He turned to see the girl with the epicanthic eyelid folds there. She was holding her cheek with her free hand, blushing slightly, eyes wandering.

"Oh, thanks," said Kamijou casually, taking it.

The Amakusa girl said, "N-no, not at all!" and beat a hasty retreat. Then came the other voices, from which she shrank away: "The towel plan again, Itsuwa?!" "Go to the next step! Blend into the confusion and grab his hand!" "Argh, you're taking too long!" "No, maybe Itsuwa's charm is in not making any progress?" "You will clash with the priestess in time, but for this, we are all behind you, Itsuwa!!" Kamijou wondered to himself what they'd been discussing all this time, noting that he was the only one anyone gave a towel to.

Of course, not all of the Amakusa members could fit at the same table, so they created other tables for the rest of them and walked over toward them as they talked among themselves.

After all was said and done, they began to pool their information and held a war council.

"First we'll start with the fleet, where that person named Agnes is being held." The first one to speak was Index. "I believe it's probably the Queen's Fleet, which guards the *Queen of the Adriatic*. Is that correct?"

She got it right in one shot. Lucia and Angeline looked at her, startled. Kamijou was somewhat used to this, but times like these made him really realize how unique the girl was.

"Guard...? Wait, so that whole stinking fleet is just extra?" said Tatemiya, in less of a suspicious tone and more of an astounded one. His expression looked like he'd just seen a trinket that reeked of the nouveau riche, but Kamijou couldn't blame him. The fleet was already enough of a threat just with that.

"Y-yes. We don't know what exactly the *Queen of the Adriatic* is, ourselves...But we think it's *so amazing that we can't even understand it.*"

"After you defeated us during the *Book of the Law* incident, we were reprimanded and removed from the front lines," continued Lucia. "We were made to work in the Queen's Fleet under the guise of repaying the debt we created for the Roman Orthodox Church... But all we were given was direct orders, so we didn't know what we were actually contributing to at the time." She loaded up Angeline's plate with only vegetables and handed it to her, causing the smaller nun to look like she was about to cry. Of course, the taller sister didn't care.

"When you say *made to work*, what were you doing?" asked Kamijou with a tilt of his head.

Lucia and Angeline exchanged glances. Angeline said, "W-we were assigned to removing the wind from the seawater..."

"What? Wind???"

"Oh, well, umm. When I say wind, I mean it in the magical sense."

..."*Wind in the magical sense*"? thought Kamijou, his eyes shrinking to the size of little dots. He had no idea what the difference was. He was about to say, *Hey, what on earth is that even supposed to mean?* before Index cut in.

"Hmm. Wind means it was the early steps of alchemy. So it wasn't physical work but mental work?"

"Then one of the four aspects," Orsola said. "And if you were removing that, then..."

"That might mean they were making you purposely create something unstable," Tatemiya continued.

The people from the magical side kept throwing out comments among themselves, and the Amakusa members around them were nodding along in understanding. Kamijou seemed to have lost the chance to ask his question. The obvious bit of knowledge that "any moving air constitutes wind" came to mind, but that was all his brain could think before exhausting itself.

"The escort ships all seem to be using seawater, so I assume they were likely being used for another spell," mentioned Lucia.

"B-but I can't think of anything besides the Queen of the Adriatic."

Kamijou, driven out from the ring of the conversation, tried to dive back into it. "But, err, the Queen of the Adriatic? I feel like I've heard that term somewhere besides in respect to the Roman Orthodox Church," mused Kamijou, putting salad with lots of little octopus legs on his plate.

Index answered him. "The Queen of the Adriatic is one of Venice's nicknames."

"Hmm? That means it's some sorcery deeply related to Venice, right? Like an ocean spell that their branch in Venice created or something."

"It is that, but..." Orsola tried to give Angeline's plate some fresh ham, but Lucia politely refused the attempt, saying that she couldn't baby her. "...Originally, though Venice and the Roman Orthodox Church are both on the Italian peninsula, there is a period in history when they were on extremely bad terms with each other."

"Huh?" Kamijou frowned.

Orsola continued. "The city of Venice was first created when those who opposed others invading and controlling them fled to the Adriatic Sea. Even after that, their independent spirits left an extremely strong society there; the city even went so far as to reject all counsel given to them to join under the Roman Orthodox Church or the Byzantine Empire."

Index, eating her buttered, stir-fried Manila clams, said, "Historically, a trader brought the remains of Saint Mark, one of the Twelve Apostles, onto the island of Venice in 829. By doing that, their stance became one of independence for the sake of protecting his rest. Maybe the Venetians wanted the Vatican to see them as equals, since they were doing the same for Saint Peter."

Lucia nodded as well. "Venice gained much fortune by trading salt and other commodities. Meanwhile, they repelled countless invasions from larger nations like the kingdom of the Franks and Genoa. The city had enough military strength to overtake one nearby city-state after another, such as Padua and Chioggia." She paused. "That's how they ascended to being a strong, seafaring nation, not controlled by the Papal States despite how close they were to the Church's base of operations."

Next to Lucia, Angeline put some chopped black porgy on her plate. "Apparently, Venice was directly excommunicated numerous times by the papacy over how high-handed the city was. Normally, that would be a death sentence, but the city paid it no mind and continued to expand anyway...The Roman Orthodox Church never knew when the city-state would bare its fangs at them, so they wouldn't have given them the gift of a giant fleet spell like that. In fact, it was..."

"...a special, huge fleet of ships made to fight against Venice," said Kamijou quietly, his fork pausing in midair.

"Yep." Index nodded. "The Roman Orthodox Church at the time felt they were experiencing a crisis, so the Queen of the Adriatic is what they put together so they could bury Venice with one strike if it came to that. A large-scale anti-city spell wouldn't be able to handle a fleet intercepting it, so the Queen's Fleet was created as a defensive network against the Venetian navy."

A huge spell that could wipe out an entire country at once. The fact surprised Lucia and Angeline more than it did Kamijou or Tatemiya. They had probably just been confronted with what they'd been doing this whole time and where they'd been doing it.

"...So they brought out some really old equipment, eh? What are they planning to start, here, with something so ridiculous?" Tatemiya shook his head and gazed out at the off-white lights floating on the distant sea.

Index made a difficult face. "The large-scale spell, the Queen of the Adriatic, can only be activated against Venice. The reason is simple. They were scared of it being stolen and pointed back at them."

"Th-then they're actually going to destroy Venice?!" Angeline's face paled.

This time, though, Orsola frowned. "The Roman Orthodox Church and Venice's rivalry was a thing of centuries ago. Right now, it's a world-renowned tourist attraction, and the Church should be benefiting greatly from it as well. I cannot conceive a reason to come here all of a sudden and destroy it."

"…Maybe there is one—a big enough reason to attack Venice," said Index into the silence settling around them.

Kamijou gulped audibly. "The Queen of the Adriatic spell is hundreds of years old, too…Can't say it as well as Orsola, but why now?"

"Hmm…You would think they would be trying to show their authority to outside powers."

"But the Roman Orthodox Church is already the biggest faction in the world, isn't it? Did something happen with them recently to make them have to do something like this…?"

Kamijou paused midsentence for a moment.

And then he said, "…The Croce di Pietro?"

Lucia and Angeline were taken aback at the unexpected term. Index and Orsola, who knew the details behind that, shared Kamijou's expression.

Only Tatemiya seemed to be completely oblivious. "That was the top-tier Soul Arm of the Roman Orthodox Church, wasn't it? They used it to attack Academy City during the Daihasei Festival, and it didn't work one bit. Only natural they'd be a little panicked."

That wasn't all it took for the science side to defeat the magic side, but it must have had a measurable impact on the Roman Orthodox Church. Their strongest trump card had no effect, so where did that leave their other cards?

"But even if they are showing that they're panicked, why'd they end up going after Venice? And what the heck was the idiot thinking who planned all this…? Index, do you get anything out of using the Queen of the Adriatic? As in, taking control of towns, like the Croce di Pietro?"

"There's nothing like that. The Queen of the Adriatic's only value is in destruction. It's basically the divine judgment exercised at Sodom and Gomorrah—its effect is that it robs everything of its value. I don't think it's going to end up creating anything of value."

"Sodom and Gomorrah...," repeated Tatemiya, tilting his wine-filled wooden cup. "That one about the archangel, the POWER OF GOD, raining down arrows of fire?" He started to speak as if he was flipping through a book. "An angel was ordered to deliver judgment on a city of immorality, but there was one pious family there. So before the angel destroyed it, he told that family to run away. And he gave them one rule. But on the day of the destruction, the wife broke that rule, so she was destroyed along with the town..."

"Yep. The Queen of the Adriatic first identifies Venice as a city of immorality, then rains bolts of fire down on it. By doing that, it'll destroy everything from the city's center to its outskirts. That's the first stage." Index's voice was flat. "The second stage goes after the people and objects who had left Venice, on top of that. People off on vacation, pieces of art donated to museums, the culture forming the foundation of Venice—it takes away all that stuff. Even the Venetian branches of academics and history might instantly disappear..."

Those were chilling words.

Just the idea was unimaginable, making the sheer scale of it stand out all the more.

It was completely out of the realm of normal imagination.

"Sister Agnes...," said Angeline suddenly. "I don't think she knows anything. If she knew what the Queen of the Adriatic was for, she would never keep quiet about it. Maybe you won't believe me, because we attacked you before, but battling professionals is one thing. I can't imagine Sister Agnes being okay with killing normal Roman Orthodox followers who don't know anything about magic."

"My image of her is not so embellished," continued Lucia, "but it's likely true she doesn't know the details. Considering the situation, the Roman Orthodox Church doesn't need to explain it to her; they just need to use her and discard her. She is the key, and that is all they see her as. A tool." Her voice was bitter.

Kamijou felt like he understood both their opinions, but he looked next to him and saw Index frowning just a little. As if she'd noticed something about what they were saying that bothered her.

Tatemiya exhaled quietly. "Well, anyway, guess we gotta get Agnes Sanctis out of there before the spell goes off. Which is obviously way more easily said than done. I mean, if you're saying they're gonna blast Venice out of existence, my heart's not going to let me do nothing about it."

Lucia and Angeline couldn't help but fall silent at his realistic words.

"Do we have a concrete time limit here?"

"...No. But now that the fleet has assembled, we most likely don't have much time. An enormous amount of energy is required to maintain it. And once the sun comes up, it would stand out far too much. Even with a ward against humans, against something that size..."

"U-until now, the ships had each been doing their own preparations separately. And the actual number of ships was only a fraction of what's there now...But considering they just now made a big move, I don't think they would purposely wait for a long time."

"...Which means we've gotta get a move on, eh?" said Tatemiya with a hint of tension in his voice.

"Hey, this is a sorcery problem, right? Why can't we ask the English Puritan Church?" asked Kamijou. He didn't understand the specifics, but he was pretty sure Necessarius, the group Index was a part of, was made to handle issues like this.

But Tatemiya shook his head. "We already did. London's pretty far away. And this isn't some sorcerer's society we're looking at here. It's the Roman Orthodox Church itself. The real thing. If the English Church brings its full force to bear and crushes them, that could cause fissures and problems all across the world. This is already their home territory—if any other religious group starts putting together a large force, they'll find fault with it."

According to him, even the fact that they'd helped Kamijou and the others had been a veritable tightrope act. He gritted his teeth in frustration at how the only conditions piling up were disadvanta-geous. But on the other hand...*It's not over yet. **That means that we, at least, can walk the tightrope.***

For example, even without calling extensive reinforcements, he believed they could use only the forces present now for legitimate self-defense and just barely have enough of an excuse to cover it.

That was probably why they'd used Tatemiya and Amakusa to save Kamijou and the others, and possibly why they weren't trying to cut off their connection with Lucia and the other sisters without giving them a chance to explain.

The vicar pope moved his plate and cup on the table to the side, then pushed a big plate full of salad in Orsola's direction.

"So here's the situation."

Tatemiya put a wooden container filled with salt into the middle of the open space with a *click*.

"This is the Queen's Fleet. Right now they're ten kilometers off the southern coast of Venice. They're far from the main island and also fairly distant from each of the outlying islands. They're in a good spot; nobody will happen to see them, even if they don't use a ward-ing spell."

Next, he took the container of sauce and placed it farther back, about thirty centimeters away.

"And here's our current location. It's another ten kilometers south. We can't see the light from the Queen's Fleet from here. In this direc-tion, we see the sandbar of Lido at night. It's a long, thin island that goes from where we are in Chioggia to the main island of Venice."

"Its casinos are famous," said Angeline, giving trivia unsuited for a sister and earning her another push on her head by Lucia.

"And..." Tatemiya picked up a wooden fork. "About five and a half kilometers out from the Queen's Fleet, given the size and angle of the cannons, is probably their search range. If we enter this circle, their cannons will start firing at us and won't stop."

Scriiiitch! Tatemiya drew a circle in the wooden table. Centered on the container of salt, the edge of the circle was just about halfway between it and the sauce container. It was like a line of battle.

"In reality, they're not gonna start firing as soon as we get into range. There's probably a good dead zone from around four to five kilometers out."

Tatemiya drew another ring inside the first. It was starting to look like the rings to mark age in a tree trunk. Then, with a *pak*, he tapped the fork's tip on the five-kilometer line.

"Simply speaking, we'll need to move this close to get into the Queen's Fleet. Our ship'll be gone as soon as they hit us once. They've got a little under one hundred, and each has thirty or forty cannons to a side. They're all pretty close together, so they can't all fire at once…but the cannon fire will still pour down on us like rain."

Scratch! Tatemiya drew a straight line on the table from the salt to the sauce, then started tapping the fork on the inside of the circle marking their firing range.

"So the question is, how do we charge in while avoiding that?" he asked. Then he continued, "Though if we did charge in, we'd have to fight even more enemies on the ships themselves."

Everybody gulped.

There was a term called *fusillade*. It referred to a wall made of incoming fire. He was asking how to slip past a thick, solid wall with no holes. It was an impractical proposition.

"Five kilometers…I guess that's three minutes by train?"

"…Man, your examples are hopelessly homely," Tatemiya said, rolling his eyes.

He explained. "Five kilometers on land is totally different than five kilometers at sea. Try putting a warship engine in a car. Might actually fly into the sky. Well actually, the car would probably break just from the weight."

Many thought of seafaring vessels as slower than cars or airplanes, but that was because the water put up a lot of resistance to being displaced. Going straight there was five kilometers, but it *felt* like many times that. It dragged out the distance, meaning they'd have to make their way in little by little while avoiding the incoming fire.

The more he heard, the more depressing it got. It was enough to ruin his appetite.

"Excuse me. Why don't we dive underwater and travel there in secret, like you did before?" Orsola asked at length.

"...U-umm, when we broke out, we did sort of the same thing. We used the seafloor coaster to flee. But that's exactly why..."

Lucia put the nail in the coffin Angeline had set up. "The Queen's Fleet's commander is no fool. He won't let it happen a third time. The leader is called Biagio Busoni. He holds the rank of bishop, but many say his guile exceeds even that of cardinals. I believe he is rethinking his sea-control systems to deal with underwater combat as we speak."

Biagio Busoni.

"I hear he is particularly good at moving several pieces rather than using his combat prowess on its own. But I'm sure he isn't simply sitting there being protected by the escorts. Creating a perfect defensive line like this proves he can almost physically feel the movements of his enemies. One doesn't gain the rank of bishop very easily."

"??? Wait, so how important is a bishop?"

"A...A bishop can order around a thousand of us nuns to act almost on a whim," said Angeline, not in a self-deprecating way but in an entirely normal voice.

Tatemiya clicked his tongue. "So we're just lucky we don't have that many people after us, eh? Either way, back to the topic, the issue seems to be how versatile the Queen's Fleet's combat strength is. They don't need to stop by a naval port to resupply, since the ships are all made of ice. They're a real pain, man."

Kamijou wasn't sure the religious group that just made a submersible out of pieces of paper had any room to talk, but facts were facts. The great fleet was originally made to avoid the entire Venetian navy. Maybe they weren't on the right track, thinking they could stand up to it with one or two little underwater vehicles.

Lucia and Angeline clenched their teeth in frustration. An outsider giving an objective viewpoint on their combat potential must have made them realize again where they stood.

"But...Still, we must go," Lucia said, her face hard.

Tatemiya scratched his head. "Hey, now."

"I will not ask you to come with us. Asking to borrow a ship would be insolent of us as well. We have a spell to create a seafloor coaster. We really don't have any choice but to use that to get inside."

"I-it isn't like we have *no* chance of winning...," Angeline added timidly. Fear was clear in her eyes, and her shoulders were shaking. Still, she didn't stay quiet. "If we string the seafloor coaster through the water like tree roots...we might be able to stop the fleet from moving. Or we could try to poke holes in their hulls and force them aground—"

Tatemiya cut in. "It only takes one of those rounds to sink our ship. But those ice ships are hitting one another with dozens of 'em, and they just heal up all the damage. I don't think breaking them's going to put a dent in their fleet."

Lucia and Angeline fell silent for a moment. The only things Kamijou heard were their stifled breathing and the sound of waves.

Finally, Lucia spoke. "...Then what would you have us do?" Her teeth were clenched. "Nobody desires the destruction of Venice. At this rate, Biagio's insensible commands will have Sister Agnes used and tossed away for this insensible 'Queen of the Adriatic.' She'll be left an empty husk, wordless and motionless. Are you telling us to sit by and watch quietly as it happens?" She shut her eyes as she talked. "Why do you think we follow her? Sister Agnes is the one nun who is so faithful in her service to the divine that it gives even *me* chills. The treasure a church needs is not money or riches—it is people like her. I will not think someone I have acknowledged is at all deserving of such an end...no matter what the case may be."

"For me...faith doesn't decide my actions as much as it does for Sister Lucia." Angeline smiled a little and continued. Not so anyone would agree with her—just to say what she thought. "Everyone's reasons really depend on the person. Sister Agnes has saved me many times in the past. It wasn't just one or two times in my life when big things happened. She's constantly been saving me. I don't want to say good-bye to her without repaying her somehow. And if I'm going to repay her, now's the time."

"..." Kamijou fell silent for a moment. No—he was moved to silence. The words of Lucia and Angeline hadn't been compelling at all. In fact, they sounded more like a rejection of the others here, an attempt to place them farther away from the rest.

But...

That was just it.

"Hey, Tatemiya. *Why don't you give it a rest?*"

"Eh?" Tatemiya frowned.

Kamijou continued. "All this stuff about chances of winning, strategies, practical problems, getting five kilometers in, dying if we take one hit...We get all that, you know? That's not what this is about. Isn't whether we want to help Agnes really all we should be discussing right now?"

Lucia and Angeline looked at him in surprise.

Index's shoulders fell as she breathed a heavy, tired sigh. Orsola lightly rubbed her back to comfort her. They both knew about this side of Kamijou, since they had been personally privy to it.

"Tatemiya," he said, using his name as the one person representing all of Amakusa. As if aware of that, all of its young men and women looked at him, too.

"Agnes Sanctis isn't a perfectly good person or anything. But *she purposely gave up her own chance of being rescued* in order to let her friends escape. She's about to be used for the Queen of the Adriatic, but she doesn't know what it's for, either. They're going to take advantage of her feelings, use them for their own purposes, and then destroy her. She'll end up like an empty shell, and then we *really* won't be able to save her, and then the curtain will fall. What's important is whether we *should* rescue her or not, right? And won't that prevent all of Venice from being destroyed, too? Isn't there only one thing to do now?"

Kamijou didn't look away. His eyes remained fixed on Saiji Tatemiya as he spoke.

"If you don't want to save her, I'll go there alone if I have to."

"Hah," Tatemiya laughed. *Crick!* He stabbed the wooden fork into the table. "Seriously, now you're making me out to be the bad guy here..." He clicked his tongue in frustration. "Shit, that stings. That wasn't what I wanted to say. *We figured out all that a long time ago.* That's why I was asking what we should do next. If being reckless hasn't been working up till now, then we have to find a way to force it to work." He shook his head, fed up with all this. "We had a plan ready from the outset."

Everyone present, Kamijou included, was surprised.

"Whether or not you all agree to my proposed plan depends on whether you think it's a good idea. I won't hear any complaints if we mess it up. Well, if you're complaining, it's already too late, anyway. What I wanted to know was if you all had the balls to do it. And you came in and took my legs out from under me!!"

Tatemiya fired a really disappointed glance at Kamijou, then looked around. His allies, those young men and women—his treasured friends—were around him. The vicar pope spoke to them next.

"Well, that's what it adds up to for us. We're all living through this and coming back. If any of you are thinking you don't want to die today or that you'll carry out your own brand of justice even if you die, you should quietly leave now. No compromises. If we go to a battlefield, we're all coming back. Understand?"

There were no objections. Their silent affirmation represented their shared intent.

Tatemiya asked the next question quietly, like a teacher asking his idiot students a question. "What's the teaching that our priestess taught us?"

All the members of the Amakusa-Style Crossist Church responded with a shout.

"The hand of salvation for the unsaved!!"

5

After Kamijou, Amakusa, and the others boarded the submersible, it began to move slowly north over the Adriatic Sea—and toward the Queen's Fleet. They stood on its deck as it floated above the water.

Tatemiya's weapon of choice was called a flamberge: a giant sword over 180 centimeters long. The double-edged blade featured a wave-like construction, evidently for widening wounds. Unlike normal weapons, it wasn't made of metal. Kamijou didn't know what the pure-white blade was made of.

"This thing is better suited to muddy battlefields…Guess I'll just have to be resourceful, eh?" said Tatemiya to himself, sticking the sword down into the ship.

I guess weapons change based on the place and situation, thought Kamijou. He couldn't imagine the reasons why; he used just his fist no matter where he was.

Lucia was holding a giant wooden wheel, like one a horse-pulled cart might use. The weighty-looking object had been created using Amakusa's paper talismans.

"I do sense something of a unique 'scent' to it…" She gripped the wheel and slowly swung it, testing how it felt to her body. "…But I can use it. This should be more than enough to use the offensive techniques modeled after Saint Catherine's Legend of the Wheel."

By Kamijou's memory, she was good at making the big wheel explode and using the rain of splinters to attack.

On the other hand, Angeline had a small cloth bag filled with gold and silver coins. She had used the blunt weapon before as a flail, relying on its heavy strikes to attack. "Ah…I can still put in more. But it'll hurt if I put in this much…M-maybe just a few more…"

With particular attention, she put in another couple of coins, then crooked her head to the side and took them back out of the bag. Lucia approached, her face one of irritation.

"Sister Angeline!" she said. "Why are you being so stingy while making your weapon?! Put in at least this much more! You have to give them what for!!"

"Wa-wah! But if I hit them with this, it'll do more than hurt them!"

"If you want to talk things out, then you must start by preparing an environment in which you *must* talk things out. If we could put our hands up, unarmed, and hold a conversation with them, nobody would be having a problem in the first place!"

As Kamijou watched from a distance the noisy argument between the two sisters, he sighed a little. "I feel like…I've been misunderstanding the Roman Orthodox Church."

"Different strokes for different folks, in terms of Roman Orthodoxy…is not quite how it works," said Orsola quietly, standing next to him. "If someone is in the wrong, it is not the right thing to eliminate that one person. Everyone possesses many things. The negative side of the Church that you witnessed is something I, too, possess… I, myself, once caused a lot of trouble for everyone from Amakusa by not trusting them completely."

Is that how it works? Kamijou mused. "…I find it hard to compare you to a bad person, though."

"Now, now. Women have many sides to them, you know," said Orsola with a smile, her words sounding both somehow dangerous and somehow erotic. Whether it was her clothing or her words and actions, the sister was always—unconsciously—overemphasizing certain things.

Then Index slid in between them. In her hands was a staff. "Here! I borrowed this from an Amakusa person, but I can't use Soul Arms that need you to temper mana, so I think it's better if you have it."

"Oh," said Orsola, taking the staff. It was made of silver. A small carving of a crouched angel sat on its tip. The six wings extending from its back shrouded it like a birdcage of its own making.

It was the weapon Agnes once used. Amakusa had been the ones to temporarily take Agnes's unit into custody after she surrendered during the battle over the *Book of the Law*. Maybe they'd acquired it at that time.

Then Kamijou noticed that Index was staring at him. "Wh-what is it, Index?"

"…" Index was silent for a moment. "Nothing really."

"What?! Why are you turning away and being all irritated, then?! Not that I *enjoy* your usual biting overreaction, but such a cool and collected reaction is hard for me to take in its own way!!"

Kamijou's shout garnered no response from Index as she stormed away. Orsola watched, then sighed and said, "…It's because you don't look after her well enough."

Now that she mentioned it, he and Index were actually supposed to be eating local pasta and going around to famous locations right about now, making all sorts of fun memories. Next thing he knew, this was happening. He thought to himself that Index might have been the one *most* excited about this trip.

"You condemn your 'rotten luck' quite often, but you have no intention of stopping now, do you?"

"...I'm like an idiot father too wrapped up in his job."

The submersible proceeded ever onward. He thought he could see the off-white glimmer of the Queen's Fleet growing slightly stronger.

"This should be a good spot. Let's get started."

Tatemiya took a bundle of paper bound by a rubber band out of his pants pocket.

Kamijou frowned. "Start what?"

"Taking on this Queen's Fleet of theirs is a bit much for one ship to handle, y'know? So, well, we're just gonna make ourselves a bit stronger. Check this out."

Tatemiya took off the rubber band and flung the entire bundle of papers overboard with a *rustle*. All the Japanese papers were strewn about like confetti as they danced through the air and fell to the dark water's surface below. Finally, the thin paper melted into the seawater.

Boom!!

As the papers expanded with the moisture, they created stacks and stacks of lumber, which then came together to form a sailboat. Unlike those in the Queen's Fleet, the minor details of its construction felt more Japanese than anything else. The new ship was thirty meters long, seven wide, and a little under twenty high including the mast. Compared to the one-hundred-meter-long ships in the Queen's Fleet, it looked pretty meager.

But more than one or two ships appeared. Several dozen came up out of the water at once. As the boats expanded, they pushed and jostled against one another, seeming to force themselves into existence. One bounced into the submersible Kamijou was on as well, and the ship shook to the side.

Kamijou regarded the sight with blank amazement. "…We've got a fleet, too? Why even bother with a plan in the first place? Can't we just ram it into the Queen's Fleet?"

"You're thinking a wee bit too highly of me. And take a good look. These things aren't warships like theirs are. No cannons anywhere, see?"

"…?"

He was right—they had nothing that resembled cannons. The walls and ornaments on the ships also looked pretty delicate, weak to impact. Did that mean they were really just sailboats? "What are you going to do with such weak-looking ships?"

"Here's how it goes. Warships ain't the only things that fight on the sea. Our Amakusa religion developed in secret by blending into our location and its customs. That means, of course, we've studied English history, too."

Tatemiya grinned and continued.

"You ever heard the story about how the English sank the Spanish's infamous invincible armada?"

6

Ship 43 of the Queen's Fleet was an intelligence ship specializing in reconnaissance. Sister Agatha, who was permanently stationed there, was standing before the giant wheel at the very front of the ship's deck when she gasped. There was a small table on either side of the helm, and several documents made of ice were stuck to them. On the thin ice tables, modeled after old parchment paper, were displays containing various real-time information: everything from maps and charts to the ship's status.

One of those stood out. The ice document displaying the nautical chart of the water in and around the Adriatic began to give a warning ring. Below the cloud of chess-like pieces representing the Queen's Fleet, several new pieces appeared and began to approach at a high speed.

"Bishop Biagio!!" she shouted.

"I see it," came a voice that seemed to vibrate the air itself. "Give me the details."

"Thirty to forty ships detected approaching from the southern Venetian Bay on the Adriatic! Their speed is…very high! They will arrive at the main ship's position in a little over fifty seconds!!"

A little less than five kilometers remained between them and signs of the ships that had appeared. Calculating from the distance and time showed that they were moving at approximately 360 kilometers per hour. But the fundamental basis of speed on water was different than that on land, due to the big difference between air resistance and water resistance.

The speed was, by all rights, absolutely impossible. Even the science faction's high-speed craft could reach only about ninety kilometers per hour. One would need a whole lot of power to move 360 kilometers per hour over water, and too much of it could cause seawater to force its way into the ship. Their enemy was forcing it to work in spite of that.

"Can you sink them?"

"Ships Twenty-Five through Thirty-Eight, deployed south of the *Queen of the Adriatic*, are in position to fire. If other ships change position while those ones are intercepting, we may be able to prevent them from slipping by."

"Be quick about it. They're after the *Queen of the Adriatic*. Do not allow them to make contact."

"Understood!" declared Agatha as she relayed the situation and targets to all the other ships. New ice documents floated up to the tables on either side of her, displaying things such as the Queen's Fleet's positioning and firing lines.

Four and a half kilometers to the new ships.

"The sighted group of ships will make contact with this fleet in fifty seconds! Sink them before they reach us!!"

No sooner had she barked the order than one explosion after another began to pound on her eardrums. The Queen's Fleet had just fired a whole slew of rounds.

Agatha called up another ice document, watching as several thick columns of water arose on the night sea and projected on the paper's surface. A few of the enemy sailboats began to sink, one after the other.

But they weren't stopping. They used their own allied ships as springboards to bounce across the water's surface, drawing even closer.

Are they using the ships in front as a shield...?

Agatha began to feel doubt. But still, they didn't look like they were protected by special armor or defensive spells. The enemy boats were going down easily, not attempting to dodge the cannonballs as they approached. Not even trying to take evasive maneuvers, even though more than ten of them had already taken direct fire.

The distance between them closed in the blink of an eye.

It was only a few hundred meters now, and the enemy ships had yet to fire a single bullet.

...*Wait.* Agatha looked again at the enemy ships displayed on the ice document.

And then she gave a surprised start. Those ships *had no cannons.*

"Which means...All ships, defensive maneuvers! The enemy, they're...!!"

But before she could finish her command to all the ships...

The wooden boats didn't slow down as they plunged toward them at an insane speed, mercilessly stabbing into the sides of the Queen's Fleet's escort ships. But they didn't stop there. The wooden boats began to emit light from inside them, and all of a sudden, there was a big explosion. It was like the entire boat had been a giant bomb.

Kaboom!! came the roar.

The surface of the water whipped about madly, and Agatha shouted out, her body now pressed against the helm. "Those are fireships—unmanned warships built to self-destruct!!"

As he listened to the explosions, Tatemiya quietly closed his eyes. "Fireships were the first unmanned weapons made to travel across the water, before torpedoes were invented. Normally you use pretty small boats for it, but when faced with the Invincible Armada, the

English navy loaded up their actual big ships with explosives and rammed them, unmanned, into the enemy."

Kamijou had to sigh. "And while they're distracted by all the nonsense here, we go right up next to them? That's a pretty messy plan."

"Sister Agatha."

"Agh…Y-yes, sir!" answered Agatha to Biagio's voice, her ears pelted with one exploding fireship after another.

"If their goal is to stop the Queen of the Adriatic's activation, then I doubt their attack will end on the perimeter. They have something else. Figure out what."

Agatha's eyes flew over the ice documents on the table. The information from the sea charts and maps was blurring heavily in response to the explosive impacts, making it very hard to read.

If the fireships aren't their main plan…then their flagship is somewhere else. But…

She changed the magnification, but though she checked five kilometers, ten kilometers, and twenty kilometers out, there were no such ships to be found nearby. Maybe three civilian cruisers were on the water, but those wouldn't be it.

Agatha considered zooming out even farther, but then her hand stopped abruptly.

…*"On" the water?*

Several ice sheets disappeared. In their place arose one, standing up on its side, with a sea chart on it. A block of ice, with the same width and depth as the sheet, appeared on the table. It wasn't displaying the sea horizontally: It was a vertically oriented map.

In other words, it was searching toward the seafloor.

"There it is! Giant structure spotted eighty meters south and forty meters below the Queen's Fleet…It's the submersible again!!"

"We've been noticed…," said Tatemiya, suddenly raising his head.

As if in response, the voices of the Amakusa members controlling the submersible came back to him.

"Enemy cannons confirmed! Estimated firing angle: thirty degrees! They're clearly aiming underwater!"

"Movement detected from enemy ships in the south. They appear to be taking a formation to prevent us from rushing them!"

Artillery warfare was invisible—or rather, by the time you saw it, it was already too late. You couldn't normally move around in sea combat as quickly as you could in the air, so it was essentially impossible to evade or shake off enemy attacks at these speeds.

Therefore, the basis of marine warfare was to find a place where you could shower the enemy in attacks and not be fired at yourself. It was a theoretical battle, and one that actually started before any cannons fired. With the natural state being the lack of a reaction, and any reaction immediately spelling defeat, the battle was a mental one, marked by heavy silence.

And...

"Several firing axes are aiming at the submersible!"

"They're handling both vertical and horizontal axes! This is sooner than we thought! At this rate...!!"

"This is the worst...," muttered Tatemiya bitterly. "All hands, brace for impact!! Watch for enemy fire! If this ship takes just one of them, it's—"

Before he could finish, a storm of explosions took away all sound.

"Successful hit on the submersible! Its movement speed has decreased!!"

"Good," responded Biagio to Agatha, his voice a little less tense. "The same trick won't work three times. We were prepared for an anti-submarine bombardment."

What he'd used were shells that froze all the seawater in close proximity. The submersible was now surrounded in thick layers of ice, unable to move. And because of the ice's buoyancy, they could do nothing and wait for the submersible to rise above the surface on the artificial glacier. Then, they could bombard it with normal shells and destroy it for sure.

"Approximately sixty seconds until the enemy ship completely surfaces. In the meantime, we'll prioritize the remnants of the fireships..."

"Sister Agatha! It's an emergency!!"

Then, a different voice from Biagio's cut into the communication. It was one of the sisters she worked with.

"The enemy has boarded Ship Twenty-Nine! Based on their equipment and spell usage, it has to be Amakusa!!"

"What?!" Agatha doubted her ears.

Then she looked again at the ice sheets on the table. An unmanned fireship had rammed into Ship 29 before...but when she looked at it, it was undamaged. If the fireship had exploded, the ship would normally have been heavily damaged...

That meant one thing.

"They prepared one ship that wouldn't explode at all, boarded it, and then blended in with the other fireships as they rammed it... Are you saying that submersible was a second-level decoy...?!"

Touma Kamijou jumped from the "moored" wooden boat to the ice ship. Following closely, Index, Orsola, Lucia, Angeline, Tatemiya, and the members of Amakusa all began to board one after another.

"Don't think about taking over every ship! They have way more people than we do, anyway! Just think about destroying the core of their operations!!"

"Their flagship...Where's the *Queen of the Adriatic*?!" Kamijou looked around, then spotted an even more giant ship than the others several hundred meters away. But there were over ten ice ships in the way just in its shadow.

"We'll handle making bridges between the ships! Anyway, you all get to the flagship..."

Another voice overlapped with Tatemiya's. It was a woman's, like someone announcing something to the ship. "All passengers of Ships Twenty-Nine, Thirty-Two, and Thirty-Four, evacuate immediately! If you don't have the time, go into the water! Our fleet will now destroy those three ships, then re-create them!!"

"Shit!" spat Tatemiya. "They're gonna wreck these ships again! Hurry up!!"

Tatemiya scattered a wad of papers into the surroundings. They expanded vigorously, then began to change shape into a wooden arch bridge stretching from ice ship to ice ship. However, before they could cross, there was cannon fire from nearby. It didn't need to be a direct hit for Kamijou to nearly fall over onto the deck from the shock wave of the blast alone. "Urgh!"

Even groaning like that was wasting time. The giant ships here and there began to collapse like earth. Ship walls were ripped away, falling into the sea and raising thick columns of water.

The spray made it onto the deck. One of the masts, so thick he wouldn't be able to put his arms around it, bent under a strike from a cannon.

"Index!!"

Kamijou grabbed Index's hand, who was shrinking in fear nearby, and ran, pulling her out from underneath the falling mast. *Ka-thud!!* The pillar fell over. Miraculously, it created a bridge that went to the ship nearby.

Kamijou didn't hesitate to jump on.

The Amakusa people, beginning with Tatemiya, climbed atop the wooden bridges they'd prepared and began to disperse onto the other ships.

He held Index's hand as they crossed the sea and moved onto the adjacent ship. He looked back to see Orsola, angelic staff in hand, also following the mast and making it to the ship they were on. A moment later, a second wave of cannon fire slammed into the previous ice ship, causing it to list. The broken mast forming an arch was dragged away and into the sea.

"Touma, what about everyone else…?"

Most appeared to have used the wooden bridges Amakusa had prepared, but he saw several jumping into the water. He unwittingly clenched his teeth in frustration.

Next to him, Orsola said, "They each possess a talisman that will allow them to create bridges and ladders. They decided they should head for the water for now because it would give them a chance at victory."

Her opinion could be called rather hopeful, but he had no choice but to believe in it for now. In either case, there were over ten meters from the deck to the water. Kamijou's hand would never be able to reach them.

"Damn it! Let's crush the *Queen of the Adriatic* fast!!"

But just as he was about to make for the Queen's Fleet again, there was a *fwump* as a new set of footsteps caused him to stop in his tracks.

Standing on the big, stagelike deck were dozens of sisters. Like Lucia and Angeline, each wore a mainly black habit with yellow skirts and sleeves attached—they were the laborers of the fleet. And part of Agnes's unit as well.

The sisters more than likely knew why Kamijou and the others had come here, but they didn't say a word to them before brandishing their weapons. Some looked like weapons and some didn't— they possessed everything from swords, axes, and staves to Bibles and torches.

Those sisters were the only ones here.

Overseers were supposedly on board as well, but they were nowhere to be found. Maybe it was their plan: to leave combat to the workers and flee on their own to a safe place. Considering their strategy was to sink entire enemy ships, though, that didn't seem to be working well for them.

"…You know what'll happen to Agnes, right? And you're still not gonna take our side?!" shouted Kamijou.

One of the sisters, however, shook her head. "Unfortunately, we do not have time to let emotions get in the way of our jobs," she declared, representing all those present.

"I'm sure they don't actually think that," said Orsola to him, truly sounding pained. "Even they probably have yet to realize it. However, they are certainly loyal to Miss Agnes and serve under her. She is their leader, and they believe she will overcome this for them. It must be painful. They're wishing, deep down, for her to turn things around."

"…" They were not allowed to express themselves with words, so they were sending out an SOS using a different method. A situation where they had to hurt each other, contrary to how they felt. When he thought about that, Kamijou's fist naturally tightened.

As if in response, the dozens of sisters all took a step forward.

Only seven meters separated him from the wall of enemies.

And then it happened.

Whoosh!! A small shadow flew over Kamijou's and the sisters' heads.

He looked up. There, flying ten meters in the air, was a thrown cart wheel.

"Sister Luci—?!"

Before one of the enemy nuns could finish saying her name…

Bang!! The wheel exploded with force. Its trajectory had been an odd one, avoiding only Kamijou, Index, and Orsola as all the little wooden splinters shot straight down. It rained destruction. The sisters tried to use their weapons and spells to guard against it, but their entire front line still staggered.

"Over here!!"

He turned to the shout and found Lucia and Angeline, who had crossed over to this ship by a different route. The edge of the deck was right behind them, and a bridge made of wood linked it to a nearby ship.

A moment later…

"Passengers of Ship Forty-One, evacuate immediately! If impossible, to the water! The main fleet will sink that ship and re-create it afterward!!"

Tension broke out around them. He didn't have to know the details on their ship numbering to know they meant *here*.

"Quickly!!"

Lucia shouted, urging them toward the bridge, but it was then that the scared sisters all moved at once.

Not to flee—to make sure Kamijou and the others couldn't do the same.

"You…All of you, idiots! If you have the gall to do this, then why don't you try to save Sister Agnes?!"

With a wave of her hand, Lucia reverted the wooden fragments scattered nearby into the shape of a wheel. With that in hand, she dove toward the sisters.

But before combat began, the roar of a cannon shot ripped through the air.

"Gwahh?!" cried Kamijou as it slammed against his eardrums. With the thunderous roar, a cannonball from the escort ship right next to them stabbed into their ship. The entire deck began to sway heavily sideways—it had been a direct hit.

And the second wave wasn't far behind.

This time, the cannons creaked as they pointed farther up, as though targeting the deck this time.

The cannons' bores pointed right at Kamijou's group. The black holes stared at them like the eyes of monsters.

Just then…

"Vieni! Una persona, dodici apostoli, lo schiavo basso che rovina un mago mentre e quelli che raccolgono!!" *(Come! One of the twelve apostles, tax collector and humble slave who destroys sorcerers!!)*

The shout came from Angeline.

The four coin bags she carried responded.

Red, blue, yellow, and green. The heavy pouches sprouted wings in four colors, and each rammed into a nearby mast like an iron fist. The strike focused on one point, crushing the pillar of ice at its roots. The giant mast swayed and began to fall.

One moment later.

A barrage of cannon fire pelted the toppling mast. The bombardment aimed at Kamijou's group had just barely been blocked by Angeline's quick reaction.

The mast, its role as a shield over, burst apart from the impact before it hit the deck.

Its fragments scattered in every direction and rained down on them. Fragments each as large as a refrigerator.

"!!" Lucia lifted her giant wheel overhead and immediately caused it to explode. The wooden splinters collided with many of the mast's icy fragments, but it couldn't repel all of them.

What chunks of ice made it through headed for the Roman Ortho-dox sisters.

Toward the group of nuns once called Agnes's unit.

When Angeline saw that, she began to run for the sisters despite their being her enemies.

"I…Where are you going?!" Lucia blasted a shout.

Ignoring the amazed nun, Angeline called back her four coin pouches, then she tried to drive away the giant masses of ice pouring down.

But the coin pouches' cloth ripped, and the coins went flying everywhere.

"Withdraw, Sister Angeline!!" Lucia shouted to Angeline; there was nothing she could do anymore. Lucia looked around and saw the boy named Touma Kamijou running toward her. Most likely to tackle Angeline out of the way.

However…

Angeline didn't step back.

Not that she couldn't—she took another step forward. She clenched her teeth and rammed into the chest of the sister closest to her. The girl, dumbstruck and unable to move, bounced backward and started to fall to the deck.

After Angeline had seen her to safety, she tried to duck for cover.

But the refrigerator-sized chunk of ice landed right next to her a moment before she could.

Upon colliding with the deck, the ice sprayed another rain of boulder-sized fragments.

Boom!!

With a dull noise, the girl's small body flew into the air.

"Si…!" shouted Lucia, as if watching something unbelievable. "…Sister Angeline!!"

The sisters nearby wavered for a moment as they saw Lucia about to run for the short, fallen sister. But then, perhaps remembering their mission, they brought their weapons up, when just then…

"Man. This is the dumbest shit I've ever seen! I'm disappointed!!"

Tatemiya and the members of Amakusa had made a wooden bridge from a nearby ship and jumped, moving between Angeline and the sisters to form a wall.

He brought a wad of papers out of his pocket, then threw the entire stack at Lucia. "An escape submersible. Doesn't offer much, but it's better than sitting in the middle of enemy territory. Don't use just one. All you gotta do is spread out some fireships and mess up their detection capabilities, and you'll have a lower chance of getting sunk!!"

Lucia ran over and stuffed the papers in her sleeve. It was all Tatemiya could say; Agnes's unit wasn't weak or dumb enough to let her simply use the talismans. If she panicked and brought out the submersible, the other ships could focus their fire on it, sinking it.

But now wasn't the time for that.

There was something more important than their mathematical probability of victory.

"...Sister Lucia. Your hands...They're shaking."

"Of course they are!!"

"That's...silly. I wouldn't die in a place like this, ma'am..." Angeline squeezed out each and every word. "...We'll all...go back together, right? Sister Agnes, and us, and those people over there fighting...Everyone means...everyone."

Creak-creak. The cannons on the ship next to them moved into position again. They were preparing for a third wave. But Lucia wouldn't take her eyes from Angeline.

"So I...won't die. You promised, too, ma'am...so I won't, either. So please...Sister Lucia. Don't worry about enemies...or allies...Won't you fight with us...to just protect...everybody...?"

"..." Lucia gritted her teeth. With a *ka-boom*, the nearby escort ship fired at them.

The attack, however, did not crush their flesh.

Something blocked the immensely powerful cannon fire: a single right hand.

Reaching out from the side to block an unwanted guest, the completely regular boy's hand caught the magically launched ice cannon-ball and crushed it with the power of his five fingers.

"Do it, Lucia. Promise," he said. "If I can help, I'll blow away as many of these bullshit illusions as I have to. So promise her! Say it, so she knows it was a good thing she was here! So she can believe it was worth enduring the pain!!"

"Yes." She looked at Angeline and quietly said, "I promise you I will protect everyone. So you must fight your own fight as well."

The small nun smiled a little at her voice.

More cannon fire struck the ice ship, rocking it. Kamijou's right hand couldn't block all the shells—there were too many. It wasn't safe here. It wasn't safe anywhere. After Lucia squeezed the fallen Angeline's hand, she stood up with it still grasped in hers. She couldn't use the wheel like that, but it didn't seem to bother her at all. It was simply a display of intent: that she would fight alongside her, even if it put her at a disadvantage.

The sisters began to move forward to follow Lucia as she retreated.

But Amakusa and Kamijou's group formed a wall between them.

They were all staring in the same direction.

The flagship, the *Queen of the Adriatic*, was just a few ship crossings away.

INTERLUDE FOUR

Not...yet...

Her mind was hazy and Lucia was holding her up, but she could still think.

I don't...want to give up.

She heard explosions and the sounds of swords and axes clashing, but she could still think.

Sister Agnes...did everything for the Church. When she was rewarded for taking on dangerous jobs...she would have more Bibles printed. She would go to all the old churches...the ones nobody came to anymore...and smile, saying she'd offer what help she could...and give them to the priests...

Her entire body was stinging with pain from the icy fragments hitting it.

One of the mast's scattered fragments had struck her on the forehead, and it felt like her brain had been shaken.

Sister Lucia...even when she wasn't working...she'd always go up to the bell tower at church. That way she could come running if even the slightest thing was wrong. She spent so long up there, waiting, that it almost seems like her home now...

Exhausted tears fell.

Not because it hurt. It was pure, simple frustration.

Everyone else...all of them had good traits. Not one person in our

*group...is a bad person. So why...? Why did this happen? I don't...
want these villains. I don't want to have to fight because...someone
drew a line on the scales of good and bad,* she thought, her limbs
swaying limply.

All she wanted was this.

Help...

She endured the pain.

Tears forming in her eyes. ·

*Someone, please rescue them...my precious friends...from this...
worthless darkness...*

CHAPTER 5

The Queen of the Adriatic

La_Regina_del_Mar_Adriatico.

1

"It won't be long now."

Biagio Busoni looked up from the ship's bottom.

"Soon this job, too, will be over. Good heavens—to think crushing a single city would be this much trouble. The *Queen of the Adriatic*...I would have liked to take a nice, long look around it for its antique value before this was over, rather than just putting it to use."

Each side almost twenty meters long, the room appeared perfectly square. But upon closer inspection, the walls were tilted ever so slightly inward. It wasn't a cube but a quadrangular pyramid. If you looked up along the walls and at the faint, bulb-like, almost-white light with which they glimmered, you could see its pinnacle far overhead. The ship was only twenty meters from its bottom to its deck, but here on the inside, the ceiling appeared to be over one hundred meters high.

"...Hmm. It hasn't quieted down yet."

As if in response, the whole body of the flagship, the *Queen of the Adriatic*, lightly shook. Not only once. The rumbles came several times in sequence. The escort ships hemming in the flagship were firing on other allied ships, one after another, like cannibals. And yet the roar of artillery continued. That meant the enemy was crossing over boat after boat, approaching this place. The roaring sounds mercilessly beat against even this, the deepest part of the flagship, enclosed by thick walls of ice.

There was a problem with this as well.

The men overseeing the Queen's Fleet, unlike the sisters who formerly hailed from Agnes's unit, were unsuited for battle. It wasn't a matter of quality but simply of variety. No tactician would fight on the front lines with a weapon in hand. That was also the reasoning for having so few of them: merely a few dozen or so.

That by itself he could tolerate. The issue, however, was that the sisters at his beck and call weren't used to shipboard combat. They were placed on these ships purely to do physical labor. This result could only be called inevitable—they hadn't received any naval training—but...

That is why I declared that they station a marine unit here in addition to the management. And they...

The people above him had seen only the Queen's Fleet's capabilities before deciding on their own that it was safe and they didn't have to call in extra soldiers. They hadn't considered that the fleet's purported invincibility could change based on the type of battle... *So above and below, it matters not. Useless trash, all of them.*

Biagio's eyes swiveled to the side, his head not moving. "Fairly stimulating, isn't it? Is it always so calm around you?"

"..."

The question was directed at the only other person in the room, a girl.

A perfect sphere of ice seven meters across sat in the room's center. The middle was empty like a bubble, but when the Rosary of the Appointed Time, the ignition key for the Queen of the Adriatic, activated, it would fill up with ice. It would freeze the compatible nun, and then he would use it to magically *break* her along with the sphere itself. Right now, she was resting against one of the sphere's outer curves, as if clinging to it.

Her name was Agnes Sanctis.

A girl made to wear a revealing habit that appeared torn.

She didn't answer Biagio's words.

Or perhaps she couldn't answer them. Why was there a battle happening? Who on earth had come all the way here and for what? Her expression said she was too busy thinking about these things to pay attention to anything outside her.

"That's the face," continued Biagio. The dozens of crosses on the four necklaces hanging at his upper chest jingled. "Simply brilliant. Your expression, shamelessly hoping for someone even at this late hour. Your heart, which dares to say your position is a good one. Yes, that is how it must be. When a lowly sinner looks at me with a face of morbid realization—that is what I dislike the most. All animals should be doing is creeping along the ground. Vanity, however, is a right reserved for *humans*."

Along with a grin and the superficial words came a bared malice.

Agnes shot Biagio a glance. "...And what do you think I'm clinging to?"

"Oh, you don't need to tell me—I know. I will not ask you again. Hmph. I was disappointed when *she* pushed this task upon me, but as it allowed me to see this, I will put up with that as well."

Agnes looked away from him out of hatred.

He watched her, satisfied. "This is where your hopes will be crushed. A cog in the machine has no need of emotions."

2

There were only around fifty members of Amakusa.

On the Roman Orthodox Church's side, however, were at least two hundred and fifty just counting sisters. Thinking normally, they should lose based on numbers only. But they were fighting aboard ships. Everyone could never gather in one place, which seemed different from the fundamentals of land combat. In any case, Amakusa was closing the distance and focusing on super-short-range attacks, allowing them to rotate smoothly through the chaotic battle. However, the numerically superior Roman Orthodox Church found their movements hampered by their allies and their own weapons. Amakusa was fighting fully aware of how to turn overwhelming numbers into a disadvantage. Their few members had probably learned it during their battles with many enemies.

The situation was, coincidentally, similar to the *Book of the Law* incident.

There was only one distinction: whether Agnes Sanctis was to be defeated or protected.

"Go! Do whatever it takes to get that kid out of there! We'll distract their main force for ya!!"

Kamijou ran, spurred on by Tatemiya's words.

The flagship was already within three escort ship crossings.

While Amakusa was holding back the sisters, Kamijou, Index, and Orsola jumped from ship to ship. Out of them, Orsola was the only one who could use the wooden-bridge spell they needed. Each time, after chanting an incantation more clearly and carefully than normal magicians, she threw another bundle of Japanese paper.

The flagship, the *Queen of the Adriatic*, was right in front of them.

The source, protected by many an escort vessel. The sorcery device binding Agnes Sanctis and its spell to destroy Venice in one shot. If this ship was the central command location, would Biagio Busoni, whom they hadn't yet seen, be here?

"Let's go! Index, Orsola!!" shouted Kamijou, running over a wooden bridge and stepping onto the flagship.

The deck was enormous.

The Queen's Fleet already featured ships a hundred meters long, but this one was gigantic—twice that size. The ice walls were shining brighter than the others, too. It was like the entire ship was made of silver awash with moonlight. And if the decorations spoke to the other ships' functions as vessels of war, this was like a resplendent palace. Even the railings and doorknobs seemed created by a craftsman, and various statues of angels and the Virgin Mary lined the ship's edge at regular intervals. He didn't feel like going to the ship's bow, but the statue attached to the end was probably a famous piece of artwork.

"There doesn't appear to be anyone here…," said Orsola, gripping her angelic staff and looking around. "This feels similar in construction to the pleasure boat that the doge, the one in charge of Venetia, used. A ship used for the national event, the Marriage of the Sea."

"In other words, the boat has magical properties," said Index. "This ship also serves as the central control for the whole Queen's Fleet. By endlessly changing this ice ship's decorations and their locations, it can control any of the specific boats directly."

Kamijou took a careful look around as well. "Which is why the sisters don't come here and why they're not firing the cannons recklessly. I bet this flagship is the only one they can't easily fix with seawater. If not, they wouldn't need to have all these escorts around it."

Index reached for the nearest door to get inside the ship, but it wouldn't open for her. She looked to see the crevices between the door and the walls closed up tight with ice. It was essentially a wall. "Wait just a second. I'll try undoing the door's magical lock—"

Her words were interrupted in the middle, however—when Kamijou took a step forward. "You don't need to be so squeamish about it. All this thinking stuff is really starting to get to me!!" he shouted, seeming truly fed up with it, pounding on the middle of the ice door with his right hand as hard as he could.

Bang!!

Not just the door but the walls around it were immediately blown away. His fist had left an open hole, a square three meters to a side, around where it hit. "Well, that was impressive," he said.

"I believe it's because unlike the escort ships, the walls and floors here all have magical meaning."

Which meant he didn't only unlock the door—he had totally busted up a bunch of other mechanisms, too.

Beyond the destroyed entrance would probably be a beautifully adorned passage, like the outside of the flagship. But the space inside also came to a clean end, the passage stopping three meters away. He hadn't just punched through the square; he'd dug into a solid cube. There were statues of angels and wall lamps there, some still kind of hanging on the walls.

"It's made of blocks," answered Index simply. "It's set up so that only the minimum required parts are cut away to prevent as much damage as possible. Even with your right hand, Touma, you can't destroy it all at once."

This wasn't how it had gone when he'd touched parts of the escort ships. *So then her theory is right—the whole ship is always changing shape, and that's how it controls the rest of the fleet*, he thought.

There was no time for questions, though.

Shwaa!!

Ice surged up like a mountain from under the deck to above it. To either side, in front and behind them, to surround them. It started to crack apart, revealing finer details. As the ice was shaved away, what lay in its place was a three-meter-tall suit of western-style armor made of ice.

And not only one or two.

Twenty or thirty of the ice armors had instantly surrounded Kamijou, Index, and Orsola.

"Inside!" shouted Orsola. "Those exist to protect the ship. They should hesitate to attack and accidentally destroy its interior!!"

The words had barely left her mouth before Index had grabbed Kamijou's hand and ran. He had been about to take the armor pieces on with his right hand, but in his surprise, he found himself dragged along, almost losing his balance. Dozens of them took in hand their swords and axes, all made of the same material, and moved.

A whirlwind groaned, and the air split.

With a deafening roar, multiple sword slashes intersected. They grazed Index's fluttering hair, stabbed right by Kamijou's face, and passed over the head of Orsola as she ran, crouched. Kamijou almost stopped breathing. But that didn't mean he could stop his feet.

Before the next attack came, the three of them rolled inside the ship using the entrance of the bored-out cube.

The interior was just as disgustingly intricate as the exterior. Angel statues lined either side of the passage, and each of the lamps hanging on the walls was changing its shape, little by little, separately from all the others. Everything from the doorknobs down to the screws looked like it had been created with the pride of a craftsman or an artist. Ships made only of ice didn't even need screws in the first place.

"This should be—"

Before Orsola, still sitting on the floor, could say any more, a cluster of ice armors flooded into the entrance.

"Shit!!" Kamijou stood up off the floor, grabbed the hands of Index and Orsola, who had sunk to the ground, and less dragged and more *swung* them farther into the ship.

Ga-gee!! came a sharp noise.

Several of the giant armors had jumped into the entrance at once, so they got jammed in there. Many blades stabbed through the chests and guts of the armors that had stopped, and they shattered. Then, plodding over the completely broken ice sculptures, new armors made their way into the passage. They pressed toward them like the shock wave from an explosion where Kamijou and the others had just been moments ago.

"They're still coming…?!" shouted Index.

But now Kamijou managed to predict the ice armors' priority… *They want to get rid of my right hand at all costs.* One of the walls of the entrance had already been destroyed. He didn't know exactly how it worked, but they seemed to have decided the Imagine Breaker was a threat. *Which means…!*

Just as Kamijou came to an intersection in the passage, he clenched his right hand into a fist. "Index, Orsola! You two go on ahead!!" he shouted, flinging both the girls into a side passage and then running straight down this passage.

"Touma!" Before Index could make her next move, all the armors ran after Kamijou. A few of them tried to go for Index and Orsola.

"Whoooaaa!!" Kamijou dragged his right hand across them, destroying them and causing the rest of their gazes to focus on the young man. They hefted their weapons, and all the automatic ice guardians flooded toward him.

3

"Sister Angeline! Are you all right?!" Lucia cried behind her as she gathered the fragments of the burst wooden wheel to her hand.

"...Yes, ma'am."

Angeline had managed to prop herself up against one of the ice masts in a sitting position. Her coin pouches had been destroyed, so right now she was fighting with her hood, stuffed with coins like heavy rocks.

She wasn't actually in any condition to fight. Even on a real battlefield, the correct decision would be to have her pull back from the front line for now. That was why Amakusa's current leader had given them the submersible talisman, but the sisters wouldn't allow that. And to shake them off, Lucia was no longer even able to cradle the injured Angeline.

Lucia stood her giant wheel in front of her, threatening them.

The ring of sisters pulled back just a bit. There were about thirty of them here, but considering their formation's density compared to one enemy, this might have been the most heated battle site right now. Their strategy was to ensure their defeat of the weaker forces first. Lucia and Angeline were well aware of that, too.

How can we get through them...?

These sisters knew the intensity of Lucia's attacks, so they didn't approach carelessly. But because they understood how her attack worked, they wouldn't back down fearing a bluff.

"Passengers of Ships Twelve, Seventeen, and Nineteen, evacuate immediately! Head for the water if you can't! The fleet will now sink those ships and reconstruct them!!"

She was used to hearing that broadcast.

At the same time, she heard this. "This is nonsense! Quit playing around with the wounded!!"

The members of Amakusa, beginning with Tatemiya, crossed a wooden bridge from a nearby ship and rolled in like an avalanche. The situation changed greatly, and the ring of people around Lucia and Angeline began to break up. Of their group, a girl named Itsuwa took a position next to Lucia, wielding her Friuli spear.

Now was their only chance to regroup. "Sister Angeline!"

"Y-yes, ma'am!!"

Angeline wobbled to her feet and away from the mast. Lucia stood in front of her, then had her wheel explode into the sisters' lines to carve a path for them.

4

Touma Kamijou was far from an excellent student.

He had a rough handle on his own abilities because he was rather used to nighttime street brawls. He felt like he had a real chance of victory only when it was one-on-one. One-on-two got dangerous, and in a one-on-three, he'd run straightaway. This wasn't because he was especially weak; it was just because numbers were more important than individual strength in fights with no rules. Needless to say, his lone fist wasn't enough to cross the power gap when it was one-on-twenty or -thirty.

Once the battle started, he would be sunk in five seconds.

However.

Those were rules for when actual people were fighting one another.

"Ooohhhhhhh!!" Kamijou's breath split through the wind.

It was one thing if his opponent was a proper human, and they'd fight until one or the other lost consciousness. *But if he only had to touch them to win*, even Kamijou still had a chance.

The armored horde charged down the narrow passage, scraping against one another as they went. Kamijou's right hand swung almost completely horizontally against the advancing enemies. He was ignoring power—it didn't matter how lightly, he just needed to get his hand on them.

Their movements creaked to a halt, as though their gears had been jolted out of place. Before Kamijou could make sure they were down, the subsequent armors, now just lumps of ice, smashed into them with their spears and hammers, securing the passageway.

"Urgh!!" Kamijou quickly withdrew. He could stop them from moving, but there were still ice remnants on the floor. He'd be buried alive if he fought in one place for too long.

And so, he repeated the process over and over.

Unfortunately...

"A dead end?!" As Kamijou continued to back away, he tossed a glance over his shoulder and finally noticed that there was a wall there.

He glanced back. The armors, looking like several people balled up into one, were pressed against one another, filling the passage, as they came for him.

He couldn't defend against that. He could block an attack, but he'd be open to the ones after that.

"Uohh!!"

Kamijou immediately leaped to the side. The width of the passage was cramped, so the only thing there was an ice wall.

But he stuck out his right hand.

A cube portion of the ice wall shattered. Index had been right—the walls of the flagship were different from those in the escort ships. Kamijou dove into the hole at about the same time the armors crashed into the dead end. All of their mighty force and weight had gone straight into the wall, and their bodies shattered from the impact. Tons of little specks of ice danced into the air like mist.

Kamijou didn't have any time to watch the spectacle. He looked around the room inside the wall, and after getting a handle on its layout, he stopped moving.

It was like a second-floor seat in a theater. Though the long rows of translucent seats extended several dozen meters each, it was only a few meters deep. If you went up to the elaborately designed railing, you could see the floor below. Like a splendid opera house, but instead of the stage and audience being far below, there were many chairs and desks lined up in a fan shape. Sort of like watching the Diet assembly on television.

It was clearly not something one would think a warship would have. It wasn't needed for a battlefield with a clear chain of command. Maybe warships were out of the sorcery factions' element, or maybe it actually held symbolic, magical meaning and was used as a meeting place. In either case, Kamijou couldn't figure it out.

Nor did he have the time to.

Roar!! An ice armor plunged into the big hole Kamijou had made. He grunted. He couldn't flee any farther. He was reminded of the railing behind him, and then he clenched his fists before instead jumping straight for the ice armor.

It swung its equally icy great sword horizontally. The thick three-meter-plus lump of ice flew at him from his right to rend his flesh.

"Ohhh!!" Kamijou responded by trying to strike the sword with his right hand.

Then, suddenly, the ice armor's legs broke apart on their own. It began to fall backward and diagonally across an axis on its thigh portions.

The great sword's mowing path changed to match—from a horizontal one aiming for his gut to one thrusting up toward his neck from below. As if to go around his right hand protecting his stomach.

Shit...!! The burst of wind from the sword blew away the cold sweat on his cheeks. "Uooohhh!!" He crouched with all his might.

Several of his hairs touched the sword. They weren't severed without resistance; instead, an intense pain shot through him as though the sword had pulled out a piece of his scalp with it. He heard a terrible tearing noise.

But he had still dodged it.

Enduring the pain and continuing the motion of his crouch, as though letting himself fall, he swung out his right fist. He aimed for the armor's chest as it fell backward, its legs having broken by themselves, and his fist connected before it hit the ground. The piece of armor stopped moving and shattered the moment it hit the ground.

"...Is it over?"

He stayed alert for more as he caught his breath, but that seemed to have been the last one. He crept slowly out of the hole, on guard for the possibility of an ambush, but he needn't have done so. He returned to the passage from the big hole he'd made.

*Damn it. I hope Index and Orsola are okay. The quickest way to meet up with them is probably to break the walls and floors...*On the other hand, the enemy could be alerted to such destructive activity. The timing of the ice armors' appearance seemed to confirm that. From what the sisters had said, this flagship was slow to regenerate. Plus, it was used for controlling the rest of the fleet and other ceremonies, so they couldn't use the cannons or enemy sisters to eliminate Kamijou's group on the inside unless they were really careful. But that applied only to the current moment. If the flagship actually seemed like it was going to sink, they'd probably move some personnel here regardless of the risks.

He thought for a moment. *Whichever way, the important part is... If I get to Agnes, the enemy boss's first priority should be to deal with me. It's going to happen sooner or later. Not enough reason for me to hold my right hand back!!*

After quickly coming to that conclusion, he went to punch a nearby wall with his right hand when suddenly a soft electronic tone sounded from his pants pocket. It was his cell phone's ringtone. *Wait, my cell phone?* Kamijou quickly checked his surroundings, and after making sure nobody was following him, he took it out. He was a little surprised it was even usable out here on the sea. How close were they to the shore?

He took a look at the screen and saw that, unbelievably, it was from *Index.* He pushed the Call button and put the phone to his ear. He held it in his left hand so his right was free. This device was something he was used to using, but he felt a lot of weirdness in his finger movements because of it.

"Oh, I appear to have gotten through to him."

"...Oh, it's you, Orsola. What are you borrowing Index's cell phone for?"

"I decided this would be the most expedient way of contacting you. Where might you be at the moment?"

"Well, I'm not really sure..." He glanced around, but there were no signs or markings to use. Well, it was the opposite. There were extravagant pieces of art overflowing in this place, so he couldn't actually use any of them as a guide. "I kept having to run away, and there were twenty or thirty of those ice armors, so I was focused on them. I'm not really sure where I am at the moment."

"...You speak of such tremendous things with ease, as usual. For my part...I am currently running away with Miss Index. It seems there were more of those guardian ice sculptures..."

"..." Index and Orsola didn't have a power like Kamijou's Imagine Breaker. Neither of them seemed very familiar with magical combat, and if it came to a straight fight, they'd be in for a real tough time against those ice armors. "Orsola. I'm at the intersection where we split up. Which direction are you from there?"

"Which direction?"

"Yeah. Doesn't have to be exact."

"Well...I believe we are to the north."

"Got it," answered Kamijou. *I'll be right there.*

Cell phone still in his left hand, he hit a nearby wall with his empty right hand. *Bgweee!!* The wall and decorations vanished, a cube-shaped hole appearing in their wake. Kamijou went inside the wall he'd destroyed and kept on breaking through the extravagant cabin walls. He was completely ignoring where the hallways and walls actually led.

"Also, Miss Index says she has something to tell you—"

A familiar voice interrupted them, as though she'd gotten between Orsola and the phone. "Give it to me, here! Touma, can you hear me?!" she called. "Touma, I heard a little from Orsola, but is one of the Queen of the Adriatic's triggers a different spell called the Rosary of the Appointed Time?"

"Yeah, apparently...Wait. Didn't we talk about that during the strategy meeting?"

"I don't think we heard the details. Are you doubting my memory?"

He couldn't really say anything to that. The girl had memorized every last bit of 103,000 grimoires down to the letter, so she wasn't mistaken. Kamijou broke through another ice wall and jumped out into another passage. "Yeah? I didn't hear much, either," he said. "It doesn't seem like Lucia and Angeline had much information about it handed to them."

Orsola replied. "They did suggest that in order to use the Rosary of the Appointed Time, they would have to purposely destroy Miss Agnes's mind."

Then he heard Index come back with a worried voice—worry was highly unusual from her when they were speaking of sorcery. "...Touma, that extra spell isn't needed to activate the Queen of the Adriatic."

"Wait, what?" Kamijou stopped in his tracks. He kept watch around him but still paid most of his attention to his cell phone.

"The Queen of the Adriatic is an antique-class spell. Before I explained how it was made to suppress the maritime city-state of Venice in a single strike, right?"

"Yeah, what about it?"

"Think carefully. That means they would need to activate it without having to wait. If they wasted time finding someone suitable and making all these huge preparations, they wouldn't be able to stop Venice from invading."

"Oh," said Kamijou. She was right, now that he thought about it. The fleet's size had fooled him, but this spell was fundamentally for countering an attack. If it didn't have the ease of use to be triggered when an enemy attacked, it would be pointless.

"The Queen of the Adriatic can be activated by itself. Then does this troublesome Rosary of the Appointed Time spell really exist? At the very least, not one of my 103,000 grimoires mentions that it's necessary. And I can't think of any reason the Roman

Orthodox Church would want to attack Venice right now, either."
Index paused for just a moment. "When it was completed, the
Queen of the Adriatic was so powerful that everyone said there was
no place to use it. Venice had enormous influence—it was the door-
step of international trade. If they were too careless, they both could
have ended up defeated. That's how people thought of it back when
it was the most necessary. I can't think of any reason anyone would
want it *now*."

"But it didn't look at all like Miss Lucia and Miss Angeline were
telling a lie."

She was right. Agnes did actually hold the key to the Roman
Orthodox Church's plans. If they could have used the Queen of the
Adriatic at any time, then the reason for their hesitation must have
meant that the Rosary of the Appointed Time hadn't been fully prepared yet.

The Rosary of the Appointed Time. Lucia and Angeline had no
doubt it was the activation key, but even they didn't know the details
behind the Queen of the Adriatic.

"Then the question is why they're using it with the Queen of the
Adriatic. Index, do you know what kind of spell the Rosary of the
Appointed Time is?"

"Hmm...I think it's not so much a spell name as the name of a
project only used in the Roman Orthodox Church. It might be hard
to figure out with just that. But the terms *Rosary* and *Appointed
Time* both simply refer to the measurement of time."

Kamijou stepped on a small piece of ice, then broke the next wall
with his right hand. "Rosaries are those things sisters wear on their
necks, right?"

"The string through it is actually crucial for more than just Crossism. The act of putting fifty-nine small beads on it is a Catholic tradition. Those who go on pilgrimages to holy places all over the world use
these beads as a tool to tell them how many prayers they've offered."

"...So a rosary, for an appointed time—*they're counting down*.
That makes too much sense."

Kamijou didn't know whether his words actually reached Index and Orsola.

Because...

Bang!!
A sudden sharp sound accompanied the ceiling tumbling down.

"!!" He grunted and immediately jumped back. That, however, wasn't enough to escape the rain of icy material. The surrounding pieces of the ceiling had been caught in a circle around the point of impact, creating an upside-down pyramid shape that turned into a giant blunt weapon.

"Shit!!" He didn't waste any time in thrusting his right hand out from his side. The ceiling he tried to destroy was gouged out in a cube shape. Then the rest of the ceiling collided with the floor, slipping right by Kamijou's body and sparing him. The shock wave hit his ears, and a small fragment hit him in the back. He forgot to take it easy with his left hand; his cell phone creaked in its grip.

He didn't have enough time to press the buttons on it. He briskly shut the phone and shoved it in his pocket, taking a few more steps back.

Fine particles of ice danced in the air, a fog-like dust before him. At the center of it, where Kamijou had just been standing, now stood one man, the hammer who had broken the ceiling.

It was a Caucasian in his forties, clothed in magnificent garb.

Though it was grand-looking, it didn't have any of the cleanliness Index's had. It was a pile of rich-person interests that happened to be clinging to him. Four necklaces were around his neck, forming concentric circles, each with dozens of crosses attached to it. The polished gold and silver of their make gave off a glare. It was like he'd painted them with grease from meat, as though his tenacity was being reflected into a slimy light.

The man's movements appeared highly strung as he ran a finger over one of the crosses at his neck. His eyes were on Kamijou, but his irises were continually moving ever so slightly.

"…That right hand…"

Surprisingly, he had spoken Japanese.

"Hah. Jealous?" responded Kamijou for lack of anything else to say.

The man's face wrinkled up in a silent display of slight repulsion and irritation. "I find it difficult to accept. Not only its nature, which rejects the grace of our Lord, but the fact that you are also wielding it as a weapon. If you had but heard the word of God a single time, the natural reaction would be to immediately strive to gain His grace, even if it meant cutting off your arm."

His words were chilling. Not the meaning of the words—but the sheer density of the emotion in them, like yellow fat, pulled out and crushed.

"Do the words of man not mean anything to you? I suppose you are merely a heretic ape. I've gone through the trouble of speaking the same language, and I receive only words of poor character. Then I, Biagio Busoni, will say the last rites of this enemy of the Lord. I simply cannot stand to see an ape pretending to be a human."

"So you're Biagio, huh? That means you know where Agnes is."

"Knowing and telling are two entirely different things."

The man who called himself Biagio crossed his arms.

Kamijou heard a soft metal *keen*. Biagio's hands gripped two of the crosses at his neck.

Whoosh. He then tossed both to Kamijou.

"—These crosses indicate rejection of immorality."

Boom!! The two crosses expanded. Their rate of expansion was equal to a flying cannonball. In the blink of an eye, the crosses had turned gigantic, three meters long and forty centimeters thick, before they attacked him. It was like a metal blast of steel bars.

"Ooahh!!" Kamijou punched away a cross walling him. But he could get only the one. Meanwhile, the tip of the other cross hit him like a boulder, sending him hurtling back.

Whump!! The sound of impact echoed.

He was immediately slammed down and slid a few meters away. He scrambled to quickly put his hand on the ground, but the ice floor reacted to the movement. *Ba-gan!!* It carved out a cube, and Kamijou fell down to the passage on the level below.

The entire ship's interior was made of ice, so nothing was there to cushion his fall. He clenched his teeth, enduring the pain from his entire body, and then—more carefully this time—he pushed himself up with his left hand and got to his feet.

Biagio's voice drifted to him from the hole above.

"When the evil dragon swallowed Saint Margaret, she, too, is said to have caused her cross to grow and rend its body from the inside. The crosses standing atop church roofs also have the role of annulling enemies without and creating a safe space within…Something like this."

From the hole in the ceiling came a few more crosses, thrown in like grenades. *Ga-bah!!* They instantly expanded in midair.

They looked less like crosses than laser weapons springing out in four directions. Kamijou hastily rolled down onto the floor before the four tips of the crosses, now metal beams, scraped right past his nose and got stuck in the walls and floor. There was no semblance of organization in the pattern. They randomly divided the passage with straight lines.

Crap…I need to get out of here before I can't move anymore…!!

Kamijou went to use his right hand a moment later, and the voice came to him from above again. "On the other hand, the cross's weight is able to cure people of their pridefulness. Saint Lucy, maiden of light, though one thousand men and two cows pulled her with a rope, moved not a step. The young Saint Christopher, known for his fantastic strength, nearly buckled under the weight of the Son of God whom he shouldered…Something like this, once again."

Grr-gah!! A rift opened in the ceiling.

From the broken ceiling came raining down small crosses, mere centimeters long. However, their speed was equivalent to a cannonball...No, they were heavier, like their rate of gravitational acceleration had been increased a thousandfold.

Kamijou rushed the giant cross blocking the passage and basically rammed into it with his right hand. He rolled forward, not stopping to see if the obstacle had shattered or not, but one of the superheavy crosses scraped past his shoulder. *Gshhh!!* Pain tore through him, like his joint would have dislocated from just that.

"...! Gahhh!!" Nevertheless, he used his right hand to destroy the nearby wall, diving out of the passage and into a cabin. He would have to move at random now, in an attempt to evade Biagio's aim as much as possible.

"Please don't destroy too much. It takes time to repair."

The ceiling broke apart again, and another handful of crosses rained down toward Kamijou. Despite their small size, they had incredible weight, and it was like iron nails breaking the cabin to bits. Rather than jump, Kamijou pressed his back to the wall, managing to barely evade them.

Biagio jumped down from the opened hole.

Thud!! He stomped on the floor, sending ice particles flying up like mist.

Kamijou, his back still to the ice wall, said, "You tell me not to destroy anything, but you don't seem to have a problem going all out."

"I believe I know which things I can break and which things I can't. You, however, are acting haphazardly. Yes, like an ignorant amateur made to take care of antiques. I understand you're taking it seriously, but first, you must learn."

Biagio's face betrayed a hint of irritation behind his relaxed demeanor. According to Index, this flagship controlled all the escort ships. The ice ornaments were continually changing tiny parts of their shapes, which all seemed to be interlocking signs...Was Kamijou's right hand doing damage to the fleet's control system?

"Hmph. Guess it's true that this junker doesn't recover as fast as the other ones. I thought I'd finally slipped into the boss room. Kinda disappointed that it's weaker."

"The *Queen of the Adriatic*'s original potential outweighs the other escorts by over two hundred times. However, if I divert power to its recovery, it will affect the other's completeness."

"The other?"

"The Rosary of the Appointed Time. I cannot imagine you don't know about it at this point."

"..."

The Rosary of the Appointed Time again. Index had said it was an additional spell not related to the anti-Venice suppression spell the Queen of the Adriatic was triggering. Biagio might not have been telling the complete truth, but he *was* attached to it despite the disadvantages. It must have meant enough for him to do that.

"Whatever. I'll beat you and drag out of you where Agnes is, and then it's over. Not gonna think too hard about it, so I'll just finish this."

"Poor words—ones that run contrary to the will of the Lord."

Biagio removed seven crosses from his neck.

Like a parting gift, he hurled them up into the air.

"—Then my crosses shall reject your immorality."

5

They couldn't stay on one boat for longer than a minute.

From an ice escort ship on the verge of sinking, Saiji Tatemiya used a wooden bridge he had made to cross to the adjacent ship. In front of him he could see a new escort appear up through the water in place of the ship that had just sunk.

"Ahh, damn it all! There's no end to this!!" he shouted as he took down a few attacking former-Agnes-unit sisters with the flat surface of his flamberge's abnormally long blade. Then he used a bundle of papers to call from thin air a surfboard-like plank. He started strapping the unconscious sisters by their stomachs and backs to the multi-person board.

The ship would be taken down by cannon fire in a moment.

Still, just from the problem of how many he had to deal with, it seemed impossible to get all the fallen sisters on there and move them. So Amakusa had prepared these "life preservers," able only to prevent the downed nuns from drowning. If they were rash and called in a giant wooden ship, it would just end up fodder for the cannons.

I know we'll pick them up later, but it still doesn't feel good leaving the sinking ships behind. He swore under his breath and listened to the next broadcast, which essentially said this ship was also going to be fired upon. Most of the fleet seemed to be on autopilot. Therefore, no matter how many people he defeated, it wouldn't affect the fleet itself from moving in the slightest. Two hundred sisters strong were scary as a simple fighting force, but the biggest threat was still all that cannon fire. Until they did something about that, they'd never overturn the battle situation in any significant way.

Amakusa had no choice but to hang on and endure until everything was over.

Damn. If I could, I'd rather bust up as much of that flagship as I can... He didn't, though. If Amakusa's main force headed for the flagship, the big army of sisters would move the same way. If their principal battlefield changed, Kamijou and those with him would be the ones caught up in it.

"Well, not expecting any credit is the basis of our foundation, anyway." Tatemiya waggled his wavy-bladed sword. "Nothing else for it. We'll tighten things up here and make it easier for ya!!"

With a shout, he jumped into a part of the deck where a bunch of sisters were clustered.

6

"—Then my crosses shall reject your immorality."

Roar!! The seven crosses each expanded explosively. They felt to Kamijou like a raging metal inferno dancing all over the place in the direction the crosses pointed. He slammed his right hand into the wall he was backed against. It was destroyed in an instant, leaving a cube-shaped hole, and he wasted no time falling into it.

Thwack, thud, bam, crash!! One after another, the thick cross tips crunched into the floor, walls, and ceiling like steel beams.

As Kamijou continued to roll over the floor, he shouted, "Piece of shit, doing whatever you want!! You think you have any right to do as you please to Venice?"

"Unfortunately, your conjecture is mistaken. *My aim lies elsewhere.*" Biagio laughed quietly beyond the barrage.

"What?!"

"I won't tell you without cost. What benefit would that bring me? But, well…At the very least, *it's far more interesting than what you're thinking.*"

Kamijou groaned and clenched his teeth, springing back to his feet using the momentum of his roll. He made his right hand into a fist. Then, going back along his escape route, he ran toward Biagio, trying to close the distance in one stroke.

But before he could, Biagio continued his discourse. "Now, crosses have many meanings, but most of them were added only after the Son of God was put to death. Crosses themselves existed before that, but their roles from those previous ages were mostly wiped out by Crossism—after all, they were the traditions of immoral heretics." He chose a cross he liked from the dozens at his chest and nervously ran his fingers over it. "Of them all, there is just one that survived from those past generations. The oldest way of using them in religious history, and one that the most important figure in Crossism, the Son of God himself, was directly related to. And that was as…"

With his right hand, Kamijou destroyed the giant cross standing between them. A step before he made it close enough to Biagio, the ostentatiously dressed man tore off the cross and raised it above his head.

"*…a tool of execution.*"

*　　*　　*

Biagio's voice was scornful, low but lacking solemnity.

"—Simon carries the cross of the Son of God."

Wobble.

The moment he heard those words, Kamijou's vision began to spin.

"...Eh?"

He felt an impact near his right shoulder. Pain shot through him. He shook his head; his entire vision was like a motion-blur picture. Only upon feeling the hard floor against his cheek did Kamijou realize...that he was lying on his side. It took a few moments for his brain to catch up with the phenomenon that had just occurred.

What...the...? Had something attacked him? But he couldn't understand what had been done to him in the first place. Until now, he'd been able to defend and dodge because he at least knew he was being attacked. Now it was different. He couldn't even grasp when the hell the attack had come.

Certain death. The words stuck to the back of his lurching mind.

He tried to get up, but his arms had no real strength. He tried to roll onto his stomach and push himself up, but he just collapsed with a *thud*.

There was a blank in his mind. As if to redirect his attention outside, a faint metallic sound began to ring.

The sound came from dozens of crosses colliding with one another in midair.

"—These crosses indicate rejection of immorality."

With a low voice came the continuous sounds of pounding flesh and the crushing of the ice floor.

7

Index and Orsola ran down a passage of the flagship, the *Queen of the Adriatic.*

It appeared on the outside to be close to twice the size of its escorts, but the passages were about the same width...No, that wasn't it.

Statues of angels carved out of the walls lined each side of the passage in place of the normal pillars, with an elaborate carving of a scene from the Bible on entire doors, as well. All the artwork was compressing the otherwise wide passage.

A magnificent palace, a majestic castle—these terms no longer did much to describe what they were seeing. Only extreme metaphors from mythology, like a shrine built of gold or a pyramid constructed of diamond alone, fit this place. And just being shown something like this in reality seemed like enough to cause heartburn.

As Orsola ran down the straight passage, silver angel staff in both hands, looking around, she said to the nearby Index, "…It is eerily silent in here."

"The ship has its role," answered Index softly. "I think they didn't expect enemies to get inside the flagship. They probably made the flagship specialize in smoothly controlling the escort ships, since they should have eliminated all enemies in the first place."

"Which means…," continued Orsola, her footsteps echoing down the passage, "…the other nuns aren't following us because even they, despite being allies, haven't received permission to board the flagship? To prevent them from snitching, maybe?"

They ran farther and approached a staircase. One set of stairs led up, the other down, but Index immediately ran down. Orsola had to hurry a little to catch up.

"Wait! Do you know where Miss Agnes is?!"

"Of course!" replied Index immediately. "I know most of the *Queen of the Adriatic*'s functions. I don't know what the Rosary of the Appointed Time is like, but if they're intervening with the Queen of the Adriatic, there's only one place they'd do it! It's the best place for it!!"

The staircase was long and coiling, like in a giant steel tower. After an extended flight downward, they eventually reached the bottom.

"This is…," whispered Orsola.

It was like an auditorium. It was a wide-open space, and at the front stood double doors that were twice Orsola's height. She didn't know how thick they were, but they seemed thicker than her, too. The staircase they'd come down wasn't the only entrance to the auditorium—dozens of passages all connected here, as though concentrated on the room.

Such a strange construction. It ignored the fundamentals of boat design. Realizing a design like this required distorting the placement of all the pillars and crossbeams in the ship. And they had forced it to work, which meant one thing.

"It looks less like this room was planned for this ship..."

"And more like the ship was shaped around the room."

Index stepped toward the big doors in front. She brought her face near it, then went to touch it with her palm and stopped right before.

"This door here...It has a defensive spell on it. Probably following the tradition of Saint Blaise. The part where heretic soldiers chased the saint across a lake, and they all drowned, since they couldn't walk on water."

"Which would mean...whoever touches the entryway without permission will be dragged into the ice, perhaps?"

Even inside the flagship, they hadn't run into anyone. The thorough emptiness possibly meant that Agnes and Biagio were the only ones who could open this door.

Index gave Orsola a sidelong glance. "Yep. *If they do it like they're supposed to, anyway.*"

"That is what it would mean."

Index managed the 103,000 grimoires, and Orsola was a grimoire and spell-analysis expert. They had both thought of the same thing already, and it wasn't the word *impenetrable*.

Index sidled up as close as she could get to the door and observed it again. She began to analyze everything from the surface design patterns to the thick ice interior of the door's construction. Orsola held her angelic staff at the ready in case Index by chance found herself on the wrong end of the door's defensive mechanism.

However...

Crash!! Upside-down ice pillars bigger than a person came up through the floor around them. Ten or twenty of them, in fact. They steadily formed shapes as though an invisible blade were carving them.

"These…"

"Rather than the nuns, they have these?!"

They were ice armors—but not only them. Two wheeled cannons were there as well. Not just the armors but even the cannons all moved on their own, the cannons' wheels shifting and creaking into place as they took aim.

Orsola grunted and reflexively readied her angelic staff. Combat wasn't her specialty, but Index didn't have any weapons at all, nor could she use magic. It would necessarily fall to Orsola to fight these, but…

"GYAH!! (Gather your aim here!!)"

…before she could, Index shouted something and threw herself to the side. The armors and cannons realigned their aim toward her. It wasn't their defensive capabilities; it was like a strong magnet was drawing them to her.

Index kept going, jumping into one of the nearby passages. "You get Agnes! I'll draw them away!! I'll be okay. I can sense human intent in these guardians' thoughts. My spell interception can interrupt it!!"

Index had speculated that these ice sculptures had been created by the overseers of the Queen's Fleet. However, they hadn't completely taken their hands off the wheel. They probably had information reports and intervention points programmed into them once every few minutes to determine whether they needed a course correction. They were reminiscent of the golem Sherry Cromwell controlled, Ellis. If they weren't fully autonomous, there was room for her to slip inside—because no matter how advanced the sorcery, there was a person controlling it.

"Wait!!"

Before Orsola could argue, there was a gust of wind. All of the guardians had shot past Orsola on their way to follow Index, who had disappeared down the path. Like a dump truck passing at a high speed, the guardians pushed on the air and turned it into wind. There was a loud *roar*, and Orsola shut her eyes out of reflex.

When she opened them again, neither Index nor the armors nor the cannons were anywhere in sight.

"Miss Index!" shouted Orsola, her angelic staff in one hand. She waited but never got a reply.

8

Agnes Sanctis, nestling up against the ice sphere, listened to the sounds outside.

"..."

The sounds of artillery. The clashing of swords. The explosions of fireships. The shouting of people—and the noise of brawling she'd just heard right outside the door.

All of it was happening with her at the center.

The battle raged on, its only purpose to see whether Agnes would be taken or protected.

She thought it was ridiculous.

It was as though everyone was worried about her. That clearly wasn't possible, but that was the sort of misunderstanding it offered.

She had thought this was the highest she could reach.

She had thought if she went out there, she could only go down.

But...

Was it still all right for her to depend on someone else?

Was it still all right for her to hold on to hope?

"..."

Agnes Sanctis, her mind hazy, thought.

And then...

...she shook her head.

She heard a *slam*.

It was the sound of the double doors made of ice crashing open, the ones that had closed in this unnaturally perfect pyramid room.

Agnes looked there. It wasn't the boy she'd met on the escort ship that time earlier. However, it also wasn't someone she'd never seen in the Queen's Fleet before.

"Orsola…Aquinas?"

It was a sister wearing a jet-black habit. It was still the same one as when she'd been driven out of the Roman Orthodox Church, and by some joke, she was gripping Agnes's staff, the one they'd confiscated, in both hands. Breaking the magical defenses placed on those double doors was no small feat. And she was slightly frazzled and out of breath—maybe she'd pushed her concentration to the limit to do so.

And yet she showed no sign of tiredness in her expression.

Moreover, upon seeing Agnes's face as she leaned against the sphere, her expression lit up a little.

"I'm…," said Orsola. Agnes's ears heard the voice of a saint herself. "I'm glad you're safe…"

Saying such a thing—maybe it meant Orsola knew the situation Agnes was in. At least as much as Agnes did herself. Maybe that was why, after seeing Agnes safe, she looked so relieved.

After all Agnes had done to her.

Because of all she'd done to her.

"…Why?" asked Agnes, dazed. "You know all about what's going on here, right? You wanted so badly to get out of the Queen's Fleet. You didn't want to stay somewhere so dangerous. You learned how unreasonable this facility is. That's why you took me up on my plan, isn't it? So why the heck are you, of all people, back here—and with that face?"

"You think too highly of me," said Orsola, smiling painfully. "I couldn't know everything just at a glance. The mechanism behind the Queen of the Adriatic was something Miss Index told me, and I'm still processing it. And I still know next to nothing of the Rosary of the Appointed Time." She gripped the silver staff in both hands. "…If we had, nobody would have suggested to flee, alone, leaving you here after you kept silent to save everyone else."

"Yes, that's why...," Agnes answered softly, noting just how remarkably out of the ordinary this person standing before her was. "That's why I'm saying it's strange. Yeah, I made myself the bait to save Sister Lucia and Sister Angeline. *But that's all I did.* There's no way everything will be fine after this is over, is there? Are you satisfied with that?"

Each and every word that came out of her mouth made her more miserable.

But she continued anyway. "You remember what happened with the *Book of the Law*! I was the one who chased you all the way to Japan, captured you, and beat you to a pulp! Normal people would have just left me here!! Are you seriously saying, after all that, that you want to let it be water under the bridge?!"

"Is it necessary for me to spell out the answer to that?" asked Orsola quietly. "Did you not remain silent about everything, directing us to Miss Lucia and Miss Angeline, *because* you knew everything? You thought that if we knew, we would necessarily come to stop you. If you still want to hear my answer in clear terms, then I will give it to you."

She looked at Agnes.

"In the end, I don't know the answer. I am still in training, after all. What is right, and what is wrong? I certainly don't have the confidence to decide that myself, nor do I have the knowledge or good sense required to influence another person's life.

"However," she continued, "at the very least, Miss Lucia and Miss Angeline stated that they wanted to save you."

"..." Agnes fell silent.

"Miss Lucia said that after they retreated to a safe place, they would still come back to save you. Miss Angeline said she was scared of one of her own being hurt and even hesitated making her weapon...I do not believe there was any falsehood in their words. They were more perfect people than anyone in that place. I cannot hold a candle to them."

Her slowly spoken words didn't have any compelling power behind them. But despite that, Agnes caught her breath.

"Do you have a complaint against what Miss Lucia and Miss Angeline said?" asked Orsola to the small nun. "Do you think their words are not enough—even though they said, faced with a hopeless situation, threatened by countless blades, that they wanted everyone to be together and happy again?"

"..." Agnes returned Orsola's look for a moment. Her lips trembling, she opened her mouth to say something.

But then a man's voice interrupted them.

"Impossible. Can you innocently believe the Roman Orthodox Church is keeping quiet about that?" said the voice. "This is a problem for us as well. Sister Agnes, do not flee from your duty so easily. Yes, the Roman Orthodox Church has two billion members. Even if you die here, the plan will not be interrupted. I will just need to search for another compatible person. However, do you have any idea how difficult it will be to wade through two billion people? It would be annoying, yes? And I do so hate annoyances."

They were shallow words that brought everything to nothing.

Orsola turned around to where the voice came from.

A man, forty years old, clad in extravagant clerical vestments, appeared. He wore four necklaces, from which many crosses jangled, and a twisted, lopsided smile plastered on his face.

Biagio Busoni.

And...

His right hand was splattered with blood.

Likely not Biagio's. He had no obvious wounds, and he showed no signs of pain in his face.

"...Then what exactly is that blood from?"

"How cold. Can't spare any worry for me, eh? And I've already answered that question. I hate annoyances, remember? So, well, *I swiftly took care of that one.*"

"..." Orsola tightened her grip on the angelic staff she was holding.

But even Agnes, watching from afar, could clearly tell she wasn't used to combat. She was the sort of nun who did battle on desks and paper—fundamentally different from Agnes and Biagio. It wasn't a question of strength or weakness but an entirely different premise to start with, like trying to cross the South Pole the way you'd walk across a desert.

Biagio must have discerned that at first glance, too. The relaxation remained in his expression.

He didn't even assume a combat stance.

"I would like to avoid such acts here if possible. Things are a bit delicate, you see. Why do you think something like the Queen's Fleet was prepared to strengthen the perimeter? Because it wouldn't be good if it could be damaged easily."

"...The large-scale anti-Venice spell. You had such willingness to reclaim the glow of this obsolete antique."

"Hmm, that appears to be your shared opinion. But that is incorrect. What we're trying to do is *not* that anti–maritime city-state attack spell. *It's something beyond that.*"

"You seem quite relaxed about it," said Orsola.

She's not very good, thought Agnes. The usual play was to gauge the distance while distracting Biagio with conversation.

"Well, yes. Nothing will come of talking about it. I can at least be relaxed about that. And it is my style to treat those about to lose their lives with the utmost courtesy. As much as possible, anyway. Oh, yes. I said the same thing to the boy before. Or should I say I explained it? He was difficult after he became more resistant, but it was still tolerable for me. I would ask the same degree of selfishness from you."

"..." Orsola reflexively took a step forward.

Biagio, however, didn't move.

It was like he was saying he didn't need to pay attention to his enemy's motions.

"Right, but where were we? Ah, yes. The Queen of the Adriatic. As I'm sure both of you already know, the spell was created specifically against Venice. It destroys the city with one strike but cannot be used in any other way. The reason is simple: Its creators were scared of it being pointed back at them if it was to fall into enemy hands."

Biagio ran a finger along one of the crosses around his neck. "The Queen of the Adriatic was completed in the ninth century...about the time the remains of Saint Mark, one of the twelve apostles, were smuggled into Venice. The Vatican—then the Roman Papal States—protected the remains of Saint Peter, and the spell was created by the Roman Orthodox Church now that Venice had created an equivalent religious environment."

Orsola suddenly frowned. She was growing more aware that this wasn't the time to be talking about it, but she asked a question anyway. "Are you lying to me? The development of Venice began around that ninth century. If the Queen of the Adriatic had been functional since then..."

"That's right. The most prosperous time for Venice was yet to come. In history, we can see that it conquered all the nearby city-states, like Padua, Vicenza, Mestre, and Chioggia. You know that, right?"

"...Are you suggesting you can guide my thoughts with commonplace knowledge?"

"There are actually many reasons for those invasions, but one of them appears to have been the Queen of the Adriatic. At the time, the Venetian government couldn't discern where the facility for the large-scale spell was. They had no choice but to keep crushing everywhere that seemed suspicious. After they'd gone that far, you would think the current Roman Orthodox Church would have used the Queen of the Adriatic...But they were probably too afraid in the end. Venice was incredibly powerful. If it was lost, they could incur significant blows, especially to their economy."

"..."

"However, as a result, Venice amassed many war expenditures from their invasions. In the end, it's said the city-state faced economic hardships and was nearly driven to ruin, which was unamusing. Of course, the invasions were not only to find the Queen of the Adriatic...but they did accomplish that objective."

"A large-scale destructive magic that they didn't use, letting fear of it destroy a nation...But...," said Orsola.

Biagio smiled. "Yes. The Queen of the Adriatic could only be used against Venice. No matter how attractive the strength it boasted, it had no meaning as long as they couldn't unlock the target restriction. Right now, Venice is a healthy tourist destination—the Roman Orthodox Church has no reason to disfavor the City of Water."

Orsola was about to ask why—and then froze.

What Biagio had just said *had a hypothetical, hopeful part buried in it.*

"Yes. I see you've realized it," declared Biagio Busoni.

"*To remove the targeting restriction on the Queen of the Adriatic. That is what the Rosary of the Appointed Time is for.*"

Orsola caught her breath. Agnes, too, opened her eyes wide—apparently, she hadn't been told about this, either.

The bishop went on anyway, a hint of a smile creeping onto his face. "What a long road. Well, I did not create the Rosary of the Appointed Time, but *she* did. We certainly had a time of it. The Queen of the Adriatic, this magnificent weapon, was sitting in front of us—to think it would take so long to use it properly! Because of that, it was left alone for centuries!!"

"No...!!" Orsola said despite herself. "Are you saying you will use the Queen of the Adriatic to destroy the city you've found to be a problem?! Waving around a large-scale weapon that could destroy in one strike the city of Venice, known as a strong maritime city-state, a cultural melting pot, and a powerful nation of sorcery?!"

"City? No, you misunderstand. It would be more accurate to call it the *world*," said Biagio, amused—as though even now, he was performing in a children's musical. "Ha-ha! The Queen of the Adriatic isn't just for a city. It destroys everything related to that city. If it were to destroy Venice, every painting and sculpture from it would be destroyed as well! Even the school of academia of Venice might disappear as well. But wait. What do you think would happen if we unleashed it on *a city representing the world hostile to us?*"

The world hostile to them.

The city representing it.

Orsola put the two together and realized what Biagio was saying. "You mean Academy City?!"

"That's it exactly, Sister Orsola! The Queen of the Adriatic will eliminate all the effects that city has created. All of the world's scientific technology has been affected by Academy City. Even if only by small things! If all that is destroyed, the half of the world of that detestable *science*, the entire science side, would be eradicated!!"

She shuddered.

The way Biagio spoke was as though he believed there was no humanity except in the places he saw. The ones living in the places he wasn't present in—they looked to him like only vaguely human shapes in a picture.

The destruction of the science side. That wasn't simply cutting away one half of the world map. People would actually die.

"Are you saying that if you destroy Academy City, it will make everyone happy?"

"No, I don't think that. There will be those on the sorcery side hurt by this as well. The Puritans of England, the Catholics of Russia—and perhaps even other religions such as Buddhism and European mythology. But we must only go forward. We must only eliminate all those in the way! Eventually the impurities will be cleansed, and the Roman Orthodox Church will be the last one standing!!"

"You are a…!!" Orsola started.

The Queen of the Adriatic, created to stop Venice if it went out of control, had no need for a reload function to fire a second time. But judging by the way Biagio spoke, it was possible they had overcome even that. *Or perhaps the odd work Miss Lucia and the others were being made to do in this fleet…That might have been them preparing to eliminate the issue of reloading…*But Orsola kept that to herself.

As she shivered at the thought, Biagio sighed and continued to speak, his voice slowing just a bit, as though his interest had waned.

"How dull. When did religion descend to the level of a mere convenient tool? Was there a mistake in the burning of Sodom and Gomorrah? The science side points to religious courts and inquisitions as a misinterpretation of Crossism, but *that* is the true misunderstanding. Why must God endure for His people? If there are those who create a disadvantage for Him, there should be no dissatisfaction in eliminating them. It is like burning out weeds. If you complain about burning the grass around them in the process, nothing will begin."

If such a spell was wielded with thoughts like that, how much damage could it cause? It could evolve into a situation where he would destroy an entire city just to broil one single enemy human. It would be the greatest tragedy in the history of Crossism.

Biagio gave Orsola a sharp look. Then, in a shrill, excited voice trembling with joy, he said to the shuddering nun, "This is the dearest wish of the Roman Orthodox Church. That's why I cannot have you acting violently in here. And I certainly cannot agree with you taking away Sister Agnes."

"I'm the one who cannot agree!" Orsola swung the angelic staff with force.

Biagio exhaled, disappointed.

"I believe I just told you not to act violently."

The outcome was decided the instant those words left his mouth.

Orsola began to speak an incantation to activate the angelic staff, but she was too slow—or rather, too polite with her speech. In combat, all you had to do was get the meaning across, yet she was using enough concentration as she began constructing the spell as one might in finishing the face of a sculpture. She wouldn't be in time with that.

But all Biagio had to do was touch one of the crosses around his neck.

"—These crosses indicate rejection of immorality."

As he spoke the words, he removed three crosses from their

chains, which flew toward Orsola at an easy pace. On her guard, Orsola tried to bat them out of the air with her staff, but...

Boom!!

An instant before, the small accessories expanded explosively. It was like an actual explosion—their rate of expansion resembled an air blast made of steel. The attack was like a steel pile breaking down a door, and it easily flung the angelic staff from Orsola's hands.

Agnes, behind her, gasped. Two more crosses attacked her as she stood, now unarmed. The second cross expanded at a position above her shoulders, flying down vertically to dislocate her joints. As her upper body bent over at the impact, the third cross exploded toward her curled back. There was a sound like a sledgehammer hitting a wall, and strength deserted Orsola's legs, sending her slamming down on the icy floor.

And still, she tried to stagger back to her feet.

"Ha-ha! Stop this, Sister Orsola!!"

Biagio hadn't taken a single step. He was so close to the completion of this too-long project, and his face wore only a smile.

He removed one cross from his necklaces and hurled it. Like a bouquet of flowers thrown into the ocean, it flowed through the air in a wide arc over Orsola's head.

"—The weight of the cross cures pridefulness."

Brr, came a noise like the midair cross vibrating.

Instantly, the cross gained thousands of times more gravitational acceleration and shot straight past Orsola's neck. The ice floor lost out to the impact and exploded, lifting upward. Her facedown body, right next to where it happened, began to slide even farther to the side.

And still.

Without a weapon, her entire body beaten, Orsola's fingers twitched.

In rebellion.

"Ku-ku. I did tell you to stop. The title of bishop is no mere honorific. We are able to wield many powers by unlocking the myriad of meanings behind the cross. If you would kill me, then come with the intent to demolish an entire cathedral! The English have their Walking Church, but even without that, I alone rival such a sanctuary!!"

Then Biagio took his eyes from Orsola.

He spoke to Agnes, standing behind her.

"It is a bit early, but let us get started, Sister Agnes."

"Huh...?" Agnes returned Biagio's look with a blank stupor.

The bishop didn't display any particular aversion. "Amakusa is up on deck. They and Sister Orsola here are eyesores, but not enough to decisively affect the Rosary of the Appointed Time's unlocking of the Queen of the Adriatic's restriction. Hu-hu. I've had enough of this craving. Did it want to make me die of patience? We will start this now and leave our names in history, Sister Agnes!"

With Biagio's words, the ice sphere Agnes rested on began to change.

"Let us begin the fitting. Once your mana is synchronized with both the Rosary of the Appointed Time and the Queen of the Adriatic, it will be over. Let us finish this quickly and deliver the good news to the Vatican!!"

A big hole opened in the sphere like eyelids parting ways—as though to invite her inside.

"...! I will...not let you!!"

"You would resist in such a state? Or do you wish to have yet more of your freedom stolen?" Biagio didn't even spare Orsola a glance. He stroked the crosses at his neck with a finger. "Let us begin. Be glad, Sister Agnes. You will gain the honor of having buried the most enemies in the history of Crossism. It is what you have longed for all this time! Ever since you began wielding that angelic staff!!"

"..." Agnes listened to Biagio's words and nodded awkwardly. Her downcast vision showed the angelic staff lying nearby.

His words were not wrong. That had actually been the reason for her action of chasing down Orsola during the incident regarding the *Book of the Law*. To bury the enemies of the Roman Orthodox

Church. That was all. If those children hadn't come to stop her, Agnes would have reveled in her killing of Orsola.

The elimination of enemies threatening her had been what Agnes wanted.

But.

"Those...enemies you speak of—does that not include Miss Agnes herself...?!"

Orsola, whom she had once nearly killed, moved so that she could shield Agnes.

Her body couldn't even move properly with the damage it had sustained.

Agnes watched Orsola, taken aback.

Biagio laughed at Orsola's words. "You really are an English Puritan now, and not of the Roman Orthodox Church. That is why you panic. If you were of our Church, there would be no need to feel apprehension with the Queen of the Adriatic before you."

"And you really never act on anything but suspicion and jealousy. The very model of us Roman Orthodox disciples. If scales of self-interest are all you possess, then you cannot understand how a person would act on emotion. And even if you could, you wouldn't believe it."

Agnes had heard those words before, too. That was when she knew that this nun, Orsola Aquinas, hadn't changed since that day.

"I said I cannot accept you using Miss Agnes and discarding her to realize such a hideous goal! Why can you not believe the fact that I can't endure you hurting so many others by doing so?!"

"...I see." The smile on Biagio's face quietly disappeared. He toyed with several of the crosses at his neck. Then he plucked one of them. "I retract my previous statement. Even if the impediment is small it must still be crushed."

Orsola stiffened. Not only at the realistic threat. This nun probably wasn't used to someone directing such a thirst for blood at her. She had lived her whole life mostly unrelated to such a world.

Agnes thought to herself. Why was she going this far? If she had been from Academy City, she'd understand. If she had been a resident of the science side, she'd understand. It would be threatening her directly in that case. If she didn't stop Biagio, it would be more than her lifestyle at risk: She would directly lose her life in the end.

But that wasn't the case. She wouldn't die even if Academy City was destroyed. If Biagio targeted English Puritanism, then she could simply turn coats to another group, another religion, like she had when she cast off Roman Orthodoxy. At the very least, Biagio was telling her he wouldn't kill her right away if she didn't interfere with the Rosary of the Appointed Time.

Why was she standing against it?

Why didn't she want to prolong her life even a second longer?

"Crossism teaches one to love thy neighbors—but there is no mercy at all against such distant enemies," declared Biagio, fingering one of his crosses. "Such is clear upon looking at the legends of the saints adorning the calendar pages." The power in his finger was smooth and accurate like a snake. It looked like he was serious now.

She would die. Agnes knew it.

So she spoke to Orsola from behind. "...Please...move aside. Either way, you can't stop Biagio. If you don't resist, you don't have to die."

Agnes hadn't wanted to say those words. It was what almost every heretic priest said to the saints in legends as they were about to die, to try to tempt them to give up Crossism.

But.

"I have...no reason to do that...!!"

As though she were a saint appearing in a legend, Orsola Aquinas refused.

The answer had been immediate.

Her voice had been shaking. She was in pain, but it was probably also due to the tension, the unease, and even the fear. But Orsola had answered Agnes immediately. She hadn't thought it through very much. She believed it didn't need much thought, and the words left her mouth right away.

"It's over, Sister Orsola," announced Biagio.

His voice was unhesitating as well, though likely born of entirely different reasoning. Biagio Busoni would now kill Orsola. He would simply follow what was inside him, believe it was absolute and just, and refuse to listen to anything else.

Orsola would die.

"They were more perfect people than anyone in that place. I cannot hold a candle to them."

She would die, likely without being able to put up anything close to a fight.

"Do you have a complaint against what Miss Lucia and Miss Angeline said?"

Orsola, who had no power and said those things to Agnes.

"Do you think their words are not enough—even though they said, faced with a hopeless situation, threatened by countless blades, that they wanted everyone to be together and happy again?"

Orsola, who hadn't worried about only Agnes but even about Lucia and Angeline.

The one who had said those things, right before Agnes's eyes, would be—

"Ha-ha! Laugh, Sister Agnes, as your dream is realized through destruction!"

The instant she heard Biagio's words, Agnes's awareness burst.

Grrkeee!! There was a loud roar of metal on metal.

"…What is this?" asked Biagio, but Agnes didn't answer.

The angelic staff, which had been on the floor a moment ago, was now in her hands. She reached her arms in front of Orsola and, by plunging the lower tip of the staff into the floor an inch in front of the nun, stopped her from moving.

The cross from Biagio, which had explosively expanded, its tip like a metal beam, collided with the angelic staff. It had been aimed right between Orsola's eyes. If it had been on target, her entire head might have just vanished. Agnes, gripping the staff, clenched her teeth against the force of the impact.

Agnes spat on the floor.

Then she came around Orsola and violently swung the angelic staff before leveling it. The action had none of the politeness Orsola's had.

"Tutto il paragone. Il quinto dei cinque elementi. Ordina la canna che mostra pace ed ordine." *(All creation in harmony. The fifth of the five elements. Deploy the crosier, symbol of peace and order.)*

It was as though that rough treatment was actually a sign of her faith in the staff.

It was as though she was implying that she believed it would take more than that to break it.

"Prima! Segua la legge di Dio ed una croce. Due cose diverse sons connesse!!" *(First icon! Obey God and the laws of the Cross. Connect foreign objects and people!!)*

Biagio, however, wasn't even watching the weapon being aimed at him. There was a bigger problem. When she had ignored his question, his face had quickly reddened.

"Sister Agnes!! I asked you what you are doing!!"

"Hah. It's just what you think it is," Agnes spat ever so weakly upon seeing the enraged Biagio, smiling—yes—like a villain. "This is all wrong. Can't believe I actually still *want* to look after Sister Lucia, Sister Angeline, and all those other sisters! And thinking about your shitty orders making them fight pisses me off so much!!"

Even as she shouted, she didn't withdraw a single step.

Biagio's temple twitched unnaturally. "You...impudent..." He clenched his teeth before tearing off one of the many crosses at his chest and thrusting the hand gripping it into the air. "Watch your mouth, you *God-damned* sinner!!"

Bgwee, came a strange noise.

A moment later.

"Ah...guh?!"

Agnes heard a cry from behind her. She whipped around to see

Orsola collapsing to the ground. She was sitting now, face covered in greasy sweat, but as soon as she shook her head to clear it, the act appeared to defeat her, and she fell over onto her side.

"Apes, every single one of you, screaming in the words of man..." The bishop's mouth split sideways. "—Simon carries the cross of the Son of God!!" The words came out like an explosion.

Before Agnes could realize what happened, her vision *started to spin.*

"Wha...at?!"

By the time she suppressed the incredible urge to vomit, she had already lost her balance and dropped to her knees. She tried to rise but almost collapsed to the floor like Orsola had.

And then...

Biagio approached her and delivered a firm kick to the kneeling Agnes's jaw. The tip of his hard shoes digging into her jawbone caused an explosive pain. Her small body bent over and began to fall backward.

"Gah...ah...!!"

She got the hand with her staff to the floor, but it had no strength. It was like she was exhausted from doing push-ups; she couldn't lift herself up. Not even the angelic staff, which she'd used so much it had her finger marks on it, would help here.

A...spell...That...attack...

But Agnes still didn't give up.

She moved her head, starting to get a handle on the situation she'd been placed in.

Most...likely...

Judging by the words in the incantations, Biagio had just used sorcery based on the legend of the time the Son of God was hung on the cross. But the Son of God had been killed with his hands and feet nailed to it, and neither Agnes nor Orsola had any such wounds.

Which meant one thing.

There are legends regarding the Son of God and crosses from before His execution. When He was burdened with the heavy wooden cross that would crucify Him and made to walk the hill of Calvary...

"...But I thought...the Son of God...didn't have the strength left to carry the cross. Instead of Him...a man named Simon...carried the cross...to the site of the crucifixion. Is that wrong?"

Biagio's eyebrow twitched. Then he grinned. "So you realized it."

"*To have one shoulder the weight of all that equipment...That is... what you attacked us with. This can't be...your weight alone...It's probably...the weight of all the equipment...worn by those on the Queen's Fleet...concentrated into one place...and converted into attack power...*"

One would think the combined weight of at least two hundred fifty people would crush a human, but it was only the weight pressing down on her—there was no *acceleration.*

There was a torture method where the torturer placed a heavy weight on the person's gut region—and surprisingly enough, the recorded limit for doing so was over four hundred kilograms. Humans were more resistant the slower the weight was applied.

"Orsola fell faster than I did because the attack is aimed from high to low. It's like a knockout punch, since normally the highest part of the body is the head."

"Splendid. You certainly are different from a certain other heretical ape." Biagio, though, sounded all too easy about his trick being exposed. "But just because you know about it doesn't mean you can block it!!"

He tore off another one of the crosses on his chest before lifting it over him. At that moment, the "weight" concentrated on Agnes's body came at her.

She thought she was going to black out.

If she did, it was all over.

Agnes was a crucial part of the plan, so he wouldn't just kill her. Orsola, on the other hand...If Agnes stopped her resistance now, he'd deliver the finishing blow to the unnecessary nun.

And yet, despite knowing that.

Even though she knew that.

The highest part of her body was being targeted—so she raised her staff overhead, but the attack sent waves of intense pain through her fingers, nearly breaking their bones. The angelic staff clattered to the ground. She couldn't help but pull her hand away, and then the impact pushed down on her head once again.

Biagio laughed scornfully at the meager display of resistance. "Ha-ha! What are you doing, Sister Agnes?! You think your frail little hand can block my attack? You should have brought more muscle with you!"

"Kh…!!"

She was almost out of strength, and yet Agnes still endured it, clenching her teeth. As if ashamed at her powerlessness. Biagio plucked off another cross at his chest to apply additional pressure to Agnes's head, but she still reached out for the angelic staff on the floor, and—

"That right? You think this right hand will do the trick, then?"

Bgwee!! came the sound of something breaking.

It came from behind Biagio. From the double doors leading into this giant pyramid room. A square of it—no, a cube—was blasted away, and someone stepped into the room.

He raised his right hand over his head…

…and drove away the weight attack approaching from above.

Biagio turned around, then yelled at the intruder. "You…you heretical monkey…!!"

"Yeah, you should have checked the body, stupid. My right hand's a little tougher than you seem to think!!"

The young man didn't say a word about Agnes. Why was she protecting Orsola? What was she thinking, doing something so out-of-place?

But thankfully, he didn't ask any of those things.

He probably didn't have the time to, given that Biagio loomed right in front of him.

And it was only natural to think his own strike had been more to save Orsola than Agnes.

And yet…

Agnes couldn't help but feel like she'd been saved.

She couldn't help but feel like Touma Kamijou had come to save her.

"Owoohhhh!!" he shouted, running straight for Biagio.

Biagio plucked off a cross and, with a somewhat impatient look, clicked his tongue and stepped back.

And then he unleashed another weight attack.

It had likely been a snap judgment based on his faith in his trump card and his surprise at Kamijou having crawled back to him. His ability to come up with a method of attack so quickly based on the threat level showed that he was very used to real combat.

But there was an exception for everything.

"Too slow! I won't fall for that again!!"

The boy instantly brought up his right hand and repelled the weight attack with a single swing before stepping right up close to Biagio.

"No…?!" Biagio hastily reached for the next cross…

…but before he could, Kamijou's fist buried itself in the middle of Biagio's face.

Crack!!

The sound of flesh slamming against flesh, of bone slamming against bone, echoed far and wide.

9

After making sure Biagio was unconscious, Kamijou relaxed at last. He turned back to Orsola and Agnes. "Great. While Biagio's out cold, let's tie him up and take his crosses. I'm worried the battle might still be going on up on the decks. Oh, and Agnes?"

"Y-yes?" stammered the short sister, appearing to think she was in for a scolding now.

"Thanks. If you hadn't protected Orsola, things would have been real bad."

"..." Though she was being thanked, Agnes's face was one of disbelief. Then she turned her cheek away with a "hmph" and fell silent.

Kamijou's eyes narrowed in frustration. "(...Damn it. What a waste of a compliment.)"

"(...If that is seriously how you think, then my, are you a cute little child.)"

"(...Uh, what? Ow! Hey, what'd you hit me for?)"

Orsola, keeping one hand pressed to her cheek, was hitting him over and over with her other.

Kamijou, as he desperately fended off the blows, said, "Oh right, the Queen's Fleet—er, even bigger, the *Queen of the Adriatic*. What should we do to break the whole thing? Agnes, you were the one they were going to use for the Rosary of the Appointed Time, right? I want to get rid of that value. I want to totally destroy the Rosary of the Appointed Time and the Queen of the Adriatic so they can never be used again. Is there, like, a core or something?"

"Umm..." Agnes paused for a moment, then looked over at where Biagio lay. "The *Queen of the Adriatic*...or rather, strictly speaking just this pyramid room we're in now—I don't think it could be replaced. I don't think modern technology could make this anymore, so if we wreck all its functions, they shouldn't ever be able to repair it again."

"However, wasn't the Rosary of the Appointed Time an additional spell that didn't originally exist in the Queen of the Adriatic? I would believe this giant pyramid is the Queen of the Adriatic, whereas the Rosary of the Appointed Time is something else."

So it's up to my right hand, Kamijou resolved, looking down slightly toward his fist. Wasn't his job to think about sorcery stuff? "Okay, so if we just bust one of them up, that's fine, right? If it can't be replaced, then let's start with this room." He faced Agnes and Orsola again. "For now, once we destroy the Queen of the Adriatic, it'll be over. The ship will sink...The ice will turn into seawater again, though, so I guess we'll just have to find Amakusa and get out of here."

Agnes groaned and cringed a little. "So Amakusa *is* here, too."

Orsola gave her a glance, then continued. "The main problem, though, is what to do once we've alighted from this ship. I cannot show the proper path to everyone. We will need to think on our own about what to do after…"

Her words never reached the end.

Rattle. Suddenly, Agnes's knees gave out.

"Agnes?" Kamijou reached out his hand in haste, but he was a moment too late. She collapsed to the floor, his hand passing right over her. The angelic staff in her hands clattered to the floor with a strangely reverberating sound.

"Gah…!" Agnes fell on her side, then curled up into a fetal position. "…Egh…gaaaaaaaaaaaaaaaaaaaaaaaaahhhhhhhhhhhhhhhhhhhhhhhhhhhhhhhh!!" She screamed, gnashing her teeth.

He didn't know what had just happened. But it was plain to see from her expression of overwhelming pain that this wasn't a joke. Kamijou couldn't guess at how much it hurt, but a muddy sweat burst out all over her face at once.

"Agnes!! What's…?" Kamijou said before seeing something odd out of the corner of his eye.

Biagio Busoni.

The bishop, who had just been unconscious a few moments ago, had wobbled up onto one knee and was now glaring at them. His bloodshot eyes rolled around frantically, casting doubt as to whether they were actually focused on anything. Highly viscous drool dripped from the corners of his mouth.

And…

His right hand, as if about to tear open his chest, grabbed every one of the crosses attached to his four necklaces. His hand trembled unnaturally.

Orsola stooped down to cradle the fallen Agnes. "The Rosary of the Appointed Time…Was *that* what it was? Have you done something to Miss Agnes through a Soul Arm?!"

Had the Rosary of the Appointed Time been fully prepared already? But if that was true, why had Agnes been left alone this whole time? Kamijou had no knowledge of sorcery, so he couldn't fathom a guess, but just from the situation, he naturally believed the preparations were incomplete.

But Biagio grinned. With excitement and tension, heaving hot clouds of air, he said, "Hah, the Rosary of the Appointed Time? Can't use that without adjusting it first. Right now, I can still *only use* the Queen of the Adriatic for its true purpose." His eyes wavered, then locked on to Kamijou. "But its *power* is all here already. Did you never use your head? The Roman Orthodox Church feared this being stolen and pointed back at them, so they added all sorts of tricks to the targeting system and the Queen's Fleet. So if it actually was turned over to the enemy, what do you think they had in store as a final, last resort?"

The Roman Orthodox bishop then told them, amused, even though it would affect him as well.

"A self-destruct mechanism."

"Biagio!!" Kamijou screamed suddenly.

He didn't give a damn about how it worked. This guy was trying to bring everything down because his plan had failed. By turning Agnes's mind into an empty shell, at that.

He grunted. The nearby illumination slowly dimmed like a movie theater right before the movie started. With nearly all of the pyramid room's light gone, they heard a shrill, grating sound. It was coming from right above them—and it was the sound of several of the equilateral triangular panels making up the walls slowly popping out.

A single ray of light shone down from the pinnacle of the pyramid far overhead.

It bounced off dozens of the prisms jutting out of the walls, and after reflecting, refracting, diffusing, and converging, it created an enormous pattern in midair.

It had not created a simple flat plane but a dome-shaped canopy.

It was like a planetarium—a glittering night sky created by man and for his convenience.

"...Don't think you're getting away." Biagio looked up to the ceiling and laughed in scorn. "This is the large-scale magic device the two hundred and fifty sinners on board this fleet have been reinforcing through alchemical methods. Simply destroying bits and pieces of the walls and floor will *not* stop this!!"

As if to answer his voice, the distorted canopy began to shine more brightly. As if to indicate with absolute calm to a human that the tool was now in standby mode.

Orsola frowned. "This isn't good...If an attack spell with the power to blow away an entire city-state runs out of control...Simply the explosive force, barring any magical effects, will travel no less than ten kilometers out."

Ten kilometers.

That was a distance his imagination could keep up with. Orsola supplemented her explanation. "...I do not know exactly where in the Adriatic Sea we are, but if we traveled north from Chioggia, we are near Venice...and *it will likely be caught up in it*. Other neighboring cities such as Adria and Padua could be in danger as well..."

"Not only that."

He didn't know what was different about a magical explosion. But say it really did torch a radius of ten kilometers, a tactical weapon.

If that was true, the victims wouldn't be limited to only the range of the blast from the explosion. A huge amount of seawater would instantly vaporize, and all the hot gas would immediately extend to cover an even larger area. The vapor would be hundreds of degrees Celsius as it swarmed out for dozens of kilometers, and that would boil people alive. Plus, the water vapor would change the atmosphere's temperature, creating an extreme difference in air pressure. Broadly speaking, it would spell the birth of a supergiant hurricane. Then, to drive the nail into the coffin of the towns already torched by the siroccos of water vapor, the violent winds would uplift buildings.

It would be a massive chain of destruction.

Kamijou swore to himself. Queen of the Adriatic? Who needed that when *this* was all it took to blow Venice out of existence?

"Ah...geh...!!"

He heard Agnes's cries.

The cold, starlike light made her complexion look worse than it was.

Kamijou rubbed his right hand over the writhing Agnes's back, but it didn't seem to undo the effects. It probably wouldn't stop until the crosses in Biagio's hand were destroyed.

Then he heard a creaking noise.

It wasn't from Agnes. The entire ship was beginning to creak.

The ship's construction was under tremendous stress from Biagio's reckless command. When it reached its limit, it, along with the rest of the Queen's Fleet, could be blown away.

"Orsola, take Agnes and get above deck! You had a submersible, right? Get Amakusa to retreat into it, too! And try to convince the Roman Orthodox people if you can!!"

"Y-yes. But what about you?" asked Orsola, wobbling awkwardly yet still cradling the trembling Agnes in both hands. She politely held the angelic staff, too.

Kamijou moved his eyes from Orsola to Biagio. "Someone's gotta stop him, right? I'll meet up with you later. So go, Orsola!!"

"But that's…?!" Orsola cried out of reflex, but Agnes's moans cut her off. On top of that, Biagio was slowly bringing his fingers to the crosses around his neck.

They had no time.

"Promise…Promise me you will!"

That was all Orsola said before running for the exit. Maybe she decided she couldn't do anything here, or she was thinking about how to give Agnes some sort of first aid.

Only Kamijou and Biagio were left in the giant pyramid room.

Inside the creaking ship, the bishop spoke.

"…This is why I didn't want to do this."

His eyes bloodshot, he slowly rose from his kneeling position. The damage from where his solar plexus had been rammed into shouldn't have gone away yet. But still, with twisted determination alone, Biagio began to support his own body weight with his legs.

Beneath the planetarium of his own making, he said this. "Damn *that woman*. A great cause? Leaving my name in Roman Orthodox history? I *told* him it was too soon for this immediately after hearing the plan. I'm already done for. Now I can only wait to be erased as a sinner. The Church's pride, the Queen of the Adriatic, one of the Ten Rites of the Holy Spirit along with the Croce di Pietro...If I lose something so important, I will never be given a chance to redeem myself."

"So you're taking everything with you? What's that going to change? All you're really doing is trying to make yourself feel better without improving anything!!"

And many other people would be involved in his wallowing in self-pity.

The sisters of Agnes's unit, forced to fight on Biagio's orders. The young men and women of Amakusa, who were trying to stop them without bloodshed. Lucia and Angeline. Orsola and Agnes. Tatemiya and Index. All of them.

By the order given by this man-made canopy...

...using the giant ship in its entirety, everything would be destroyed with overwhelming destructive force.

"What...are you saying?" Biagio Busoni grinned. His courageous smile stretched across his face. "Who would not feel danger in this situation? Where you have fought so many of my soldiers, sunk so much of this fleet, and saw to it that the bishop Biagio Busoni will perish? Your strength alone, along with your connections, can already be labeled a threat to the Roman Orthodox Church. There is not a soul who would disagree with my choice. I will make the end grand. I would give up the entire God-damned Adriatic coastline if it was to overcome such an enemy!!"

His thoughts were the polar opposite of Touma Kamijou's.

He struggled not to move forward but to turn back.

Not satisfied with defending but with taking.

Not stopping the pain before it got to others but forcing it on everything around him.

"Biagio..." Kamijou clenched his right fist without a sound.

The bishop didn't care. He spread his arms wide, declaring, "...Yes, that's the expression. That fortitude of yours is the threat to us. And that is why I will crush you while I have the chance. It will be the final achievement I can offer to the Roman Orthodox Church!!"

"Biagiooooooooooooooo!!" shouted Kamijou, sprinting for him as fast as he could.

Biagio didn't even retreat—instead, he placed both hands on the many crosses hanging from his neck. He made a gesture as though he was praying, but it didn't look the slightest bit holy. All Kamijou could sense was the sludge of his clinging tenacity.

Kamijou made it to close range and wound up to punch him in the side.

"—The cross indicates rejection of immorality!!"

The crosses in his hands explosively expanded. In an instant, they became giant metal shields bigger than a coffin, stopping Kamijou's fist's movement.

The power in his right hand blew the cross shield away like it was sand.

Biagio, behind it, took five crosses and flung them over Kamijou's head.

"—The cross's weight cures pridefulness!!"

The small accessories, given immense gravitational acceleration, crashed down toward him like cannonballs.

Kamijou didn't even bother looking up. "Ooohh!!" *Stomp!!* He took another step forward.

Toward Biagio—toward the safe zone he'd left as Kamijou drew closer.

Then he let loose with his fist.

He put every ounce of strength into his right hand for one decisive blow to the man's face.

"?!"

But Biagio crossed his arms to guard his face. Kamijou felt him punch his hard bones, but the damage had been directed away from his core.

The motion wasn't meant as an impromptu defense.

Because Biagio had the shields for which he used the giant crosses.

Which meant…

"—The cross indicates rejection of immorality!!"

Behind the bishop's crossed arms were one cross held in each hand.

They exploded right in front of Kamijou.

Pop!!

It was pretty much a counterattack: The tips of the two crosses, now the size of steel beams, dug into Kamijou's right shoulder and gut. He didn't even have room to clench his teeth before being whacked straight back. After bounding a few times across the ice floor, he continued into a roll.

"Guh…" He coughed. He wasn't breathing right. Within one second, his whole body had burst out into a sweat. The pure pain wasn't as big a priority as the bile rising within him. As he tried to get up, he felt like he was leaning over to the side.

But he still got himself up again.

When he moved his fingers, the pain in his shoulder shot through the rest of his arm.

Biagio watched and smiled. His expression and emotion weren't directly related, and to prove that once again was the fact that his smile was an infinitely shadowed one. "I am surprised you can get up after that…I gave you enough of a shock to rock your heart…" He wasn't unhurt, either. Biagio rubbed his nose, which had been punched. "Why do you struggle so? Is Sister Agnes on her own such a meaningful reward to you?! It's just one nun—she's going to die, anyway! Our organization is enormous. It consists of two billion people and spreads across one hundred and thirteen countries. You cannot defy us in any real way…And also! That woman already has no place that will welcome her!! Why don't you understand that, you fucking heretic monkey?!"

"…I will…never understand." Kamijou clenched his teeth.

She threw away her only chance at being saved to protect Lucia and Angeline and the rest. He didn't know exactly what was happening, but she had stood up to Biagio with angelic staff in hand to defend Orsola. And she'd been right to do that for her.

Two billion people, 113 countries? Enormous organizations? They meant less to him than the leaves on the trees.

This guy was already about to ignore even the Roman Orthodox Church's ideas and strike one final time in desperation. Agnes's mind would be broken, and everyone who came to the Queen's Fleet would die in the explosion. It was the worst possible outcome—and Kamijou wasn't going to have any of it.

Biagio Busoni's words were shallow.

If they were enough to get him to give up, nobody would have come here in the first place.

"You piece of shit. Nothing you say's gonna convince me...!!"

And so, that was all he shouted.

He didn't get into an endless dispute. Both Kamijou and Biagio were unwilling to continue the relay race of this conversation. Now Kamijou would punch him and end things—that was it.

Touma Kamijou ignored his aching shoulder, spat on the floor, and tightened his right fist.

Biagio Busoni brought his hand to the many crosses hanging around his neck.

The first breath they took was the signal to start.

Bam!! Both of them began to run at the same time, trying to close the distance.

"Ooohhh!!"

Within three seconds, Kamijou would plunge into his fist's attack range.

Biagio removed one of the crosses at his chest.

"—The cross indicates rejection of immorality!!"

His palm was raised right in front of Kamijou.

In addition, his free hand was already on the next cross. Even if he let the first one be blown away, Biagio's attacks would continue. Blow for blow, the crosses were more powerful than Kamijou's fist. If Biagio tried to overwhelm him with numbers, Kamijou would be pushed back for certain.

I can't get in close the normal way. At point-blank range, Kamijou turned his attention to his tightened fist. *It's not just this attack. I need to stop his entire flow of attacks…!!*

There was no time now that he thought of it, even if he tried to prepare something.

In the end, he had to bet it all on his one fist.

The cross in the palm held in front of him popped and began its expansion.

"Biagioooooooooooooo!!"

At the very same time, he sent his fist flying at the accessory.

Not his right—but his left.

Even an amateur could tell his nondominant hand's strike was much weaker. Compared to his right fist, which he always used to punch, its speed was overshadowed.

But his left fist was different in one other respect.

It didn't have the Imagine Breaker's power in it.

"!!"

The cross Biagio was gripping bounced a little from Kamijou's left fist. With a soft *tink*, the accessory in his hand had simply changed its direction slightly.

However…

The cross, facing in a different direction than Biagio had planned, expanded very quickly.

Boom!!

The tip of the cross that had been in his hand now stabbed his jaw.

"Ghbah?!"

Biagio's body sprang straight up.

This…little…He used my own attack…!!

He could think, but he had no room to speak. The whole inside of his mouth stung with pain.

Kamijou took another step toward him.

"Ooh…"

Another step into the deepest range.

This time, he rallied all his energy into his weapon, his right fist.

"...Ooooooooaaaaaaaahhhhh!!"

With a roar, he unleashed all his force.

Ga-grak!! came the sound of metal breaking.

He hadn't aimed for Biagio's face but lower—for the middle of his chest.

Because Biagio's body had sprung upward, Kamijou's straight fist had made contact with the bishop's chest.

His fist dug deeply into the four necklaces there and the many crosses hanging from them—as though trying to plant itself in Biagio's sternal plate behind them. The chains of the four necklaces came apart and fell to the floor, and the pile of accessories shattered apart with the sound of a chandelier breaking.

Boom!! Its power gone, the bishop's body was mowed down.

Leveling his gaze on Biagio as he lay on the floor, Kamijou caught his breath. "Don't worry, I'll fight it...," he said anyway. "...I don't care if you have two billion followers or one hundred and thirteen countries. If you come after Agnes and the others again, I'll stand against you, no matter how many times it takes."

He looked above him.

In his widening range of vision, the planetarium supported by countless prisms began to fade. Like an unplugged appliance, all it left in its wake was a cold, dead hunk of metal.

In the now lightless room, a splitting sound cracked through the air.

The Queen's Fleet was beginning to crumble.

The crosses at their core had been destroyed.

At the same time, he was sure he'd prevented the giant explosion that would have caught everything in it.

The pyramid room began to break, the flagship began to tear apart, and the young man once again began to fall toward the Adriatic.

EPILOGUE

Return to Academy City

L'inizio_Nuovo......

An Italian hospital. That was new.

Many people go overseas on vacation, but Kamijou thought sightseers who unexpectedly ended up in the hospital were a rare breed. At the moment, he was on a rickety stretcher moving through a dark passage. No matter what the doctors and nurses tried to say to him, he was clueless. At any rate, his right shoulder and left hand were bandaged, and gauze stuck to his face...Or maybe that was antiseptic, because his eyes were a little blurry.

"It must be antiseptic. That's the only reason possible! Damn it, all the other Amakusa people were taking a bath spell until their skin practically glowed, too..."

"The Adriatic Sea was less cold than I thought, huh?"

"Why are you so happy about it, Index?! The two of us fell into the Gulf of Venice with the rest of the ship!! Hah! Wait, maybe you're in a good mood because I didn't leave you by yourself this time..."

"!!" Before Kamijou could finish speaking, Index got her legs tangled up and fell on the floor. "I-I'm not in a good mood!!"

"I got it, but are you okay?! Sheesh, don't go crazy over something dumb, Index. Look, you're causing problems for the nice nurse lady, too— *Dbahhhh!!*"

The moment he mentioned the newly hired blond nurse, Index bit him. "Are you still Touma even when you're on a stretcher?!"

"I don't even understand what that means!!"

The doctor subdued the nun struggling around on the stretcher and peeled her away. The nurse crooked her head to the side, not understanding what they were saying.

"Breathe in, breathe out. Touma, Touma. The doctor's saying to hold on to this," said Index.

Kamijou looked at the doctor, who was holding a cordless phone for some reason. He wondered if it was okay to have that in a hospital, but when he thought about it more logically, it seemed more normal to have a phone *somewhere* in here. He took the phone tentatively. It was already connected, and when he put it to his ear, a familiar voice greeted him.

"You go through the same things on vacations, don't you?"

It was the frog-faced doctor. The one who was always fixing him up in Academy City. Kamijou's life was one of getting recklessly injured, then going back to the starting point—or, rather, the hospital—so he had already assumed that doctor was extremely good at his job, among other things.

"What? This is rather sudden. Wait! Are you one of those nutso doctors who gives checkups to patients over the phone?!"

"If I could do that, the hospital would have already made a phone application, I'm sure. But, well, I can't, so I have to put in a request with you. You need to come back to Academy City right away."

....*Huh?*

"Well, I'm not joking, you see. You may be in an Academy City–associated facility, but I think there are many reasons we wouldn't want an outside hospital tinkering with an esper's body, don't you?"

"Umm, no, that's not...But wait! You're gonna make me get on a plane like this? For almost ten hours?! Just so you know, the good Mr. Kamijou has been pulverized!"

"Oh, no, that is perfectly fine. There should be an Academy City supersonic passenger jet at Marco Polo International Airport. You know, it can apparently go over seven thousand kilometers per hour at its maximum speed. It'll only be a little over an hour to Japan, right?"

"On a jumbo jet?! Aren't you actually talking about the mystical North American X-15 experimental aircraft?! How am I supposed to fly something that goes faster than most missiles without any training?!"

"It's fine, it's fine. I've actually piloted one before, and you only feel a little bit weightless."

"And for an hour?! I think the entire contents of my stomach are going to come right out!!"

"It's fine, it's fine. I've actually piloted one before, and you don't have time to think about things like that after the first ten minutes."

How is that fine?! Kamijou grabbed his head with his hands. "Please, wait—I beg you! I—I haven't even been in Italy for a whole day yet! I've tasted the waters of the Adriatic Sea twice—no, three times if you count when we escaped—but I haven't even taken a single step into Venice, the place I was supposed to be going this whole time!"

"Oh yes, if you've experienced that much, then I'm sure you're satisfied. Well, I can only say one thing…There's no way that will work, so give up and get back here."

That was mean and kind of apathetic!! he thought, pushed ever further to his wits' end.

And then the voice on the line said something else. "Oh, right. The cute little girl who's been around for hospital visits lately—I mentioned I would contact you, and she asked me to relay a message for her."

"What???" Cute—who was that? Right now, Kuroko Shirai and Aisa Himegami were the ones in the hospital. Himegami would know Seiri Fukiyose and Miss Komoe, and if he looked at Shirai, it would probably be Mikoto Misaka visiting…

"…Wait. Mikoto Misaka?"

"Yes," said the frog-faced doctor with a nod.

*   *   *

"I'm glad you know. She said something about 'preparing yourself for the punishment game from the Daihasei Festival when you got back,' you see."

"Gyaaaaaaaaaaaahhhhh?! I totally forgooooooooooot!!"

As Touma Kamijou began to rage in the stretcher, the doctor and nurses had to use all their might to hold him back. They must have noticed that the situation called for haste.

Touma Kamijou and Mikoto Misaka had made a little deal during the Daihasei Festival. Now, having lost, he would be forced to do whatever Mikoto wanted. If she knew he'd not only stood her up but was off in Italy for a relaxing vacation...

"...then I'll be in for hell when I get back! Now I really don't want to go! Wait, no, let me go, please! Come on, seriously, don't lock me down with professional-looking tools like that!!"

The stretcher clattered along on its way.

The phone spoke to the wailing Kamijou.

"Well, I suppose, hmm. Welcome home, Touma Kamijou."

Before the calendar date changed, during the time referred to as "late night"...

In a pocket of Lambeth, London, was a dormitory-like building for English Puritan believers. Those who used it most of all were not those without money but those who didn't want civilians to be caught up in sudden attacks. If everyone nearby was a professional, if it came to combat, they would get through with minimal casualties.

"Is that so? Good work."

Speaking in one of those rooms was Kaori Kanzaki. She had an Asian face, and her black hair, though tied into a ponytail, was long enough to reach her hips. Her clothing consisted of a short-sleeve T-shirt tied around the waist and jeans with one leg cut off. She also regularly wore a large katana at her waist, close to two meters long, called the Seven Heavens Sword, but right now it was leaning against the wall.

She wasn't talking to a person but into a telephone. It was an old rotary phone—a perfectly antique item, made of red ceramic and bordered with gold. For the record, the person on the other end was Motoharu Tsuchimikado.

"Nya. But if you wanted a report, you should have asked someone else from Amakusa. It's a bit dangerous for me to go looking for intel, you know. You do know that, right, nya?"

"R-right now I'm not a member of Amakusa anymore. Even the thought of speaking so freely with them should be called arrogance," said Kanzaki, playing with the phone cord with her index finger. She went on. "Besides, whatever the case, you were collecting information around Venice already. The timing was too impeccable. Those from Amakusa going to Chioggia to help with moving *and* the young man and the index coming to Italy together...By the report, Orsola Aquinas was mistaken as someone sent to stop the Queen of the Adriatic and attacked by the Roman Orthodox Church, but I wonder. I believe their hunch may have been correct."

Kanzaki tapped her bare foot on the floor as she spoke. The room was a western one, but Kanzaki forbade anyone to enter with their shoes on. It was, perhaps, a blending of Japanese and western styles.

"Mm, about that. There're things going on over here, too, so I can't answer that."

"Wh-what is it?" Tsuchimikado's voice had been oddly slow and drawn out, but it instead put Kanzaki on her guard.

And her hunch was correct. "...Zaky, you caused a big problem for Kammy again, didn't you, nya?"

"Pfft?!" Unfortunately, the damage was way outside what she was able to tolerate.

"Jeez. What are you gonna do now? Zaky, I think you're gonna need to do a little more than put on a maid outfit and be his servant for a day. Oh! How about this, nya? I'll lend you my angel set—a halo for your head and white wings! It's an improvement on the maid outfit! Then you can go for it, Zaky!! Wh-whoooa! A freaking angel, damn it. If such a cute fallen angel arrives at his front door, what'll happen to Kammy?!"

"Wh-why must you insist on this absurdity...?! And why would you even have something like that?!"

"Oh, well, actually...I bought it for Maika. That stepsister of mine...She said *maids aren't in cosplay* and punched me real good in the face. I gotta wonder about a girl having a punch that seems like it came out of the army, nya."

"...She is at that age, so maybe you should be a little more considerate," said Kanzaki, about to deflate entirely, before giving a start. This wasn't what they were talking about. "Wait a moment. All this was really just the leaders of the English Puritan Church and Academy City pulling some strings and getting Touma Kamijou involved so they could resolve this incident, wasn't it? Why am I at all related to this?!"

"Hmm? Zaky, you mean to say you're not grateful to Kammy for anything?"

"Urgh?!"

"Oh well. Kammy went out of his way to protect everyone in Amakusa from the Queen's Fleet blowing up, but you declared you have zero gratitude toward him and even that you weren't related to this. You've really fallen, Kaori Kanzaki. If Kammy heard about this, he'd be pretty disappointed. He's weirdly nice about things, so he probably wouldn't even be mad."

"Th-that's...You do have a point, but what more am I supposed to do?! My debt to him does nothing but increase!!"

"That's what I'm saying! The only path for you is to give your heart and soul and truly become the fallen-angel maid! Even if there are only twenty of you saints in the world, you'd better be prepared, Zaky!!...Huh, hello? Zaky, you listening? Hey, wait, I'm not done...!!"

She slammed the receiver back on its hook. She stared down at it for a few moments, dazed, and finally her face went white.

"...F-fallen-angel maid...?"

Kanzaki's eyes dropped to her uncontrollably shaking hands. Then she looked at the rectangular water tank with her tropical fish in it next to the phone. There she saw the face of the former priestess, directly confronted with a grandiose problem.

"W-would a halo be something like this? B-but a fallen angel... How would one act and speak...? Synonymous with devils, in this case female, and when presented with a male, they would be cute and mischievous..."

If the POWER OF GOD, the archangel who had partially descended to earth as Misha Kreutzev, heard that, it would probably instantly attack her. Kanzaki had no knowledge of this, though, as frenzied as her mind currently was.

And then, the sublime saint, of whom there were only twenty in the world, after a brief moment of silence, tilted her head to the side and said:

"...A-as you please, Touma?"

All of a sudden, there was a *ding-dong* at the door.

"...???!"

Her shoulders suddenly jerked violently in surprise as she quickly took the decorative plate off her head. When her small tropical fish saw her do that, they all rushed madly to the tank's rear. Kanzaki quickly scanned her surroundings, and after making sure nobody was around, she put a hand to her chest and sighed quietly before eventually looking at the door.

This dorm had a bell for visitors at the front door in addition to the ones for each room. If that had rung, then what was it? Maybe it was a delivery.

Kanzaki retrieved her katana from the wall, went to the door, put on her boots, and left the room. She headed down the long wooden hallway toward the front door.

The dorm had custodians, but they tended to be sloppy and often slept on the job. As she went to the entrance, she glanced into the nearby custodian room and saw the ladies dozing off as always. The television had been left on, so they were probably unconscious. The television had originally been brought in to *prevent* them from taking naps, but it seemed to just encourage them if nothing they liked was on.

Not that she could do anything about that, so Kanzaki opened the door.

There standing at the entrance was Orsola Aquinas.

"I-I'm home."

"Oh. Welcome back, Orsola," said Kanzaki, showing her room-mate a bewildered face.

She had no need to ring the bell, since she was a resident, but her hands were full at the moment, so she probably couldn't get her key out. Actually, both her hands held a travel suitcase, and there was a sack on her back and even a duffel bag hanging from a shoulder strap. She looked fully decked out to go mountain climbing.

"Orsola, I thought you had sent your things beforehand."

"Eh-heh-heh. My things increased on the way here."

"???" Kanzaki frowned, moving aside to let in the smiling Orsola.

Oh, thought Kanzaki, her eyebrows rising a little.

Hiding in Orsola's shadow, tugging on her habit, stood a short sister. Her name was Agnes Sanctis.

Then, as Kanzaki stood there trying to understand the situation and failing, Orsola dropped a bombshell.

"Many more will be coming later, so this dormitory is going to become quite lively."

St. Peter's Basilica, Vatican City.

In the largest and most important cathedral of the Roman Ortho-dox Church, the sound of footsteps violently split through the tran-quil air.

"Tch. So in the end, that Busoni idiot failed. And he even destroyed the core of the Queen of the Adriatic, and that can't be reproduced…I swear, who does he think he has to thank for think-ing up the Rosary of the Appointed Time, planning it out, and even managing to implement it? It defies reason. And the most unreason-able part is that now he's gone missing! I demand to know who's hiding him! Where am I supposed to vent all this stress now?!"

Two people walked through the dark interior of the cathedral—a man and a woman.

Two silhouettes were visible.

One appeared to be an older man with a stoop.

And the other one seemed to be a young female with a dynamite body.

"…Still, however, this was a bit hasty even for you. The English Puritans intervening was certainly unexpected, but even without that, there were several other barriers strewn about." A pause. "I will speak frankly. Even without their intervention, Bishop Biagio would not have succeeded. It was a mistake to expect from him any ability to deal with failure."

"Who do you think you're complaining to? If I say it, it happens. That's how the world *works*. This is ridiculous. Have you seriously not figured that out after all this time?"

"And *you*—I question whether you understand who it is you're speaking to."

The old man's presence became more dreadful.

With those few words, the old man dominated the space there. The situation was one of prostration. Not of bowing one's head because one desired it—but because one was *forced* to. Those who heard his voice would find their heads grabbed with an unseen hand and pushed down. That was the sort of dreadfulness he emanated.

And yet the female silhouette remained unchanged.

"*The pope of Rome, right?* What does that matter?"

The female silhouette answered in a casual, uncaring voice.

The space, which had initially been dominating, was now so light, as though it had been broken to pieces.

"…" The old man, whom she had called "pope," fell silent.

She didn't seem to mind. "Would you quit that? You know as well as I do who's *really* pulling the strings in the Church. You could vanish right now and we'd just find a new pope to sit in your chair. But if I go away, you won't find a replacement. Is that so hard to understand? You want to test it out?"

"Absurd," he interrupted, uninterested. "Saint Peter is the only one to whom the Lord directly entrusted the future of Crossism. Though later popes succeeded at many things, their main role was still the preservation and administration of his remains. The people, not the Lord, have chosen me. I am also fully aware of this. Therefore, do not say such things. It will irritate me if you repeat something already known."

"Yeah, and that's why you want it, too—the proof that you alone were chosen, not just by popular vote. Plus, you want to return Roman Orthodoxy to its original form—to when our paths were guided by a single teaching, not by rule of the majority."

"...I believe I told you not to repeat."

"Sorry, sorry. But the way I see it, you're still not ready. You're not *enough*. That's why you can't come to us. Oh, and all this talk about popes being voted in. I think it's plenty honorable to be elected for the spot, but that's not enough to satisfy you. Reason's real simple, too. In the age of the Son of God and His disciples' acts, Crossism itself was a majority decision by a minority group. And even though they were a minority, their strength never faltered against superior numbers. That's why you think there isn't much divine value in being elected through a majority vote. And that's why *you glare at people like me, who have that kind of value, while being completely unchained by the majority*. And yet you only amass more and more votes...It seems to be less like an ordeal and more a worry of luxury."

"!!"

A moment later, the old man's head whipped around.

Pchee!! came an incomprehensible, splitting noise.

Even faced with the mysterious situation, the female silhouette still didn't move. But their attitudes of tension and relaxation displayed the result of this inscrutable battle.

"Malice. Very good." The woman snickered. "But if you direct that malice at me, you *will* die," she remarked, sticking out her tongue.

A *griiik* sound of metal against metal.

She had a ring in her tongue. A thin chain, like a necklace chain, hung from the ring, reaching down to her hips. A small cross was attached to the tip of the chain.

"..." The old man took just one step away. With detest and a little bit of envy in his voice, he said, "...God's Right Seat. Not enough to be swayed by a mere pope, I see."

"Just the fact that you know the name of the *schema* I belong to means you're pretty high up there. Still not satisfied, I'm sure?"

She had been on the receiving end of some sort of attack, but she certainly didn't seem to care. She remained smiling. "Look this over and sign it."

"A command—to me?...Wait, this document is..."

"I'm sure you would have drawn this up yourself eventually. Maybe in two or three years. I'm just cutting to the chase. It's a pain, but your signature is worth a lot. Do it before sunrise, will you? Just write your name there and it'll be all over."

"However..." The old man seemed to hesitate for a moment. "...I still cannot accept it. If he was deeply involved with sorcery, that would be one thing—but he is simply ignorant of our Lord. Faith in false idols is a sin, but if born of mere ignorance, there is still salvation. I will have to deny that we go this far..."

"There is no negative form with me," the female silhouette said, cutting him off flatly. "Passive, imperative, conjunctive, attributive, imperfective, perfective, predicative, conditional...What else was there? Well, it doesn't really matter. But the negative form is the one thing I will not acknowledge. You do what I say to do. Whether it's Saint Peter or the Son of God, this rule doesn't change. So you *will* sign this document. Understand?"

The old man, paper in hand, nodded briefly. And slightly bitterly.

"Very good. ♪" The woman's silhouette disappeared into the dark.

Had she really vanished or just made it seem that way? The old man didn't think about it. He didn't need to analyze the technique she'd used. Whatever the case was, she would continue down her own path. Though whether that was a path that led upward, he couldn't determine.

Instead, he directed his attention to the document.

With the lights off inside the cathedral, the only illumination came from the moon shining in through the stained glass windows. The letters were almost unreadable in the near-darkness, but the old man's eyes followed them.

…*This is a bit too soon. A habit of hers, I assume.*

Still, now that she'd made the decision, it was done. As she herself had said, the negative form didn't exist for her.

Sourly, the old man decided to withdraw to his own quarters.

There was no pen here.

On the document was this:

"Touma Kamijou.

"Portrebbe investigare urgentemente. Quando lui è pericoloso, lo uccida di sicuro."

Its meaning was: "Touma Kamijou. Immediately investigate the aforementioned person, and if he is acknowledged as an enemy of the Lord, kill him without fail."

In practicality, it was a request for the Roman Orthodox Church to rally all its forces and conduct an assassination, even if it meant mobilizing the God's Right Seat.

The order would be carried out before five days were past.

AFTERWORD

Those of you who are buying one volume at a time, it's nice to see you again.

For those of you who carried all eleven volumes to the register at once, it's nice to meet you.

I'm Kazuma Kamachi.

At some point during this relaxing run, I made it to the eleventh volume. This time, well, you know how it is at this point…Still didn't get to the uniform change. The punishment game was postponed as well. This is the overseas trip arc. It was a curveball, and I took the chance to stray from the beaten path: having not Kaori Kanzaki but the rest of Amakusa, depicting a fleet battle not with cannons but with the exchange of fireships, and things of that nature.

As for the story, it's essentially about the aftermath of what happened to a certain group. The short girl and the tall girl *were* mentioned once before by name, but they were major characters here. In a strict sense, there were extremely few new characters, but I think that made it all the livelier.

On the occult side, as well, a certain two organizations were the highlight of the book. It also hit upon things like legends in the Crossist tradition and, though more discreetly, the Twelve Apostles.

The part about the fireships isn't made up; they were actually used for tactics like that. We're talking before the torpedo was really introduced, when the English navy apparently, in all seriousness, loaded up their big ships with explosives and sent them to ram unmanned into an enemy fleet. It was a huge battle, where they absolutely needed to come out as the victor—an awfully massive story, isn't it?

As always, I'd like to extend my gratitude to Mr. Haimura, my illustrator, and Mr. Miki, my editor. With the abrupt change in setting, I think it took a lot of time and effort to gather resources and materials. Thank you so much for all the work you've done. I'd also like to thank Miss Haruna Yoshimi and Miss Yuuko Fukushima for their supervision on the Italian translations.

And, even more than usual, I want to thank all my readers. I'm truly grateful you've always been with me to the last page each time.

Now then, as I close the final page here,
and as I hope you find it within you to open up the next first page,
today, at this hour, I lay down my pen.

Next time will have the uniform changes and punishment game for sure!

Kazuma Kamachi